THE EMPTY CANOE

By
Peter Georgas

Also by Peter Georgas:
Dark Blues
The Fifth Slug
The Curse of the Big Water
Theophanes Virgin

ISBN: 149913309X
ISBN-13: 978-1499133097

For
The Sebastian Joe's Regulars

Jim Thorpe usually remained at his desk until after six, not so much because he had work to do but because he would spend less time at home with Irene harping at him. She resented him for being gone so much, so wrapped up in his work that he didn't have time for her and the boys. She even accused him of having something on the side, not that he was screwing anybody--she figured he was not man enough or good looking enough for that--but rather enjoying a happy hour cocktail with a youngish secretary or assistant talking office politics. Irene was just jealous, that's all, giving up a fledgling career as a Wells Fargo lawyer specializing in mortgage fraud to raise two sons. Life at home for her was piss-awful dull, he granted her that much, but she didn't have to take it out on him all the time.

Thorpe wrapped up some calculations and closed his computer around six-thirty, walked down four flights of stairs to his Reserved Senior Vice President parking spot, his nod to exercise--ride up walk down--and from thirty feet out remotely unlocked his Lexus in the now-deserted ramp. It happened so fast there was no opportunity to react. As he approached his car, a sharp, brutal blow to the back of his head dropped him to his knees. Another blow, this time behind his left ear, toppled him to the concrete floor. He rolled on his side and lay still.

Buddy Boynton was a borderline insomniac. He worried about everything and he had good reason to. He was in the construction business, building high end homes in the south suburbs of Minneapolis: Apple Valley, Eagan and Eden Prairie. On the surface these were prosperous communities, but if one were to dig deeper, under the visible layer of three-acre lots, three-story entryways and three-car garages, one would quickly discover financial dry rot. A widely circulated rumor as to why the new Whole Foods store (aka Whole Paycheck) on Old Shakopee Road closed a year after it opened was because the heavily mortgaged residents couldn't afford the chain's upscale prices.

Buddy had a 5000 square-foot spec home under construction on Deer Creek Road and a finished one in foreclosure on Friendship Lane, both in Apple Valley. No prospects for either of them. Money came easily in the good times but when he asked Jim Thorpe, Senior VP at R&S Bank, for an extension of his loan two weeks ago, he was turned down. That's when his insomnia kicked into high gear--what had been borderline was now a frontal assault.

He had started out small like most builders, working alone remodeling kitchens and baths and building bedroom additions. He got his first chance to put up a house from scratch when an architect called him out of the blue. The architect, Karl Mittelstadt of Mittelstadt and Associates, had got Buddy's name from one of his remodel jobs--Buddy's reputation as a quality craftsman was spreading--and the two, architect and builder, hit it off. But Buddy could not build an entire house alone and so he hired a carpenter to help out while subbing the electric and plumbing. During the crazy boom years, Buddy grew fast, too fast. He incorporated as Boa Constructors with his wife Chloe taking the title of treasurer. He had a crew of sixteen. For a while he was putting up a house every fourth month--and the two-bedroom ranches grew to six-bedroom, five-bath monsters with slate roofs and turrets to nowhere. He despised the term McMansion but the shoe fit.

Now, Boa Constructors was on the brink of bankruptcy and he was desperate. He even entertained the notion of suicide--he read somewhere that if you die your debts die with you. But taking your own life? Man, that was a hard question to ask a six-foot four, two hundred pound man of pride.

He checked the time on the glowing clock by his bed: 3:45 a.m. He stared at the three until it became four, four until it became five...maybe there is another way, he thought, a way to die but not really die. He remembered reading an article in the Star Tribune a few years ago about a lawyer who staged his own death; the only clue was an empty canoe on a lake in Spicer. The guy had a huge insurance policy payable to his wife. Buddy couldn't remember how it turned out--if the guy got away with it or got caught. But it was a fascinating story.

Part I

Meredith. He disliked his name. If you were to tease him about it, he would admit to hating it. It's a name that could go either way--male or female. As a kid he beat up other kids doing a falsetto to taunt him. As an adult he got credit card solicitations in the mail addressed to Ms. Meredith Gilbert. Jesus, not Ms, MR! or, better yet, Fire Captain. Fire Captain Meredith Gilbert, Station House 28 on Penn and Sheridan, that is. Coming up on 30 years now, from rookie to boss. And retirement lay ahead. But not yet, not for a while, not as long as those knees below his panting chest kept him running a mile in 8 minutes. That's what he was doing now, running, his daily routine around Lake Harriet, before dawn on his days off, like today, running hard, breathing hard, sweating hard, making that 55-year-old body act like it was 20 years younger. When he was on duty, he called out the rig to follow him around the lake so he could get his run while the guys got theirs, a practice run riding in the cab. He could do that, he could order the rig to follow him, he was Captain.

Meredith--damn but he wished his parents had picked something else--was coming around the west shore of the lake. Quiet morning, hardly any runners but himself, the sun just peeking above the trees on the other side. Ahead was the Lake Harriet band shell and the parking lot where he had left his car, a vintage Caddie, 1990, the last year GM made his beloved Coupe Deville. A few ducks bobbed on the rippling water, nothing different, like any other day running around Lake Harriet.

Except there was an empty canoe bumping the limestone retaining wall. Nothing unusual really--someone's canoe was left off the rack and floated away--but his first-responder eyes were always looking for the overbalanced, the unexpected, that indefinable something that told him hold up, check it out. He slowed his pace and veered off the track for a closer look, running in place.

Meredith knew a little about canoes. Growing up in the City of Lakes, water was in his subconscious. His quizzical eyes took in imperfections in the fiberglass coating–a milky cloudiness here and there where the fabric mesh was visible. This was a homemade canoe and most likely a first effort. Constructed of half-inch strips of cedar that gleamed under a coat of varnish, the blond wood of the gunwales and the triangles of deck at both the bow and stern were accentuated with strips of darker wood, cherry he guessed. This canoe cost someone a lot hours and money.

He guessed the length to be eighteen feet, with room for a third passenger and lots of gear. The canoe was made for long trips on wilderness lakes. The portage yoke confirmed his conclusion. So, what was a canoe designed for big northern lakes doing on a city lake you can run around in a half hour?

Moved by an easterly breeze that picked up speed as it came across the open expanse of water, the canoe bounced on the wall in a rhythmic cadence, putting marks on the varnish. That bothered him--the canoe owner needed a talking to. The rough wall of weathered limestone was built in the 1930s, a WPA project to keep the shoreline from eroding where people gathered to hear summer band concerts. The bandstand from that time was long gone, the one now resembled a medieval castle with turrets and pennants fluttering on the pinnacles.

Meredith stopped running in place altogether when he spotted what seemed to be a blood smear on the center seat, extending over the gunwale and down the side. Under the seat was an oar. In the still shadowy morning it was hard to see detail, but it looked like it had a crack in the blade, as if it was used to hit something hard, a skull maybe. He was tempted to haul the canoe ashore for a more detailed inspection but his training told him, no, don't touch anything, this could be a crime scene. He looked around but no one was paying attention. If anyone did, that person would have assumed the graying, well-built guy in baggy running pants and a bright red sweatshirt that read from the rear in big black letters, KEEP 500 FEET BACK, was taking a breather before continuing his run.

Ok, Meredith, thought. A loose canoe. Maybe a bloodstain, maybe spilled ketchup from a Big Mac, who knows? There was a Park Board license number on the side. That would be easy enough to trace. All he had to do was call Al, the dispatcher.

"Meredith here," he said into his cell.

"Yeah, Merrie," Al answered, knowing that the nickname would bug Meredith. Firemen are like that--a daily fare of potential injury and death has to be glossed over with teasing and practical jokes to make life bearable, like the time Al bought a new Toyota Corolla. The guys kept topping off his gas tank when he was on duty, and he kept bragging about the unbelievable mileage he was getting. After a few days, they siphoned some gas out of the tank, and Al went back to the dealer mad as hell that his new car went from 45 to 10 mpg in less than a week.

"Need you to trace a number for me," Meredith said, "Park Board canoe license 76130. Find out who it's registered to."

"Ok," Al replied. "You want to wait?"

Meredith walked over to a nearby park bench and sat. "I'll wait."

It didn't take long. "Merrie, I got it, belongs to a guy named Robert Boynton, 5416 Country Club Road, Edina. Delinquent on this year's license fees, it says here."

"Got a phone number?"

Al gave it to him.

Meredith looked at his watch. Six-thirty. Shit, if he's asleep he deserves to be woken up. He punched in the number and it was answered on the first ring, a female voice, anxious, tense.

Meredith introduced himself, title and all. "Found a drifting canoe on Lake Harriet licensed to Robert Boynton, is he there?"

"His canoe?" the woman said without answering his question.

"Yeah," Meredith said, looking at it still bouncing. "Can I talk to Mr. Boynton?"

"Buddy isn't here."

Buddy, Meredith thought, Buddy Boynton. That was a familiar name. It came to him. "Does your husband own Boa Constructors?"

"Yes, but he's not here."

"At work? Can you give me his number?"

"He's not at work, he's gone."

"Where?"

"I don't know. When the phone rang I thought it was Buddy. And now you're telling me his canoe is, what did you say, drifting?"

"By the Harriet band shell. Empty except for an oar." He decided not to tell her about those red stains. He decided they weren't ketchup. "You say you don't know where he is?"

"No."

"Have you called the police?"

"No!" she said sharply, defensively. "Why should I?"

He didn't want to belabor the point that there was both, it appeared, an abandoned canoe and an abandoned wife. "How long has he been gone?"

"Since last night. He called from work saying he would be late but he never came home."

Meredith decided not to push it further. "If he doesn't show up today you'd better notify the police. ok?"

She hung up without answering.

He rose from the bench and walked back to the canoe. It was beginning to attract attention. If Mrs. Boynton doesn't call the police then he'd better. He opened contacts on his phone and scrolled down to Ben Hanson. Lieutenant Ben Hanson of the Minneapolis Park Police. Meredith was calling his home line.

A disgruntled voice answered, "Goddammit, Merrie, it isn't even time for the Today Show. What are you calling about?"

"An abandoned canoe and a missing person."

"Do I have a choice?"

"No, they're connected. Ever heard of a guy named Buddy Boynton?"

Meredith sensed Ben was shaking his head, not in response to his question but because he was pissed. "Can't this wait until I get to work?"

"I got a loose canoe that I think is a crime scene. It belongs to Buddy Boynton of Boa Constructors..."

"The one who builds those McMansions in Eagan?"

"That's the one, and his wife said he didn't come home last night. I think there is blood on the seat and the paddle has a crack in the blade like somebody used it for a bludgeon."

"You got all this before seven a.m.?"

"Sorry I took so long."

"Stay put. I'll call the Sheriff's office and find out if they want to do a sonar scan of the lake. Harriet is pretty deep. My guess is they will want probable cause before they do any body searching. Have to talk to the wife first and see if she wants to file a missing persons report. In the meantime stay by the canoe and don't let anyone touch it. We'll send a forensic team over to check it out."

Meredith sighed as he hung up. And this was supposed to be a routine jog around Lake Harriet.

Jim Thorpe liked his name even though it didn't suit him. The famous Jim Thorpe, one of the greatest athletes to compete in the Olympics, was a legend of tough muscle and smooth attack. This Jim Thorpe was, to be brutally honest, an athletic wannabe. Short of stature, round of waist, he loved to be in front of the barbecue, grilling all year, winter and summer, and it cost him. When he sucked in his gut he missed by 35 pounds. He owned a treadmill, the Cadillac of NordicTraks, which he stared at more often than he used.

Thorpe, responsible for $300,000,000 of the bank's portfolio, had just come from a meeting of Minnesota managers. R&S was a Midwest regional bank with a national headache. Too many of its loans were wrapped into derivatives and shipped off to god knows where. The number one agenda of the meeting: get rid of 10% of your personnel by the end of the year. Thorpe's commercial/housing division had a team of 33. A ten per cent cut meant he had to axe three and a third people. He was given a chart to follow, neatly organized and justified in corporate jargon by HR. There were four categories of skill: high value, superior, average, and satisfactory. His instructions were to reassess each member of his team, and drop three and a third to satisfactory, meaning you had cause for termination. His one-third pick would be added to the picks of two other departments, mortgage and small loans, and placed in what was being called in executive country the "dead man's" lottery.

Thorpe was a guy's guy. He relished hanging out with his team--some were barbecue buddies. They hunted, fished and attended Gopher basketball games together. He would rather put himself on the list than one of them but he had a family to support, two kids in college and a spendthrift wife. He called her.

"Irene," he said, "we had a managers' meeting and the news isn't good."

Always the pessimist, she asked, "You got fired?"

"No, but I have to get rid of ten per cent of my team."

Irene breathed a sigh of relief. "Have you picked them yet?"

"I just got back from the meeting. I have to give corporate my list by next Monday. I have a performance chart. The ones on the bottom get canned."

"Who are they?"

Thorpe swallowed. "My guys. They're all satisfactory."

"You can't just dump them."

"I don't want to but there are a few pricks I can live without."

"Like Hank Riker?" That's all Jim talked about after a tough day at the office—what a pain in the ass Hank Riker was. "Why don't you start out by firing him? You're the boss."

Jim thought about that. "I'd love to but I can't fire him for bad performance. He's in the high-value category."

"Didn't you tell me he made some bad loans, like the one to Boa Constructors?"

"I could start with that I suppose," Jim, said tentatively. "I wish I could hang something big on him."

"Like what?"

"Well...you know Hank."

"Rumors maybe."

"He does play around."

Irene was not one to damn someone with faint praise. "Screw him," she said, and meant it.

"Speak of the devil," Jim said quickly and hung up.

Hank came into Jim's office, a corner suite with its own bathroom. Hank didn't have either, a corner office or a private toilet. It pissed Hank off that an incompetent like Thorpe was not only his boss but also earned 100K more than he did.

"What's up?" Jim asked.

"I heard some skinny about corporate trimming."

Jim shrugged. "No big deal. Ten percent. A drop in the bucket."

"If you're talking about someone's blood, then it's a big deal. Ten per cent means three in our department."

"And a third." Jim explained the dead man's lottery.

"How do you pick them?"

"Performance."

Riker felt some relief but he remained wary. You couldn't trust a sonofabitch like Thorpe.

He decided to test the waters, try to find out what Thorpe was thinking. "We're doing ok, except for Boa Constructors."

Sensing a chink, Jim said, "I warned you about that."

Riker remained silent.

"You let your friendship with him cloud your vision."

"I don't give a shit for Buddy..."

"Well, that architect friend of yours, that Nazi, Karl Mittelstadt."

Riker stiffened. Thorpe was goading him, trying to get him to say something he might regret, like calling Thorpe an asshole, which is what he was. "Well, it's too late now, the damage is done." Riker made ready to leave. He had to get out of here.

"Another thing," Jim said, maneuvering like a predator going for the jugular. "You need to cut back on pro bono stuff. Not only money but also energy. You're spending too much time on that food bank." Jim waited a few seconds to let it sink in. "Are you still seeing that broad who runs GOD?"

GOD stood for Groceries On Demand, and Hank admittedly was involved, not because he was compassionate about the needy but because he was passionate about Estelle Graham.

Estelle ran GOD, the largest food bank in Minnesota, serving the Twin Cities suburbs of Richfield, Bloomington, Eden Prairie, Apple Valley and Eagan. It may have surprised outsiders but not Estelle that the hungry were not necessarily families who lived in "pockets of poverty" but also those who lived in grand houses on tree-lined streets named Deer Creek Drive and Friendship Lane.

Unfortunately pain had been her sidekick for most of her life. She grew up on a cattle ranch in Montana, riding horses almost before she could walk. Her dad was her hero and when he died in a car accident three days after her ninth birthday, a lot of her died with him. She married early, divorced early and, since that bitter time, lived a life of one-ness--no one entered, no one left. Everyone she worked with knew that her job was her life. And that was the way she wanted it.

Her personality was direct if not confrontational. She had learned that to succeed in the male-dominated corporate world where she always had her hand out for contributions, she had to be tough yet feminine, pushy yet polite. This worked well: it gave her separation--like that of the proscenium arch--between the audience on one side and the actor on the other. This is the way she maintained her business relationships until three months ago when it all began to unravel.

The meeting at R&S bank on Normandale on a promising spring day in May was an unqualified success. The urgency of Estelle's well-rehearsed power-point presentation was not lost on her supportive audience, junior VPs Hank Riker and Hermione Sanders, who made up the bank's Non-profit action group known in headquarters as Npag, agreed not only to increase the bank's annual giving by 4% but also, and more important, sponsor an annual golf tournament, Estelle's proudest achievement.

Hank Riker was a 12 handicapper and readily agreed to host the event, suggesting that the prestigious Olympic Hills Golf Club in West Bloomington, where he was a member, be the tournament's venue. Estelle loved the game, but played infrequently because, with her office demands, spending four-and-a-half-hours on a course was more than she could comfortably manage. Estelle and Hank formed a committee of two to plan the first annual GOD Golf Gala--there would be golf balls, towels and tees imprinted with GGG, a new Camaro for a hole in one, Callaway clubs for the longest drive and ball closest to the pin--all provided by R&S's beneficence.

At first, their planning meetings were held alternately at each other's offices. Then, as they got to know each other and found things in common--not just golf but light opera, the Art Institute and John Sandford mysteries--they began to meet over dinner. Like the frog that doesn't realize it is being boiled to death over a slow fire, Estelle, a single woman who hadn't felt so much as a warm glow in 30 years, was falling in love with a man 7 years her junior, married and the father of twins in high school.

It made her laugh to think about it. How could this be happening to her, the deliberately self-styled epitome of the cold bitch? And what was there about Hank that would make a woman's blood run faster? He wore his belt below his stomach so he could still cinch it at 36 inches, he used a comb-over to disguise thinning hair, he was not even as tall as she.

And what did he see in her, an older woman whose knees hurt from too much running around Lake Harriet, compulsively you might say, to keep calories in check. She had never considered herself pretty, though it was clear she had style and class – always an asset in business. Actually, her figure wasn't bad, and she knew how to set it off with elegant clothes and trendy hair-dos. Anyway, she could keep analyzing the situation forever and still not explain the attraction that grew between them, culminating finally in the front seat of Hank's 450 SEL—a middle-aged couple coupling on Corinthian leather in a bank-leased Mercedes!

"How are we going to get out of this?" she asked when it was over, making an effort to put herself together again.

He thought she was referring to the their cramped positions. "I'll move the seat back."

"No, I mean this...this mess we're in." She held out her hands as if encompassing all that was bad about their tryst.

"You see this as a mess?"

"Don't you?

"I see this as a love affair. Want a cigarette?" he asked kiddingly.

"Like in Now Voyager?" In her mind she pictured Paul Henreid lighting two cigarettes, one for himself and one for Bette Davis. "Be serious, Hank. We have to stop seeing each other."

"How? I'm helping on your golf tournament, remember?"

"Put that woman, what's her name? Hermione in charge. I should have asked her in the first place," Estelle said gloomily.

"Too late for that." Hank thought about Thorpe's pressure on him. He didn't want to let Hermione take over. It would make him look weak. "We have to see it through."

Estelle sighed. "Then no more fooling around."

Hank laughed.

It was obvious he wasn't taking her seriously. If she had relied on her well-honed business instincts rather than her emotions, she would have seen that he was pushing their relationship more than she was. It made her shudder to think that maybe he considered her nothing more than a conquest. She could see him bragging to his golf buddies on the first tee at Olympic Hills, I laid that frigid Graham dame, the one who's running that food bank.

Estelle looked out the side window, fogging it up with her breath. They had parked in a nature preserve off Lake Harriet, down from the canoe racks. Defeated and, to be quite honest, frightened, she wondered if anyone had seen them. His car was very distinctive.

"What if someone finds out?" she asked more to herself than to Hank.

"No one will."

"Don't be so sure." She covered her face with her hands. This disciplined, hard-working, goal-driven corporate woman who ran GOD—GOD of all things!—was an adulteress. If word got out, her career was over.

Karl Mittelstadt was second generation German. When his grandfather, Gunther, emigrated to the United States in 1902 from Bad Ischl, a Bavarian village bordering Austria, there was an umlaut over the a. The immigration official at Ellis Island was a trainee the day Gunther saw the Statue of Liberty for the first time and mistook the two dots as ink stains and so, when he copied Gunther's name onto the entry form, he left them out. With his fragmentary English, Gunther tried to explain how deleting the umlaut completely altered the pronunciation of a family name going back six generations. But he was in a new country, starting a new life, and maybe it was better, after all, to have a new name, too.

Karl enjoyed hearing this story over and over again growing up on the farm in Stillwater, milking cows, tossing hay, and rendering lard for baking. When his grandfather died at 91, he mourned the most. His older brother, Eckert, took over the family farm, allowing Karl to pursue his dream of becoming an architect. He went to the University of Minnesota and was mentored by Ralph Rapson, head of the department. Karl graduated from the U at a time when Urban Renewal was the new wave--scrap the old, even if the old was turn of the century, and erect cityscapes of gleaming glass walls. Karl, however, had never designed any of these award-winning structures. Marriage and children interfered with launching a high-end career and, instead of joining Skidmore, Owings and

Merrill to design award-winning structures, he started his own business and grabbed any commissions he could find.

A family room expansion the contractor Buddy Boynton had done in Linden Hills, Karl's neighborhood, caught the architect's attention. It was the best job of fit-and-finish construction he had ever seen. He gave Buddy a call and, as the saying goes, the rest is history. Business was good and their two firms expanded together--adding personnel, picking up new clients of the newly rich. The success bred overconfidence bordering on recklessness when they got a hefty line of credit from R&S Bank to build big houses on spec.

When business began to turn sour, Karl called Hank Riker, a VP at R&S Bank. They met for early breakfast at Zumbro's on 43rd and Upton, not far from Karl's house, in a neighborhood shopping district that was a popular destination for the swells who drove their Land Rovers in from Eden Prairie.

Riker, a banker with a lot of sharp edges, was the person whose family room addition first connected Karl to Buddy. Riker introduced the architect and the builder to Jim Thorpe, Riker's boss, for the loans that kept the business going--borrow, build, sell, pay off. This worked as long as the spec house sold before the paint dried. (The BMW dealer where Karl leased his 1 Series once told him that the best time to sell a trade-in is while the engine is still warm.)

On their second cup of coffee, Hank said to Karl, "Something is going on at R&S. The state managers met last week and Thorpe has been on a tear ever since. He's really riding my ass."

"What about?" asked Karl.

"I'm under pressure to close down some accounts..."

Karl shifted nervously. He had a bad feeling of what was coming next.

"If I don't swing the axe, my job is on the line," Riker said.

"How do you know that?"

"I know that Thorpe is looking for a reason to get rid of me, and the only way he can do that is to downgrade my performance. I have to cut the dead wood, as he calls it, in my sector, and he mentioned Boa Constructors by name. The bastard singled out Boa because you and Buddy are friends of mine. I brought your account to R&S, remember? He's trying to squeeze me."

Now Karl was genuinely worried. His firm, Mittelstadt and Associates had, over the years, intertwined expenses with Boa Constructors--transferring funds from Karl to float Buddy and Buddy to float Karl, mostly the former. Only last month Middelstadt and Associates had given Boa Constructors a hundred thousand dollars on a promissory note, pending the sale of the two houses under construction

"I have to call in your loan," Riker said. "A million and a quarter."

"The houses we have on-stream are worth twice that. The loan is secure."

"Not in today's market."

Karl sighed. "Give us some time..."

"Time is what I ain't got. Thorpe said the end of the month. If I don't get the money it becomes a negative balance and my job is, if you don't mind my German, kaput."

Karl shook his head. There wasn't a chance in hell to raise that kind of money in three and a half weeks.

When the CSI team showed up at Lake Harriet with their black cases, white plastic gloves and yellow tape, it was time for Meredith to go home, shower and plan his day which wasn't much, nine holes at Rice Creek with his brother Tad and dinner with his current squeeze, Vicki. That was pretty much standard fare on his days off. There was excitement enough on the job; no way, or reason, to replicate the rush you get on a run in his personal life. When he first started as a fireman more than 25 years ago, he was fighting mostly fires. Now most of the runs were gunshots, car accidents, drownings, domestic violence.

And fires? Not more than a third.

He'd saved a few lives for which he was proud but as a fireman you don't get a medal for saving a life. You get a paycheck. Toweling off from the shower he checked himself in the mirror. Not as trim as he used to be but he could still pull a hose off the truck with the youngest of them.

He was on the sixth hole pondering a chip shot to the green when his phone rang.

Tad, younger, taller, thinner and with more hair than Meredith, shouted at him, "Shit, can't you just shut that thing off?"

Meredith gave his brother a hush sign as if signaling that he was a first responder and he had to have his phone on all the time, which was essentially true. He answered. It was Ben. Meredith walked away from the green a few steps. "What's up?"

"It's blood all right," Ben said. "O positive, kinda rare, and not very old, about four hours."

"Not Heinz 57," he said.

"You got it."

"Talked to the widow?"

"Widow?"

"Buddy Boynton's wife."

"How the fuck can you say she's a widow? We don't have a body. I'm glad you are not a cop."

"Are you going to drag?"

"Too much to cover. Sonar. But we still have to get Boynton's wife to declare a missing person."

"Have you talked to her?"

"We have but she isn't cooperating. We'd like to get a sample of her husband's DNA to see if there is a match with the blood but we can't without her approval."

"Wonder why."

"Complicity maybe?"

"Think so?"

"You're the one who's calling her a widow."

"Mind if I talk to her?"

Ben hesitated. "What for?"

"Just an idea."

"Merrie, let me give you some advice..."

"Ben," Meredith interrupted, "how long have we known each other?"

"What's that got to do with anything?"

"Answer my question."

Ben thought back to the day the Northwest Bank branch on Chicago and 36th was held up. He was a patrol cop with the Minneapolis force then. It was February and bitter cold. Two men were holding hostages inside and Ben, along with a dozen other cops, was crouching behind the open door of a squad car, pointing his .38 police special at the front entrance when a hook and ladder rolled up, siren blasting, and parked around the corner out of sight of the front windows and entrance. Several firemen jumped down, carrying so much gear Ben wondered how they could walk. They set up a ladder, lifted it over the roof of the bank, and one of them ran up the ladder, ran, not climbed, and disappeared behind the brick parapet. Ben wondered what the hell this nut was doing. Minutes passed and suddenly the front door opened and this fireman came out arm-locking the two hold-up men, teenagers as it turned out, one 15 and the other 17, their arms lifted high behind their backs. Their feet were nearly off the ground and their faces frozen not by subzero temps but by pain. The fireman had come down the fire escape, through the back door and surprised the kids looking the wrong way. The fireman, Meredith S. Gilbert, got a commendation.

"Nineteen years," Ben answered. "We met on February 14, Valentine's Day."

"And you never sent me a card."

"Don't get cute with me. What's your point?"

"That you've known me long enough to know that I don't take advice."

"All right," Ben said, resignation in his voice. "If you contact her you do it as a private citizen. Got that?"

Meredith finished his golf round with a 45. Not bad considering he triple bogeyed one of the par threes. He waved goodbye to Tad in the parking lot and got into the Caddie. He waited until Tad drove off and then called Boynton's number stored in his phone's memory. Mrs. Boynton answered before the first ring was finished, like she was parked by the telephone.

"This is Meredith Gilbert calling back."

"Who?"

"The fireman who called you this morning."

"Oh," she said. "Do you have any news of Buddy?"

"No, do you?" he said, pretending not to know anything.

"I heard from the police."

"What did they say?"

He could sense she was holding back tears. "I don't

21

know if I should tell you but they found blood in the canoe."

"Oh my God…"

"Mind if I come over?" He had decided to be abrupt, presumptuous, let her assume he was a take-charge guy and that this was what Mrs. Boynton needed, someone to take charge. "Maybe I can help you sort things out. Just talk, you know what I mean?"

"I don't know…"

"I found the canoe, remember?"

"Like you have a vested interest?"

"Something like that."

She gave him her address.

Buddy Boynton lived on Browndale in a new house in an old neighborhood, the Country Club district of Edina, developed in the 1930s when upscale houses were clad in stone. The original house had to be a scrape, razed to make room for this 21st century modern. The exterior was stucco with windows flush to the wall, no framing, no drip caps, no sills. Even though Meredith was a fireman he got a crackerjack education at St. John's in Collegeville, where the Benedictines beat an education into him. He loved the humanities, and learned all he could about the 20th century including the Bauhaus School. This is the kind of house Corbusier might have designed, or Mies Van der Rohe or Marcel Breuer. Meredith guessed it was no more than five years old while its neighbors were eighty. It had to cost a bundle.

The lawns on the block, like all the lawns in the Country Club, blended as one, connecting expanses of perfectly trimmed Bermuda grass growing in the same direction. The ribbons of sidewalk were immaculately edged. As Meredith cut across the lawn from the angle where he had parked his car, he wondered if he should take his shoes off.

She must have seen him coming because the door opened as he approached the flagstone front steps. She held back the screen and he entered a cool interior. Was it the air conditioning or was it her?

He extended his hand. She accepted it, her slender fingers lacing around his knuckles. They remained connected like this as each took the measure of the other. Behind the frown of concern he saw a very attractive woman in her late forties, maybe fifty, her brown eyes quizzical, frank and honest. Her hair was parted down the middle, no bangs and of a color like the wood of a freshly debarked tree.

She dropped his hand and stepped back, and now Meredith was able to take her all in. She was slender, above average height, a bit on the boney side, more like a model than a housewife, but it was hard to get a true sense of her figure because she was wearing a baggy shirt and pants right out of Vogue. Designer flip-flops revealed long slender toes. One of them had a gold ring on it.

"So you are a fireman."

Meredith nodded.

"You like rescuing people?"

"If they need rescuing."

She was clearly distracted. "I'm not a good host. Can I get you something? A beer? I don't know what you like. A Coke?"

"Nothing thank you."

She offered an Eames chair. He recognized it. "Great design."

"You know Eames?"

"A little." He didn't sit, just looked around, checking the furniture, the art on the wall. There was a Maxfield Parrish, a print or the real thing? "I like your house. Who designed it?"

"Karl Mittelstadt. He works with my husband. Ever heard of him?"

Meredith shook his head. "Mind if I look around?" He started moving, looking into the sunroom and then the living room, stopping at the mantel over the stone fireplace. "That your husband?" he asked pointing to a family photo. Good looking guy if you like them tall and broad shouldered. After she nodded he checked the dining room and kitchen. He expected her to protest but she just followed him like a realtor showing a house for sale. "What kind of cabinets? Hickory?"

She seemed impressed with his knowledge. "The cabinet maker said he'd never use hickory again, too hard on the blades."

He ventured into the front hall where an open staircase led to the second floor. This time he really thought she would stop him but all she said, as if in apology, was, "The cleaning woman doesn't come until Friday."

He guessed she was proud of her house and liked showing if off. She followed him upstairs and into the master bedroom, a large expanse of bamboo flooring and a Persian rug the size of Rhode Island. Beyond was the bathroom.

"Beautiful," he said.

"Thank you."

After a pause, he added, "I totally forgot to stop at the golf course..." and looked across to the bathroom.

"Oh, please, use ours. I'll wait downstairs."

He didn't think it would be this easy. In fact, he had given himself a fifty-fifty chance. He locked the door and did his business while taking in what a hundred thousand dollars can do for a shitter. After zipping up, he looked in the drawers of the vanity and found a Braun shaver sitting in its cleansing tray. Next to it was a hairbrush with gray strands of hair trapped in the bristles. Not hers, he noted, as he pulled the strands free and wrapped them in a piece of toilet paper.

Back downstairs he found her in the living room standing by the Eames. She looked good next to it, like a fashion model in an advertisement.

"Do you have children?" he asked.

She nodded. "A son. He's in Nicaragua."

When Meredith raised his eyebrows she said, "He's

in the American Field Service community program, teaching English in a school in Managua."

"Have you called him?"

"Not yet. I don't want to worry him."

"He should know."

"I thought I'd wait a little longer. I don't want to worry him, he's so far away. Maybe Buddy will call." She seemed to be grasping at straws.

"I wouldn't wait too long. Maybe you should have your son come home in case..."

"In case what?"

He didn't have to finish the sentence. She knew what he meant.

"Look, Mrs. Boynton."

"Please...Chloe. No one has called me that since my PTA days." She permitted herself a small smile.

"All right, Chloe. But I'm sure you'd want your son by your side if you get any bad news."

5

Ben was really pissed when Merrie dropped by Park Police headquarters on King's Highway and 40th and gave him the wad of toilet paper with Buddy's gray locks trapped inside. He grabbed Meredith by the elbow and led him into the hallway, away from attentive ears.

"What in hell were you thinking?" he asked, each word separated by a hyphen of emphasis. Ben's eyes, normally hazel, had darkened to a depthless green. "This amounts to breaking and entering."

"She welcomed me into her house."

"Bullshit! You took something that doesn't belong to you, that she doesn't know about. You are looking at one to five, probably five since you ought to know better."

"You wouldn't turn me in."

"I'm sorely thinking about it." Ben looked at the wad of paper in his hand, turning it over and over. "I have to throw this away."

"After all the work I went to get it?"

"I go by the book, you don't."

"Just trying to move things along."

Ben had to smile at Merrie's brazenness. "How in hell did you get all the way to her bathroom?"

"Charm." He nudged Ben's arm. "Don't you want to know for sure if the blood belongs to Buddy?"

"Of course I do."

"So why don't you just turn it over to the lab. Those brainiacs in white coats don't give a damn where the evidence comes from; they just want to solve the crime."

"Let me think about it."

6

Dinner with Vicki was listless. The flame of their relationship had dimmed long ago. Now they were simply going through the paces. They went to fancy restaurants as though this alone would be enough to reignite passion. Tonight, their first date in a week, they were at Maude's on 65th and Penn. Even the candle on their table was sputtering.

"What have you been up to?" Vicki asked

"Not much," Meredith said, upset that this meal was setting him back seventy bucks. "Golf with Tad."

If he told her that he had also insinuated himself into the home of a beautiful woman, even seeing her bedroom and using her toilet—talk about tearing the rag off the bush. He couldn't even tell her about finding the canoe because that would eventually lead to Chloe; and Vicki, he had learned quickly, was a jealous woman. Jesus, Meredith thought, why do I get into these messes? Sooner or later Vicki would learn from someone else anyway, bits and pieces of conversations she would put together like a jigsaw puzzle and assume the worst, learning it from Ben or Ben's wife, Anne, in a casual conversation on a double-date, or even from Al at the station who was probably looking for a way to get even with Meredith for siphoning the gas out of his new Corolla.

Merrie looked at Vicki across the flickering candlelight. Her face was like cardboard, one-dimensional and flat. This did not mean she was not pretty, but comparing her to Chloe was like comparing Three-Buck Chuck to Cheval Blanc. He knew the moment he saw Chloe that she was high-born: White Bear Lake, he guessed, St. Paul noblesse oblige, not Minneapolis nouveau riche.

Since leaving her house he could not get her out of his mind. He couldn't believe that he was obsessing over a married woman with a kid out of college. Maybe it was because she was so untouchable that he found her attractive. In contrast, Vicki had been an easy catch, too easy, and maybe that's what rubbed Meredith against the grain.

They had met at Bunny's, Vicki having just moved back to Minneapolis from Las Vegas to take care of her aging mother. She was Events Coordinator for the Wedding Chapel of the Fountain at Circus Circus, and observed too many unions that did not bode well for long-term commitment – perhaps contributing to her own history of failed marriages, the last one to the night manager of Circus Circus, which lasted less time than it takes to lose a wad on the pass line.

She was toughly independent, at least she appeared that way to Meredith when they first began dating—and, mistakenly as it turned out, he was attracted to her precisely because he could not abide the clinging type. He needed to protect his free spirit, come and go when he felt like it, and be around when it suited him, not her.

Familiarity replaced mystery in a matter of weeks. At this point, Vicki and he were no different from a married couple trying to find something interesting to say. "What have you been up to?" was the high point of their conversation.

Vicki attempted to revive their moribund evening. "So how was your game?"

"What?"

"Your golf game. Did you beat Tad?"

"Oh," Meredith said, returning to the present, the boring present. "No one beats Tad."

"You always say that."

"He's my kid brother," he said as if that explained everything.

Tad had made it big in men's sports gear, starting with one store he called Ski-Six after Skeezix, the main character in the old comic strip Gasoline Alley, and now owned several exclusive shops in suburban malls.

Vicki set her fork on her plate. She wasn't eating much anyway, just pawing at the expensive roast duckling.

"You feel one down with Tad."

Meredith sensed that Vicki was seeding an argument. "That's crap."

"You have a better education."

"Tad dropped out of school to keep up his car payments, selling quilted jackets at Hoigaard's. He just worked his way up the ladder." As soon as he said that he could have bitten his tongue.

"Ladder?"

"Ok, so I'm a fireman."

"I didn't mean it that way, Merrie. What I wanted to say was that your brother knows what to do with his life."

"And I don't?"

"You are fifty-five years old and you still rent an apartment."

He knew what she was driving at. She lived in her mother's house in Hopkins, a mother who was failing fast and would probably die in a matter of months. All he had to do was move in with Vicki after a reasonable interval and his fate was sealed.

"I like to travel light."

Meredith watched her as she thoughtfully played with a strand of hair, twisting and untwisting it. Vicki was just the other side of 40, but her dark hair made her look older somehow. He was trying to think of a word that fit and it came to him: matronly.

Fortunately his phone vibrated. He checked the name. It was Ben.

"Vicki, I have to take this call." He got up and walked into the restaurant's foyer. It was empty.

"Well," Ben said, "you were right."

Meredith felt his chest swell. He didn't get much praise from Ben.

"The DNA of the blood and the hair match. It's Boynton all right."

"So he's dead."

"We don't know that."

"What's next?"

"We look for a body."

"I want to be in on that."

"Ok, tomorrow morning at six at the Lake Harriet boat landing. Wear your uniform."

7

Meredith fumed that Ben had patronizingly ordered him to wear his uniform. Ben was like that, bossy, even supercilious at times. What did he expect, that Merrie would show up in shorts and an aloha shirt? One would think that Ben ought to show more respect, if not for Meredith, at least for the two bars he wore on his shirt collar. He was a captain after all and Ben was a lieutenant. But, and it galled Meredith to admit this, a fireman's rank was not as prestigious as that of a cop. Cops copied military protocol--standing for inspections, saluting, drilling--they liked to show off. Firemen were grunts and it did little to point out that policemen and firemen both worked for the City of Minneapolis, belonged to the same pension fund, and had identical death benefits.

Meredith would be on his 24-hour shift anyway, and so he didn't have to be reminded to wear his uniform. He'd have it on. And, if the truth be told, he looked pretty damned good in it, solid black shirt and pants. The only relief were the twin silver bars on his collar and the silver fireman's badge on his shirt pocket.

He got up before five and arrived at Station 28 on the corner of 50th and Upton at 5:30. He always took the same route from Meadowbrook Manor, his apartment complex in St. Louis Park: following Excelsior Boulevard to West Calhoun Parkway, around the lakeshore to Upton which took him to 50th. The faster way was Highway 100 but he would miss the serenity that Minneapolis's chain of lake's offers while driving to a thankless job.

The firehouse was less than ten years old, disguised

as a doctor's clinic or a business office so as not to offend the neighboring bungalows. A single story of orange brick with a shingled roof and curtains in the windows. The only giveaway of its true identity was the double garage door in front and an aluminum pole with the American flag fluttering aloft. Missing was the architectural element that once identified all fire stations: the hose-drying tower that most people mistook for a belfry. Newer firehouses like this one had deep pits where wet hoses were hung to dry so they wouldn't kink and become impossible to fold up.

Merrie checked in with Al and told him he was heading for Lake Harriet. He got into a specially modified Suburban, shiny and red, with an Inspector's medallion on the door to separate it from the one the Chief drove. The Suburban was used not only for fire inspections and arson investigations, but also grocery shopping for the meals prepared in the kitchen downstairs. It was parked next to the pumper used primarily for rescue, not a hook and ladder, because No. 28 was a substation, not large enough for a big rig.

The drive to Lake Harriet took all of five minutes. He parked in a no-parking zone not because he could, but because he wanted to show Ben that he too was a man of authority. He scanned the scene at the boat landing. Ben was standing by as a water-patrol boat was being off-loaded from its trailer by two deputies. It had yellow markings signifying that it belonged to the Hennepin County Sheriff's Department. The boat was packed with rescue gear. The deputies climbed aboard, one in swim trunks, the other in uniform with a bright-orange life jacket, who manned the four-stroke Evinrude suspended over the stern. The guy in trunks who looked like he could clean and jerk 200 pounds, began methodically to dress himself in scuba gear: fins, mask, goggles, tank. He was in no hurry. There was no one to save, only a body to find.

Meredith was not a stranger to water rescue. He had seen enough drowning victims to last three lifetimes. Only rarely did he make it soon enough to resuscitate. Most were swimmers who literally got in over their heads--found either floating face down or lying on the bottom with eyes open but seeing nothing.

It was quiet, peaceful until the Evinrude came to life, spewing a wake as it moved away from shore. Meredith walked over to Ben.

"What's the drill?" he asked

"They're using side-scanning sonar, moving in an expanding grid from the canoe racks over to the bandstand."

"Where Boynton's canoe ended up."

Ben nodded. "This is not rocket science, you know. They've also got a fish locater and a drag line." After a moment's reflection he added, "I hope this is not a wild goose chase. The Director was not pleased to bring the Sheriff in on this. The cost comes out of our budget."

"They've got the equipment."

Ben nodded in agreement. "I'm giving them three hours at 500 per and if they don't find anything we hang it up."

Meredith's mind went into high gear. "Ok, if they don't find him, we've got two possibles: the muskies are having a feast or he's alive and hiding somewhere."

Ben looked over at Meredith. "This becomes a cold case if we don't find a body. I'm not using more man-hours looking for a live one."

"I can."

"You can what?"

"Look for Boynton."

Ben shook his head. "I wish I had your schedule. You've got too much time on your hands."

Ben was right. Meredith worked 24-on, 24-off, 24-on, and then a three-day break, not even adding in all the vacation days he had accumulated. He needed a hobby: find Buddy Boynton.

"Are you going to see that Boynton woman?" Ben asked.

"Right after this is over. I have to do some

explaining to Chloe if we don't find him."

Ben looked fully at Meredith as though a light bulb lit up over his head. "So it's Chloe now, is it, not Mrs. Boynton? You want to cozy up to her, right? And you can get even cozier helping her look for her old man. Am I onto something?"

"I won't involve you."

"You better not. I know you don't like taking my advice but I'll keep trying. This dame is way over your head, Merrie. Have you done background on her?"

"Just her house."

That elicited a smile from Ben. "She comes from money, I mean really big money. Her father helped launch Control Data. She can hire a whole detective agency to find her husband. She doesn't need you."

Meredith thought to himself: Let Chloe decide.

Conversation stalled as they turned their attention back to the boat moving slowly across the water, the Evinrude puttering in trolling mode. An hour went by. The sun now came fully over the lake. It was going to be a warm day. There were more in-line roller skaters than joggers on the asphalt path now--lithe young women drawing attention in tight shorts and tops--some of them slowing briefly to check out the rescue boat on the lake.

Ben was ready to give up after two hours, save the department some money, when the diver leaned over backwards and splashed into the water, leaving a trail of bubbles as he went under. Minutes passed. Tension mounted. Ben and Meredith walked down to the water's edge peering intently at the boat two hundred yards out.

Presently the diver broke the surface. He had something, all right. A body. The deputy in the boat helped the diver pull the lifeless form over the gunwale. He lay it across a sheet of canvas and covered it, and then helped the diver into the boat. The diver stripped off his scuba gear as the Evinrude started up again and the boat returned to shore.

Subdued excitement filled the air. Onlookers began to gather and Ben told them to move on, this was police business. The sheriff's deputies beached the boat and the four men formed a perimeter to keep the curious away. Ben lifted the canvas. The body was bloated but certainly recognizable. It was clothed in a business suit and tie, waterlogged shoes looking more Salvatore Ferragamo than Thom McAn.

Ben had posted a newspaper photo of Buddy Boynton on the bulletin board back at police headquarters. He looked hard at the body lying on the canvas. This was not Buddy Boynton.

8

First shock, then puzzlement. Who the hell is this guy? They decided to make only a visual inspection until the coroner arrived, which was the first thing Ben did after uncovering the body: call in for assistance. He had decided earlier not to order a meat wagon unless they found a body. No sense wasting the County's time and straining the Park Board budget even further by keeping the coroner sitting around. But now he was needed.

The victim looked to be in his forties, of average height. Meredith was used to seeing the dead, most of the time breathing their last from a terrible auto accident or from a bullet, seldom a corpse this far removed from life. It disconcerted him, looking down at a spongy bag of eyes swollen shut, lids distended, hair matted. This was a cruel mockery of a human being. He turned away.

"Take a look at that," Ben said, pointing to the man's head.

"Where?" Meredith asked, forcing himself to pay attention.

"Behind his ear, look closer. That's a wound, like he was hit with something."

Merrie bent down. There appeared to be a puffy bruise behind the ear.

The four men exchanged glances. Was this guy hit on the head and dumped into the lake? But the body was found 200 yards out--he wasn't going to float that far on his own. Had to be taken out to deep water and dumped overboard. In what? A boat? Not likely. Boats were allowed on Lake Harriet but they had to be trailered in and out. No one trying to get rid of a body was going to launch a boat and then haul it away again. The only craft allowed permanently on Lake Harriet were canoes and sailboats. Sailboats were tied to buoys along the west shore of the lake, a quarter mile away, and who was going to paddle a dinghy to a boat, hoist sail, and then dump a body?

Merrie responded to his mental question by a shake of the head. That left a canoe—at least 30 of them were secured along a rack right next to the boat landing. That's where Buddy Boynton stored his.

"The empty canoe," Meredith said, extending his line of thought out loud.

"What?" Ben asked.

"Boynton's canoe and this dead guy. Is there a connection?"

Ben motioned Meredith to walk over to his Park Police vehicle, not a squad car but a white Jeep with black police markings and a light rack bolted to its top. On the way, Meredith looked back at the two deputies guarding the body. The diver had thrown a towel over his shoulders.

"I don't want to discuss this in front of the deputies," Ben said, leaning against the fender.

"Ok, so we come out here to look for Boynton but find someone else instead. Coincidence? I don't think so."

Ben made an imaginary line on the asphalt with his toe. "I don't think so either. And that means Boynton is not just a missing person, he is also a person of interest."

"So you figure the dead man was murdered?"

Ben nodded, deep in thought.

This is what Meredith liked: trying out scenarios and seeing where they led.

"For the sake of argument let's put Buddy and this guy in the canoe together, ok? Suppose there is a fight, Buddy is cut and bleeds on the canoe, that's where the stain comes from. But he hits the other guy with the paddle who falls overboard and drowns. Panicked, Buddy paddles back to shore, jumps out and the canoe drifts off."

Ben shook his head. "Doesn't make much sense.

This guy looks like he just left the office. What's he doing in a canoe fighting Buddy in the middle of the night? Seems to me he was killed elsewhere, and brought here to get rid of the body."

"Maybe there was someone else."

"A third party?"

"Yeah. The dead guy is dressed for work. He's attacked in his office, brought to the lake where Buddy is waiting with the canoe. He paddles out to dump the body."

"What about the blood stain?"

Meredith thought about that for awhile. "Maybe it was self-inflicted," he said. "Like he was trying to divert suspicion."

"We'll know a lot more once the vic is identified and we find out how he died," Ben said.

The coroner arrived with an assistant in what looked like a hearse, but not before a Channel 4 news truck pulled up with a crew that took camera footage from a discrete distance. One of the passing joggers must have called in the news alert. Meanwhile the body was lifted, canvas and all, onto a rolling gurney and folded into the back of the vehicle. The two got in and drove away without so much as a nod.

"I guess that's what you get working with dead bodies all the time," Meredith said, "indifference."

In the meantime the deputies secured their boat onto its trailer and they, too, drove off, leaving Meredith and Ben alone, not enough of an attraction to keep the knot of onlookers from disbursing.

"I'll call as soon as I get the coroner's report." As Ben began walking to his Jeep he stopped and turned. "Merrie, in all seriousness, don't contact that Boynton woman."

"I had the distinct impression you didn't care if I did. When I told you I wouldn't mind looking for Boynton, all you said was that you wished you had my hours."

"Remember, I said, if we don't find a body."

"The body is not Boynton's. He's out in the world somewhere."

Ben could feel Meredith's frustration. "Look, Merrie, it's time you back off and let me handle this. If he's out in the world somewhere we'll find him. For all we know, he might be dead too."

9

Meredith's 24-hour shift had a dinner run: a condo building on 54th and Lyndale, across from Barton Volvo. An idiot had left a lit Weber kettle grill on the wood balcony of a one-bedroom, two floors up. The heat of the metal started the floor smoldering and actually burned a hole into the soft cedar before the crew arrived. They had it out in minutes and the only argument was, who did more damage, the idiot who forgot the grill or the fireman who broke a window, letting a fair amount of water into the living room.

Meredith didn't give a shit; he was really getting fed up with this life of saving people from their own stupidity. The run interrupted a firehouse dinner of pork chops, stewed tomatoes, mashed potatoes, Schilling's gravy, and homemade apple pie ala mode. When they got back everything was at room temperature including the ice cream.

Station 28 was well-equipped for comfort: four bedrooms and two bathrooms downstairs in addition to the kitchen, a dining room, and an open area with a sofa, two easy chairs, a 52-inch VIZIO flat screen on one side and a carpentry workshop on the other. There was even a lathe, and one of the drivers, Eddy Compton, was turning spindles on it for a crib he was making for his new granddaughter. Firemen had so much time on their hands they needed projects to keep them occupied.

Meredith retired to his room early, hoping he could sleep through the night, and found a text on his cell phone.

It was from Ben. "Call me at home."

Good, Meredith thought, maybe he has news about the stiff they found this morning.

"What have you got?" he asked when Ben answered.

"Trouble."

Meredith tensed but didn't want Ben to sense it. "Trouble is my middle name."

"It's your first and last name, too, as far as I'm concerned," Ben shot back. "Director Hamilton questioned me about the hair samples we used to match Boynton's blood."

"Oh."

"The evidence was illegally obtained, so we have to go back to square one. I really should have known better. Why the hell do I listen to you?"

"Look, Ben..."

"Don't look-Ben me! I could have been suspended. Now I've got to get a warrant, go see that broad you think is so hot, and get a fresh sample of her husband. Then forensics has to start all over again to test for DNA. Do you know how much this is going to cost?"

"If you hadn't already done the DNA we never would have looked for a body. Did you tell Hamilton that?"

"That's the only thing saving my ass. But the DNA we got would never be admissible in court. Any judge would throw it out."

"Why would it have to go that far?"

"You never know, especially with a likely murder and a missing suspect. That's why we have to redo it. Just in case."

"Have you heard from the coroner?"

"Yeah," Ben said, as if this were the furthest thing from his mind. "The dead guy's name is James C. Thorpe, a senior VP at a bank called R&S out in West Bloomington. He lives, or lived, in Minnetrista"

"Did he drown?"

"He was dead before he hit the water. Two solid blows to the head, one behind the left ear, one in back. Either one could have killed him. But here's the interesting thing: he's been in the water several days. So I went through the APB records and sure enough I found that his wife had reported him missing a week ago Tuesday."

Meredith thought back. "That was when I found the canoe."

"Right. Boynton and Thorpe went AWOL at the same time. And get this: Thorpe's wife reported him missing the next morning, while Boynton's wife is still keeping mum. What do you make of that?"

Merrie didn't want to make anything of it. "How come you didn't know that Thorpe's wife reported him missing until now?" he said, implying not too subtly that Ben had dropped the ball.

"I told you Thorpe's from Minnetrista. Who the hell knows what goes on in a township 20 miles away unless you check the reports, which is what I did two hours ago." Ben was getting defensive. "The big question, Merrie, is not why I didn't know about Thorpe, the big question is what is this Boynton woman trying to hide? Why didn't she file a missing persons like Thorpe's wife did?"

"Maybe she doesn't want the publicity. You said she comes from a rich family. People like that want to stay out of the limelight."

"Well, she's going to be in it whether she likes it or not."

10

The next morning, his shift over, Meredith left the station in his Caddie, retracing the route of pleasant residential streets he had used 24 hours earlier when life seemed much less complicated. He turned left on Excelsior Boulevard, busying up with morning traffic, and headed west on the four-lane thoroughfare, not wanting to drive as fast as the traffic. Everyone passing him was anxious to get to work. Merrie was merely anxious. He drove by the Minnekhada Golf Course and could see early morning dew on the greens behind the chain link fence. Excelsior Boulevard bisected this elegant private course, one of the oldest in the city--nine holes on one side, nine on the other. When it was laid out a hundred years ago, this was country. A golf perk for Meredith, as well as all Minneapolis firemen, was a free round on the first Monday of each summer month, June, July and August, courtesy of the Pillsburys, Heffelfingers and Crosbys who ran the Club's Board.

Meredith did not look forward to his three days off. A steady 24-on, 24-off, if there were such a schedule, would suit him much better. Being at work made his heart beat faster--runs to make, guys to share danger with and play tricks on, but three days off gave him too much time on his hands, too much time to think about where his civilian life was heading, which appeared to be nowhere. Golf with Tad and dinner with Vicki, was that all there was?

Sure, there were other things like wash the car and run errands.

As he peered through the windshield of his ancient Cad, pitted and worn like himself, Meredith had a moment of insight. He realized he was depressed. How else can he explain the fact that he didn't bother to jog this morning, or that he didn't want to go home either and spend seemingly endless hours in a two-bedroom flat, in a vintage World War II building whose brick badly needed tuck-pointing.

He parked in the lot, not in the basement garage available for a hundred bucks more a month, and walked across the lot to the back door. No elevators, hell who needed them, it was only a two-story building. The handicapped lived on floor one with their ramps and wide doors. He liked it better on two.

He stripped down and showered. He could have done this at work but he liked the privacy, not only to shower but also to use the toilet. Someone was always leaving the seat up at the station and Meredith liked to urinate sitting down--Christ, he thought, just like a woman--and more than once he didn't pay attention, sat down with the seat up, and dangled in water.

At least he could still laugh at himself.

He was on his balcony in shorts and a collared t-shirt staring glumly at the traffic on Excelsior Boulevard, killing time until his golf date with Tad, when the call came. His cell phone told him it was 12:49 pm, a blocked number that he was going to let go, probably a solicitation for the Fireman's Fund, when he changed his mind, he didn't know why, instinct perhaps, a notion that maybe this was a call not to miss, and so he answered: "Meredith Gilbert."

There was a momentary hesitation, hardly more than a second. "This is Chloe Boynton."

The unexpected sound of her voice suddenly exhilarated him, lifting him out of his doldrums like a glider hitting an updraft.

"I hope I'm not bothering you."

"Not bothering me at all."

"Your number is still in my phone's call log. Are you at work? I mean, can you talk now or should I call back later."

He wasn't going to tell her he was on his balcony killing time, waiting to head for the golf course. "No, no," he said quickly. "My day off."

"I had the Noontime News on. There was a report of a body found in Lake Harriet."

Ben had warned him not to get in touch with her but she had initiated the call, so why not talk to her, as long as he wasn't too specific? Besides, finding the body was in the news—it was public knowledge.

"I thought you might know what happened," she said

"Really? Why so?"

"I saw you on TV by the rescue boat with three other men."

Shit, he thought, that damned cameraman from Channel 4. "The police have that information. I'll give you the person and the number to call."

"I'd rather not involve the police. Can't you tell me?"

"Tell you what?"

"I'm worried about Buddy. You saw his picture at my house, remember? You would know if it was him or not. Was that Buddy under the canvas?"

A simple answer would rest her mind. How could Ben object to that?

"The police always notify the next of kin," he said. "And if they still haven't contacted you..."

She jumped in before he was finished, which is what he was hoping would happen. "Then it wasn't Buddy!" She had answered her own question.

Relief spread like an aura that enveloped Meredith as well, but the relief was short-lived. "If it wasn't Buddy, then who was it?" He had opened the door a crack and now she was pushing on it.

"Ask the cops."

"I told you..."

"Look, Chloe, I've said more than I should have."

"Have you forgotten the day you came to my house? You said you'd help me sort things out, remember? Those were your exact words."

"What do you want me to tell you?"

"Buddy's disappearance and now a body...it doesn't make sense. Not Lake Harriet, in the middle of Minneapolis. What's going on? Is there a connection between Buddy and that person who drowned?"

When he didn't answer right away she added, "Please, Meredith."

This was the first time she had used his name. It made him feel as if he really mattered to her, not as a fireman but as a trusted friend. He turned around and leaned against the balcony railing, his back to the traffic hum. He saw his reflection in the glass of the sliding door, and stared as if he were having a discussion with himself. Meredith the Fireman would maintain professional distance, but Meredith the newly Trusted Friend--who was hanging onto Chloe's every word, savoring the nuance of her voice, imagining the tilt of her head as she talked, this Meredith would weaken.

"He didn't drown."

"Who?" She seemed confused by his answer.

"The man in the water. He didn't drown. He was hit on the head and dumped into the lake, presumably on the night Buddy disappeared."

"Do you know who it was?" He sensed a vulnerable, frightened woman.

"Someone named James Thorpe..."

"Jim Thorpe?"

"You know him?" Meredith asked, not as surprised as he probably should have been.

"Not well," Chloe said, almost too quickly. "He's my husband's banker. Buddy pretty much kept his business life separate from his private one." There was a vacuum where nothing was said. Finally, Chloe asked.

"Was he murdered?"

"Looks that way."

"Do the police think Buddy had anything to do with this?" she asked.

"It can't be pure coincidence, Chloe. The police figure Thorpe was dumped into the water the same night that Buddy disappeared. Add that to his empty canoe and his blood..." He stopped himself but not in time.

"Blood? What blood?"

Meredith had never done a half-gainer with a full twist into a pool, but now he knew what it must feel like. "There was a bloodstain on the canoe," he said. "It belongs to your husband."

"How do you know that?"

"DNA."

"DNA?" she repeated. "They'd need something of Buddy's..." her words trailed off. "Is that what you were doing in my bathroom?"

"Yes," he admitted.

"I trusted you!" It was a shout of anguish. "And all the time you pretended you liked my house."

"I do like your house. But, Chloe, listen to me, this would have come out anyway. The police want a new DNA sample because what I got from your husband's hairbrush was taken without consent, and they have to do it over again. This time it will be official, but the results will be the same. It is Buddy's blood."

"How long have you known this?"

"Three days."

"You really weren't planning to tell me, were you?"

"I was told not to contact you."

"By whom?"

"Lieutenant Ben Hanson of the Minneapolis Park Police. He's in charge of the investigation. He will be issuing a warrant to search your house. I have a hunch he will look for more than a DNA sample."

"Like what?"

There was no sense sparring with her any longer.

Tell her not only all that he knew but also all that he speculated. "Computer records, business files, phone calls, anything that will connect him to Thorpe and provide a motive. Was Buddy in any financial trouble?"

"He was worried, I could tell that, but he never wanted to bother me with business details."

"Maybe that's why he disappeared. Maybe he was in trouble with the bank, got in an argument with Thorpe, killed him, and ran away."

Chloe said, "Whose side are you on?"

"What do you mean?"

"Are you working for the police?"

"I am not a cop."

"You talk like one."

Meredith wondered what Ben would think of that comment. He would have hysterics. "Chloe, I'm on your side. I want to help you."

"Then why have you already convicted my husband? Buddy would never kill anyone."

"Motive and opportunity point to it, that's all I'm saying. That's what the police are looking at."

"What if he's dead?" she said, as though asking an exploratory question rather than a personal one.

"That's what the police assumed when they searched the lake. They were expecting to find Buddy, but found Thorpe instead. You have to face the fact that Buddy is now a fugitive from justice, not a missing person."

"Either way he could go to jail."

"Well, murder is a helluva lot worse than unlawful flight." He shifted himself again, this time away from his reflection in the glass. What she had just said disturbed him. "What did you mean by that, either way he could go to jail?"

"Nothing, just thinking out loud."

"Chloe if you are holding anything back, anything the police should know, you are also facing jail time."

There was a heavy silence. Presently Chloe said,

"Meredith, can we get together?"

He looked at his watch. All he had to do was cancel his golf date. "I don't live far away. Give me fifteen minutes." To hell with Ben and his by-the-book edicts.

"Wait..." she said just as he was about to hang up. "Not at my house. Somewhere else."

"Where?"

"Marine on St. Croix."

"Why way out there?"

"I'll tell you when I see you. Meet me at the General Store at three-thirty."

11

Tad was already on the first green when Meredith called to cancel.

"Got a hot date?" Tad asked, kidding.

"Yeah, as a matter of fact, I do."

Tad laughed, knowing this was pure bullshit, and hung up.

Meredith changed into khaki-colored slacks and a white dress shirt turned up at the cuffs showing off his hairy wrists. He grabbed a bottle of Evian from the fridge on his way out.

Meredith had been to Marine on St. Croix once before, not by highway but by river. He and Vicki had pontooned with avid-boater friends of Vicki's on the St. Croix one Sunday afternoon about a year ago. It was unbelievably boring, sitting on a padded bench doing two knots and drinking tepid beer. It would have been a complete dud except for a stop on a narrow tributary below the small river town. They climbed a heavily wooded path to the Village Scoop behind the General Store, well worth the effort because Meredith enjoyed the best ice cream cone he'd ever tasted. However, he had the distinct feeling that on this trip he would not be enjoying a scoop of Black Forest Double Chocolate Chunk.

He had plenty of time and didn't exceed the speed limit except on I35 North. He off-ramped onto 36, a four-laner separated by a wide boulevard and chockablock on either side with strip malls, service stations, stand-alone retailers, office centers, and car dealerships. Passing ugly, he noted, as he passed them.

But the drive through this suburban blight was worth getting to Stillwater, what a small town ought to look like, whose only drawback, albeit picturesque and historic, was the rickety lift-bridge across the St. Croix to Wisconsin which, when raised for passing boats, stalled traffic for blocks on either side of the river. He geared down the steep hill into Stillwater, drove through town north on 38, taking in the heavily forested riverbanks along the way to Marine. He arrived around 3:15, parked on Judd Street across from the General Store in a lot facing a large triangular park. From where he left the Caddie, the main drag of Little Marine looked lopsided, with all the buildings clinging to one side of the street, as though they might at any moment slide down the hill and into the river.

He walked through the entrance to the General Store, built in the 1870s, a tourist mecca of Marine memorabilia, recalling the town's first sawmill operated by two men who named it after their hometown of Marine, Illinois. He strolled by display cases and clothing racks, killing time until Chloe showed up. *If* she shows up, he thought. What if she had sent him on a wild goose chase, to get him out of town for some nefarious reason? He shook his head at the nonsense clouding his mind. She told him she'd explain once she got here. Be patient.

He was so self-absorbed that hearing his name spoken suddenly behind him startled him. He swung around nearly in an attack position, slightly crouched, shoulder turned like a boxer, honed from years of dealing with implied danger.

Chloe stepped back, her eyes narrowed until he smiled. "Did I say something wrong?"

"No," he said, angling for the right response. "It's just that I'm not used to hearing my name coming from a pretty woman."

She was bemused, not flattered. She was dressed casually, as she was in her home, but this was public casual, to be seen beyond the confines of her front door, not private casual: a flowing skirt and blouse in light rose, covering her body loosely but yet revealingly when she moved, the flowing material clinging for an instant before changing course. Suggestive yet modest. How does she do it? Must have a private fashion consultant.

Merrie was able to make a few determinations of her figure in the mini-seconds a man is allowed without seeming boorish: legs not slim but muscled like a runner (he could see himself running Lake Harriet in the early morning hours alongside her), smallish breasts but nicely proportioned for her body build, slightly bony hips. Ok, so she wasn't Victoria's Secret but she still had a figure he would like to see more of.

"Thanks for coming."

"It's ok."

"There is a lot to talk about."

"How about the coffee shop?"

"I'd rather not. I don't want to run into someone I know."

"I thought Edina was your stomping ground."

"It is but we have a farm between here and Scandia."

"Farm?" He wondered how her husband had time for farming.

She read his mind. "My family owns it. Buddy and I use it as an escape."

Escape, he thought. Escape from what?

She motioned toward the front entrance. "Why don't you follow me in my car? It's just a couple of miles."

They went outside. "Mine is over there," he said pointing to his vintage Cadillac.

"I know. I saw it when you came to my house. It's hard to miss."

"The only thing about me that is," he replied.

She gave him an extended look. "I'm not so sure about that."

They crossed the street together. He wondered why she was walking him to his car when he noticed an Escalade parked on the other side of it.

"I drive a Cadillac, too." She pressed her remote and the big, shiny black machine lighted up in welcome. He watched her open the driver's door and climb into the richly leathered front seat, a treat for the eyes because it revealed more leg and, for the first time, her shoes—finely crafted soft suede flats that hugged her feet.

He followed her north, up quiet, two-lane St. Croix Road that was totally in shade as the tall pines lacing the right of way hid the late afternoon sun. She turned left just before Copas and followed a county road bisecting fields of knee-high corn and ankle-high alfalfa. They passed Jackson Meadow, a new town development of white houses that all looked alike except for subtle variations in surface design. Shortly, she turned into a long, winding driveway of crushed rock ending at a modest farmhouse, a big barn with a silo, and several outbuildings. What caught his eye immediately were several vintage tractors lined up alongside a tool shed: an Oliver, an Allis Chalmers, a Massey Ferguson and a Minneapolis Moline. They appeared to date from the 1930s and 40s.

After they climbed out, Meredith said, "Those are rare tractors."

"Buddy collects tractors, I collect art."

They went inside the farmhouse, a two-story clapboard frame with a peaked roof. It was simply furnished with a sofa, a rocker and an oval braided rug, not what he expected.

As he looked around she said, "This is our hideaway."

"Who takes care of it?"

"A father and son. They live in Scandia. The father is a retired farmer. Taking care of this place gives him something to do."

"Do you come here often?"

"Not anymore. When Jonathan was young we did."

"Jonathan?"

"Our son. In Nicaragua."

"Oh, yes. By the way, have you told him that his

father is missing?"

"That's what I want to talk to you about. Maybe we should sit down."

"Fine with me." Puzzled but curious, Meredith sat in the rocker, Chloe across from him on the sofa, which had large rounded arms like Pullman furniture. She tucked her legs under her, folding her skirt tight around her thighs and knees. The move reminded Meredith of a knight girding his loins for battle.

"This takes a lot of explaining."

"I'm waiting."

"As I told you, my son is in Nicaragua with the Field Service Committee. He is fluent in Spanish and is teaching English at a local school."

"Does he like it there?"

"Loves it. He met someone...." She stopped for a moment. "But that's not why I invited you here, to talk about my son."

"You still haven't answered my question. Did you tell him about Buddy?"

"I didn't have to. My son already knew."

"What do you mean?"

"Jon called to tell me that Buddy is with him in Nicaragua."

Meredith stared blankly as though he were helplessly watching a levee being breached. Everything was fine one moment and chaotic the next.

"Wait a minute. You're saying that your husband fled the country and went to Nicaragua?"

"Yes."

"So you knew where he was all this time?"

She nodded.

"You were lying to me." Meredith shook his head in dismay. "Playing me like a violin. No, more than a violin, a whole orchestra." But he had to hand it to her, he had been outconned. Maybe he stole a few strands of hair but she stole his trust, his friendship, probably his reputation. How could he show his face to Ben after he finds out about this?

"Meredith, please give me a chance to explain. I didn't expect it would come to this."

"Neither did I."

"Let me tell you what happened. A week ago Tuesday, the night before you called, I came home from the Arboretum, I volunteer there, and I found a note from Buddy. In it he wrote that he was going away for a while, telling me not to worry, that he would get in touch with me soon. He said he needed time away to think things over. The next morning when the phone rang I thought it was Buddy but instead it was you calling about the empty canoe. You must have been able to tell how worried I was."

That was true, Meredith thought. She sounded scared.

"So when did you find out where he was?"

"Later that same day when Jon called. He didn't know anything either until Buddy showed up at his apartment."

"So this was a surprise to both of you?"

She nodded.

He found it hard to believe that Chloe and her son were innocent bystanders while Boynton plotted a disappearing act. "So you're saying that Buddy set up the canoe stunt and then left town without a word to you or your son?"

"I'm telling you the truth."

"Did he explain why he did this? Why he disappeared?"

"He said he needed time to think. The walls were pressing in on him; those were the words he used. And I was instructed not to tell anybody where he was because he doesn't want to get Jon into trouble. That's why I didn't say anything."

"You are protecting a man who has run away from his responsibilities and left his wife and son to take the heat for him."

"He's still my husband, Meredith, whatever kind of person you think he is. Right now he's in trouble and I need to help him."

"How can you help him? You're in Minneapolis and he's in Nicaragua. Call him and tell him to come home."

"And then what?" she snapped. "Get arrested for murder?"

"If he's innocent he has nothing to worry about."

"Nothing? His DNA matches the blood not on just any canoe but his canoe, which you spotted floating not far from where the body of Jim Thorpe was recovered."

"But running away makes him look guilty even if he isn't."

"That means he can't come home until he clears his name."

"How do you expect him to do that in Nicaragua?"

She shrugged. "Someone has to do if for him, find out what's going on."

Meredith remembered what Ben had told him: she was a rich woman, she could afford anything. "Hire an investigator."

"I thought about that, but I have a better idea."

"What?"

"I want you to help me find out who is framing my husband."

Meredith laughed derisively. "I thought I'd heard everything but this takes the cake."

"I'll even pay you."

"I would not take your money."

"I can afford it."

"That's what I've heard. Have you even told your husband about me?" he asked, still laughing.

He had upset her. A proud woman like her needs to be taken seriously. She shot back, "Tell Buddy that a fireman came snooping around his house for DNA so he could connect him to a homicide?"

Meredith decided it was time to begin rocking. The chair with its tall spindled back and cane seat was as hard as a piece of plywood. And it squeaked, too, a welcome relief to the otherwise painful silence that had grown between them.

"I'm sorry," she said finally. "I've been under a lot of stress."

"It's understandable, and I think it is getting in the way of making wise decisions."

"I have made a wise decision. I want to hire you to find out who is trying to frame my husband."

"Look, Chloe, in the first place, I am not for hire and, in the second, I am not a detective. I wouldn't know where to begin."

"You've already begun, Meredith, don't you see? You began when you found the empty canoe. You did investigative work to find out that it belonged to Buddy. You acted like a detective when you came to my house to get his DNA. And when I turned on the television news, there you were with the Park Police and the Sheriff's deputies retrieving Jim Thorpe's body."

"A private investigator would be professional."

"And he would be obvious, too. You can do it discreetly, talk to people, ask a few questions. No one would know you were doing it for me. I'm not asking you to tail someone or take pictures behind a tree. You wouldn't stop being a fireman."

"I don't know..."

"You said you have a lot of time off. What do you do when you're not working?"

An honest answer would reveal how truly boring his life was. Well, this would certainly spice it up. "I wouldn't take any money."

"I was ready to do whatever it takes, even pay you. I should have known you would find that insulting. But you are the only one who can help me, the only one I can trust. I have no one else to turn to. Won't you do it?"

Even though Meredith was taking the time to mull it over, he had made up his mind. He would help her. It would put him at odds with Ben, maybe even fracture their friendship, but he rationalized that his friendship with Chloe was more important to him, at least for now. What made him even more convinced that this was the right thing to do was the excitement it would provide, he could feel it already affecting him, and it would also keep him in contact with Chloe, a welcome plus. He didn't let it bother him that her husband was thousands of miles away in a small South American country hiding out in self-imposed exile, and Meredith his lifeline to freedom. Jesus, what delicious irony! Well, Meredith would do all he could to help Buddy clear his name, but what if he can't, or what if he finds more incriminating evidence that would hang him? Well, he would cross that bridge if he came to it.

"Ok," he said, "When do I start?"

12

They went to dinner at a small restaurant, Costas, owned by a Greek husband and wife team. Over candlelight they studied the menu of home-cooked choices. He ordered dolmathes stuffed with lamb and she had the spanakopita appetizer. Meredith also ordered a small bottle of retsina and, with demitasses of Greek coffee, they shared a dessert of galaktobouriko.

They made small talk, which grew more personal as the retsina took effect. She told him about what it was like growing up in White Bear Lake, going to a private preparatory school, graduating from the all-women College of St. Catherine in St. Paul's Hyde Park, meeting Buddy while on college spring break in Mazatlan, raising her son, Jon.

"You were a stay-at-home mom?"

"Mostly. When Jon was little and Buddy incorporated his business, I kept his books and appointments. Buddy didn't have a separate office. He worked on the fly; it was hard to keep up with him. He was always hard to keep up with." She smiled to change the subject. "Tell me about yourself."

What was to tell? "I've been a fireman for 25 years."

"Why did you decide to do that?"

He had never shared the intimate details of his personal life with anyone. He didn't want to start with Chloe, and tell her that he once planned to be a priest and was ready to enter the seminary. Even Vicki didn't know this about him. The decision to quit broke his mother's heart but he chose a profession whose mission if not saving souls was, perhaps even more ennobling, that of saving lives.

"I only ask," Chloe continued, "because you are sophisticated. You know about art and design. I'm sure you are knowledgeable about a lot of other things, too."

"I did get a good education."

"Where?"

"St. John's in Collegeville."

"Are you Catholic?"

"Not so you'd notice."

"Me, too."

They laughed over this common juncture in their uncommon backgrounds, hers ruling class, his working class. Maybe he would tell Chloe more about himself someday, but right now it was purely business.

"Let's just say," he replied, "that being a fireman gives me time to help damsels in distress."

There was an ease between them made more pleasurable for Meredith in the way the candlelight created moving shadows on her hair.

He leaned forward, "So, how do you want me to proceed?"

"See Karl Mittelstadt. Remember, I told you he was the architect who designed my house?"

Meredith nodded. "Why him?"

"He's my husband's partner. He can tell you whatever you need to know about the business."

Meredith mulled this over. "Have you told him about me?"

"Not yet. I had to know if you were willing to help me first."

"Ok, so you're telling me I don't have a free hand? I'm already reporting to somebody?"

"Karl is completely trustworthy."

"Let me ask you a hypothetical."

"Go ahead."

"He is your husband's partner, right, someone you say is completely trustworthy?" When he got her confirming nod, he pushed on, "Suppose he helped your husband leave the country?"

"If Karl did," she responded almost huffily, "he would have told me."

"Did *you*?" Meredith asked.

"Did I what?"

"Help your husband leave the country?" He had to ask, had to hear it from her that she wasn't using him in a way he still did not understand.

"Of course not!"

The ease between them disappeared in a flash of petulance and it made him realize how delicate their relationship really was. "I hope you understand," he said, "that if I am going to help you, everything has to be on the table."

She smiled at him, almost coquettishly, as she toyed with her dessert spoon on what was left of the Greek delicacy. "Including me?"

He felt his cheeks flush. Was she toying with him, being suggestive in order to put him in his place? She could not mean what that implied, that she was available. She was using reverse psychology to suggest that he could have his way with her, even on a table, when in fact what she was telling him was: don't lecture me, I'm in charge, you do it my way or, in the vernacular, take the highway.

"I just want to know what the parameters are. You know me, the overly suspicious fireman who looks for danger when it may not even be there."

She put her spoon down and looked into his eyes. "I won't keep anything from you if that's what you mean."

"Fine. So you'll let this architect, Karl...

"Mittelstadt," she said, helping. "I'll give you his card."

"...Thanks. Will he be my contact rather than you?"

"I don't think it would be a good idea if we saw

each other in Minneapolis. We can meet here at the farm when we have to."

He was disappointed. She was effectively removing herself from active involvement, slipping into the background. His contact was to be this architect, not her.

"I won't be seeing much of you, then."

"It would be unwise, don't you think?"

13

The offices of Mittelstadt and Associates took up the entire second floor of a two-story building on the corner of East Hennepin and University Avenues. Meredith parked his Cad in an unmanned lot opposite the building--where you drop a small envelope with your license number and three dollars into a slotted metal lockbox. He ran across University dodging traffic to the entrance, skipped the elevator, and climbed the stairway three steps at a time.

He entered an office that was one big room whose open space was interrupted by riveted steel columns sprayed matte black. Drawing tables set at various angles were lined up in three rows, some occupied, some not. Along the windows looking down on University Avenue was an area partitioned off by a wall of glass. He detected no receptionist and asked the nearest person to him, a young man in shirtsleeves studying house plans, where he could find Karl Mittelstadt.

"Over there." He pointed to the partitioned area, which upon closer inspection was a conference room with a long table and chairs around it. Meredith recognized the influence of Herman Miller in the leather-slatted office furniture. A lone figure sat at the table in the end chair reviewing a three-ring binder as though waiting for a meeting to start.

Meredith tapped on the glass. "Karl Mittelstadt?"

The man he was looking at parted his hair down the middle, a style Meredith associated with barbershop quartets, and oddly out of synch with the surroundings. The architect also sported a thin moustache, which had a tiny part down the middle just like his hair.

"Meredith Gilbert," he said, extending his hand. "I called you earlier."

"Yes, sit down." His words were clipped like his moustache.

Meredith looked around. "A converted warehouse?"

Karl smiled. "A converted car dealership."

"You're kidding."

"The main floor was the showroom. Up here was storage. A big elevator brought the cars up."

"Where?"

"You're sitting in it."

Meredith looked down at his feet as if expecting the floor to move.

"It was a big challenge to remodel this space." The g came out sounding almost like ch.

"I'd say you do good work."

He bowed his head slightly. "Thank you."

"You spoke with Chloe?"

"She said I was to give you any assistance I could." He gave Meredith a wry smile. "She can be very persuasive. I tried to talk her out of it but she wouldn't listen. I don't expect anything to come of this, I guess all we can do is humor her."

Meredith was hoping to do a little more than that. "I don't think she wants to be humored."

"She's under severe strain with Buddy gone, she's not thinking rationally. And now, this ugly business with Jim Thorpe...."

"That's why I'm here. Chloe is convinced someone is framing her husband for Thorpe's murder."

Karl hunched his shoulders up as if a draft had hit him. "Murder. I can't believe this is happening." He looked at Meredith. "I do not recall her ever mentioning your name until she called me yesterday."

"We haven't known each other long."

"Just what do you do? Are you an investigator of some sort?"

"No, I'm a fireman."

This comment evoked a slight smirk. Mittelstadt tried to disguise it but Merrie's antennae were always up when it came to his profession. He'd handled these slights before. "If this building caught fire you'd be happy to see me."

"I meant no slur, Mr. Gilbert, I am only questioning what this so-called investigation has to do with you. Personally, not professionally."

This was an innuendo Merrie could not ignore either. "Just say I'm a close family friend."

Mittelstadt nodded but Merrie knew that the architect was assuming much more, that he and Chloe were beyond a mere working relationship. Let him think what he wants, Meredith couldn't care less.

"I want to help, Mr. Gilbert, don't misunderstand. So how do we proceed? Do you have a plan? I am an architect, after all. What I do is design a plan and then work from it. What is yours?"

"Just ask questions I guess."

"You guess?" Karl was obviously a rigid person who did things in logical order while Merrie liked to follow a scent and see where it led him. "I'm not building a house, Mr. Mittelstadt. I'm looking under rocks. It's not a predictable way to operate but it's the only way I know."

"All right then. What do you want from me?"

"Names. Buddy's clients, friends, enemies..."

"Enemies?" Karl seemed affronted. "Buddy has no enemies."

"Chloe seems to think so."

This guy was going to be impossible to work with. How could Chloe have put him in this position? Unless she didn't want him to get anywhere. He still did not have complete faith in her motives. However, he had to deal with the situation the way it was, for now anyway. If things got worse, he would simply call her up and say sayonara. In the meantime he would push on and, as they say in court, rephrase the question.

"Let me ask you this: How about Jim Thorpe? Did he have any enemies?"

Karl smiled. "Legion. I can't think of anyone who didn't have an axe to grind with him."

Bingo, Meredith said to himself. "Including you?"

Karl stiffened. It fit his personality perfectly. "Perhaps but not enough to kill him."

"Who else?"

Karl inhaled dismissively, clearly wishing this interview were over. "Maybe you should talk to one of his subordinates."

"Who?"

"Hank Riker. He's a junior vice president in Thorpe's division at R&S Bank in Bloomington. He would be a far more helpful person to talk to than I."

"Ok, I'll get in touch with him. Is there anyone else I should talk to?"

"Start with Hank."

Merrie left feeling uncertain about a lot of things. Mittelstadt was supposed to be, according to Chloe, his contact but he was more an obstacle than a help. Maybe he was trying to hide his own involvement. Everyone was guilty, Merrie decided, unless proven innocent, the opposite of simple justice. This meant everybody, including the achtung architect, even Chloe. He couldn't trust anyone. What had he gotten himself into?

He still had time on his car, hell it was an all day lot, he could leave it there until six, and so he decided, as long as he was parked, to drop into a nearby health food store to pick up some good victuals for a change. He had heard Ezekiel cereal was good and he could use a few bananas, some really dark chocolate, and Greek yogurt. He was charged a quarter for a paper sack because he hadn't brought his own.

He walked around the corner. It was reaching five

and the sun was on the other side of the building, which was casting dark shadows on his car, parked near the wall. As he approached he noticed a mark on the driver's side door. What the hell, he thought, some asshole had keyed his car, his babied Cadillac. How could anyone be so damned mean? He looked around as if he could still spot the culprit. Getting closer he saw that there was more than a single mark, there were several of them, a veritable binge of vandalism. Then he realized that the scratches spelled something, a message of some sort. He studied the marks, carefully following them with his fingertips. They made a word, a chilling warning.

STOP

14

Merrie got to work before dawn, while the overnight shift was still asleep. He put on a pot of coffee whose aroma stirred the sleepers awake.

"Why so early?" Al said, coming out of one of the bedrooms, wearing only boxer shorts.

"I want to show you something," Merrie said. "Get dressed."

Al looked down at his shorts. "I am dressed." He poured coffee into a mug so stained it looked like it once held 5W30.

They went outside to the parking area behind the firehouse. Meredith pointed to the Cadillac. "Look at that."

Al rested his mug on the hood, which did not sit well with Merrie, and bent down for a closer look at the scratches on the door.

"Can you rub that out?" Merrie asked.

Al moved his fingers across the scratches. "Too deep. Got to see your Maaco Man."

"Can't you at least polish it enough so you can't see what it spells?"

"Spells?" Al moved back. "I'll be damned." He winked at Merrie. "Some guy caught you playing around with his wife?"

"Something like that."

Al worked on the door with rubbing compound and a polisher while Merrie changed into his uniform. When Merrie came outside, Al was standing back admiring his work. "Looks like a Picasso."

Merrie smiled. At least the word was now undistinguishable. He could drive the Caddie like that. He went back inside and got ready for his shift, checking the call log: maintenance sheets, crew assignments--whose turn it was, for example, to go to Trader Joe's for groceries.

The day was uneventful except for a false alarm; someone called in what was thought to be a garage fire but was only an idling engine burning oil. Just as well. Merrie could not keep his mind on anything but the malicious warning. On the surface it seemed like a practical joke, nothing more than a prank, scratching a sign on his car but, given what he had involved himself in since finding the canoe two weeks ago, this was a not-so-subtle message to lay off. But who knew he was helping Chloe except Chloe herself and that kraut architect? He had a distinctive car, so anyone who had an axe to grind and a sharp object could easily keep track of his whereabouts. Was he followed to Marine on St. Croix and then to Chloe's farm? If so, what was he warned to stop doing? Who could know that he was helping her find who was framing her husband? No one. That could only mean that someone wanted to scare him off seeing Chloe. And if he didn't stop, what then? Another key job or a broken window? Or perhaps something physical against himself, or even Chloe.

He'd better call her. He got her voicemail. He really didn't expect her to answer. Given the circumstances of her life, she was in all likelihood screening calls. He didn't hear back from her until ten o'clock just as he was turning in.

She was testy. "I thought we weren't going to call each other like teenagers."

"I wouldn't have bothered you if it wasn't important."

"Something you learned from Karl?"

"It might be related. I got a warning."

"A warning?"

Meredith told her about the scratches on his car

door.

"Seems like a joke."

"I don't think so. What bothers me is the way it was done. Whoever did it could have put a note under the wiper, but he vandalized my car instead. It was intended to piss me off, and it worked."

"It doesn't make sense."

"This is what a jealous man would do. Could it be your husband never left town, had me followed, and found me alone with you at your farm?"

"That's absurd. I told you, he is in Nicaragua."

"We could clear this up right now. Let me hear it from Buddy himself. Give me his number and I'll call him."

"I asked you to help me clear Buddy's name, not question my honesty."

"What about Mittelstadt? I stopped at a store after seeing him so he had time to leave his office and key my car. I wouldn't put it past him because Karl was not very friendly, in fact he was dictatorial."

"Karl is, well, a bit Prussian, but he is loyal to Buddy."

"That would give him a good reason to warn me off."

"But it doesn't sound like something Karl would do. It's not his style. He's not sneaky."

"Mittelstadt told me to see Hank Riker, a friend of his and a banker who worked for Thorpe. Do you know him?"

"I've heard his name, that's all."

"My meeting with your architect friend was a complete bust. Maybe Riker will be more helpful. I don't start my three days off until Thursday. I'll see Riker, and call you afterward."

"Ok."

"And listen..."

"What?"

"If I'm being followed, they also know where you

are. Go somewhere else, like a B&B for a couple of days, but don't drive straight there, take a roundabout route."

"You think I'm in danger?"

"I don't want to take any chances."

"Are you still ok with helping me?"

"I've been answering alarms for twenty-five years, Chloe, I can't stop now."

15

Merrie could not have slept even if there were no alarms, but as it turned out there was a two-alarmer at a Taco Bell on France and 54th, a grease fire that got out of control when a helper threw water on the grill, splashing flames onto the counter. No one was hurt except for superficial burns on the terrified kid but the kitchen suffered heavy damage. The fire itself was over in minutes but the cleanup and putting everything back in order on the rig took an hour. Merrie was in a haze, slurping down coffee in the morning, when he got a call from Ben. It seemed a lifetime ago when he talked to him.

"We've been trying to find that Boynton woman but no one is home."

Ben waited for Merrie to respond and when he didn't he said, "Do you know where she is?"

"No." He wasn't really fibbing. He didn't know which B&B she would go to.

"We sure as hell need to talk to her. Even with a warrant I can't break into her house. The DA's office has designated her as a material witness and we've got an APB out on her, like her husband. This thing is getting more involved than I was hoping it would be. I wish I knew what was going on."

Me, too, thought Merrie.

"I told you not to get in touch with her, but I changed my mind. I want you to help me find her."

"Me?" Merrie asked, surprised and pleased at the same time.

"You're hot on her, don't deny it. So, I'm thinking,

let's put a hound dog on her scent. Ignore everything I said to you about staying away. Do what you can to track her down. Will you do that? I'll make points with the Director if I find her."

It was as if heaven had opened up and showered Merrie with blessings.

"Sure, why not?"

On the first morning of his three-day break Merrie called R&S Bank and asked to talk to Hank Riker.

"May I ask who's calling?"

Merrie was still feeling good about Ben's turnabout regarding Chloe. Now, if the police spotted him with her, he had an excuse: doing so at the request of Lieutenant Ben Hanson.

"Yes, tell him this is Meredith Gilbert. I'm a fire captain nearing retirement and I need financial advice. Karl Mittelstadt said Mr. Riker is the man to see."

"One moment please."

Riker came on the line right away. "Mr. Gilbert, is that right? How can I help you?"

Merrie made an appointment for two that afternoon.

R&S Bank was on Normandale and 78th, a typical glass-wall, suburban office building with a spacious lawn and an artificial lake with a fountain in front and a parking lot in back. Merrie counted ten stories as he walked from his car. He wondered if it was all R&S or they leased out some floors. Waiting for the elevator he discovered that the bank occupied the first three floors, the rest taken up by the kinds of businesses one finds in any suburban office directory: Intrasonic Inc., Dickenson Graphics, Cloud Nine Chiropractics and Massage. How can these two-bit outfits afford a luxury building like this one?

He announced himself at the desk fronting a hushed office with traditional furnishings, looking more like someone's living room than a bank lobby. Within five minutes he was escorted to an office along the back wall.

The carpet he walked on was actually springy. Hank Riker sat behind a mahogany desk that was so neat Merrie wondered if Riker did any work. Where were files, a computer, the telephone? Probably hidden away in the long, ornately carved credenza that reminded Merrie of the altar at St. John's Church.

When Riker stood to extend his hand Merrie could see that he had more of a stomach than he probably liked to show, which was normally hidden when he sat behind the desk in his glossy black-leather chair.

Riker wore an expensive suit, banker's gray with pinstripes, and a subtly patterned tie over an off-white shirt. All this was in sharp contrast to a black armband above his right elbow. Merrie stared at it. He hadn't seen one of those since his father wore one when President Kennedy was assassinated.

Riker noticed. "For Jim Thorpe, our senior vice president." He touched the armband reverently. "Not only my boss but also a friend. Maybe you saw in the papers that Jim was murdered. Terrible, they found his body in Lake Harriet. It was all over the news..." he trailed off, staring at Meredith's face as if he were studying it for plastic surgery. "I could swear that I saw you on Channel 4 when his body was being recovered."

Merrie nodded. "You don't have to swear. That was me."

"Of course, you said you were a fire captain. You'd be part of the recovery team. Well, what a coincidence."

"Not entirely. I want to talk to you about Thorpe's death."

Riker had the kind of eyes that burrowed rather than looked. Merrie could almost feel the heat on his face. "I thought you came to see me about retirement."

"Someday, not now."

Riker leaned back into his leather. "So you made an appointment essentially under false pretenses."

"I had to get in to see you."

"I could call security."

81

Why, Meredith wondered, do I always get off on the wrong foot with everyone? "Mr. Riker, I'm sure you want to find out who killed Jim Thorpe, right? Well, so do I."

Riker seemed to relax a bit. "We're all under a lot of stress Mr. Gilbert. I'm sure you can appreciate how this...this incident has affected the entire R&S company, not just this office but all of our branches."

"It has affected me as well, Mr. Riker, having been involved in his recovery. Karl Mittelstadt suggested that you could help me. I'm trying to find out more about Jim and the circumstances surrounding his death."

"How well do you know Karl?"

"I met him two days ago and he strongly recommended that I see you. That's why I'm here."

"I see. Well, what else can I add that the police don't already know?"

"You've talked to the police?"

"Yes, a lieutenant from the Park Police came yesterday. His name is Ben Hanson. Maybe you should contact him."

"Thank you," Meredith answered, knowing how ridiculous that was. "But in the meantime perhaps you can clear up a few things for me."

Riker seemed to enjoy talking. He was a salesman after all, not peddling used cars but the method was the same. "Only if you decide to join our bank." He smiled.

"This office is not convenient for me."

"Where do you live?"

"St. Louis Park."

Riker's smile widened. "We have an office on West Lake Street, across from the old Lincoln Del. Do you remember the Lincoln Del?"

"Everybody our age remembers the Lincoln Del, Mr. Riker."

"Call me Hank."

"I'll look into shifting my account. By the way how many branches do you have?"

"Thirty-seven in Minnesota and Wisconsin." Riker

leaned forward. "I will tell you that we were on the brink of being bought out by the Montreal Bank of Canada, a huge deal, and now because of Jim's death it has been put on hold."

"What does that involve?"

"R&S is a regional bank but by merging with a Canadian bank we become an international entity that can do business in any country in the world."

"And Thorpe's murder is a problem?"

"Major. Jim headed the committee working on the merger. Our bank took a hit on derivatives, and we are in the process of cutting staff. The offer from Montreal was a lifesaver for us. And now, with Jim murdered and the fallout from that, they can't handle the bad publicity, you know? As if that weren't bad enough, one of R&S's clients is, what do you call it, a person of interest."

Merrie played dumb. Maybe he was getting too good at it. "Who is that?"

"Buddy Boynton, the builder who disappeared just before Jim's body was found. The police are looking for him. Perhaps you don't know who he is but his company, Boa Constructors, is one of the major house builders in the Twin Cities. His upscale homes are custom built and begin at a million-and a-half."

"Was Boynton in financial trouble?"

"Like many who depend on swing loans to operate, Buddy Boynton was not immune. He needed an extension but was turned down."

"By you?"

"It was Jim's decision to deny the extension."

"How much?"

Riker cleared his throat. "That is not for me to discuss. He has a wife, you know."

"There's a Mrs. Boynton?" Merrie said, still playing dumb.

"Yes. She used to keep his books. She ought to know how much is involved."

"I see. Can you tell me about her...what's her

name?"

"Chloe." Riker looked right and left as if making sure he was not being overheard. "The police are looking for her, too."

"Do you think she might be involved in Buddy's disappearance?"

Riker shrugged. "Anything is possible."

"What do you know about her, the kind of person she is?"

"Karl knows her much better than I do. But people talk."

"About what?"

"She's pretty high-powered. Comes from a lot of money."

Meredith leaned forward as well, encouraging Riker to tell him more.

"My point is that if she has a lot of money why should Buddy have to finance his homes through our bank?"

"How much are we talking about? How much is she worth?"

"Her father was co-founder of Control Data and pulled out when the stock was peaking. She was an only child and when he died the gossip is that she inherited conservatively 50 to 75 million."

Meredith stared in shock. He couldn't be sure he had heard correctly. "She's worth 50 to 75 million dollars?"

"Conservatively. I've heard she's tucked it away overseas in various investment accounts, mostly in Switzerland. Her father died five years ago, so her inheritance could now be worth upwards of 100 million."

"What does she do with all that money?"

Riker shrugged. "Those of us in the banking business keep asking the same question. At least we know she's not giving any of it to Buddy."

"What about her son?"

Riker suddenly became guarded. It was as if he had

shrunk a size. "How do you know she has a son?"

After his careless question, Merrie had to jump-start his brain. "Oh, Karl told me that Buddy has a son in Nicaragua."

Riker relaxed back in his chair, nodding. "He went there about a year ago, some kind of teaching job."

"What do you know about him?"

Riker thinned his lips. "Best schools, Breck, college abroad. I've heard that he is a momma's boy." He abruptly looked at his watch as though he suddenly realized he had said too much. "I have to get back to work."

"One more question. Can you think of anyone else besides Buddy who might have had a reason to kill Thorpe?"

"Jim was all work and no play. He ticked off a lot of people."

"Including Buddy?"

Riker placed his fingertips on the edge of his desk as if he were about to play a piano. "Especially Buddy."

16

Meredith paused before heading back to his car to take stock of what he had learned from Riker. He sat down in an overstuffed chair in the bank lobby. A ceiling-mounted, flat-screen VIZIO was tuned to CNN with the sound turned off and supertitles crawling across the top. The bottom was filled with breaking news. The really breaking news was the fact that Chloe was worth a fortune. He was stunned. Even though he stared up at the screen he absorbed nothing.

Merrie came to see Riker expecting to shed light on Buddy but instead it shone on Chloe. That she was visibly well off was without question: a home in the Country Club, designer clothes, expensive art and furnishings, an Escalade, but people live like that with a couple of decent incomes, large debt and chutzpah. Chloe was living like a pauper compared to her personal wealth. She could easily afford a 30,000-square-foot mansion on Stubbs Bay and a 48-foot Cantius Sports Coupe tied up at the dock, not to mention a chalet in Kitzbuehl, a penthouse on Fifth Avenue, and a hundred yards of shorefront at St. Martins.

What in hell is going on? Each new revelation and he had to ask himself the same question. His brain could be immersed in formaldehyde for all the help it was giving him. He needed to sort things out, but where to start? The empty canoe? And where did that lead him? So far into a quagmire.

He thought of a word used by diplomats: decoupling. Decouple Thorpe's murder from Boynton's disappearance. Let's assume that Buddy did not go to Nicaragua because he owed money he could not pay, that Buddy did not kill Thorpe because the banker turned him down for a loan he desperately needed. So why did he go to Nicaragua? Think big, Merrie told himself, look at how much he underestimated Chloe's wealth. Is his son ok? Did something happen to the kid that he could not handle alone and Buddy rushed down to help?

As he exited the building he was reminded of the word STOP someone had etched into the finish of his Caddie the last time he left it in a parking lot. Could that have anything to do with Nicaragua? Unless it spelled PARADA, it didn't. He decided he would not decouple that warning from Thorpe's death. Assume the two are connected: whoever killed Thorpe either marked his car or had someone do it for him. Merrie looked around as if he were being followed. He was nervous. He had gotten into a situation in which there was no viable direction. There was no one he could trust, not even Ben. He was on his own.

He had to see Chloe, not just talk to her on the phone but sit down and talk to her face to face. She had to explain everything. He was due this. And then what? Stay on or hang it up? He caught his reflection in the outside mirror as he backed out of the lot, smiling ruefully. He drove home, parked and went inside. He called Chloe's number and got the predictable voice mail.

He sat around for two hours before she returned his call. "Got to see you."

"When?"

"Now, tonight. Where are you?"

"In a B&B like you said. You sound anxious."

"I am."

"Did you talk to Riker?"

"Yes. That's what I want to see you about. Tell me where you are."

"I'm at the St. Croix River Inn just outside Osceola, on the Wisconsin side of the river, 305 River Street. It's quiet and secluded."

"Where's your Escalade parked?"

"I didn't take it. We have a station wagon at the farm, I drove that instead."

"Good. I'm going to rent a car and I probably will be late, around midnight."

"Call me and I will let you in. The owners will have gone to bed."

Good, Merrie thought, he didn't want anyone to know Chloe would have a visitor. He didn't think at all about where he would spend the night unless it was on her sofa.

Meredith rented a Nissan Versa, about as ordinary a car as he could think of, and had it delivered even though it cost him an extra twenty bucks. He left his apartment building heading east on Excelsior Boulevard. He turned left on Xenwood, one-way north, just before Highway 100, turned left again and came down Yosemite, one way south, driving very slowly as though looking for an address. Satisfied that he wasn't being followed, he got on 100 north and took it to 494 where he eventually connected with 35 and then County 38. It took extra time to find the Inn, being unfamiliar with the roads, and he arrived well past midnight.

He parked down the street and called Chloe as he walked toward the inn. She let him in through a side door, which had a connecting hallway to a curving staircase. He was in a surreally quiet environment of Victorian furniture, brocaded antimacassars, ticking grandfather clocks, gold-framed genre pictures and crimson-painted walls.

Chloe was wearing a white terrycloth robe with a blue YSL stitched on the pocket, and matching bedroom slippers. In the dimmed light she seemed more ephemeral than flesh and blood. She made no sound as she mounted the stairs ahead of him. She showed him into what was an apartment with a sitting room, bedroom and bath, and closed the door so softly behind her that the lock barely clicked. A lamp on an end table was turned on, the soft light belying the tension in the air.

She put her finger to her lips. "Speak softly."

He was so edgy he began pacing. The floor squeaked.

"Please, Merrie, sit down." She motioned to the sofa. "We both can use a drink, but all I have is the scotch I brought with me." She poured single malt Glenfiddich into two lowball glasses. She sat next to him and they sipped quietly until the smooth-tasting scotch settled him down.

"I saw Riker in his office. We had an interesting talk."

"So interesting you had to drive all the way up here to tell me about it?"

"It couldn't wait. I need some answers. For one thing, I learned that you are a very wealthy woman."

"You heard that from Hank Riker?"

He nodded.

She shook her head. "I wish he hadn't said anything."

"You told me to dig so I dug. Why didn't you tell me?"

"It's not something you talk about." She extended her hand in a mock handshake. "Hi, I'm Chloe Boynton and I'm a very wealthy woman. How would that sound?"

"It would sound like you trusted me. You asked me to help you find out who is framing Buddy, but you failed to mention a critical factor that may be important."

"My personal finances are not relevant."

"Oh really? Then how come Buddy is in financial trouble when his wife is worth a hundred million?"

"We keep everything separate. Buddy has never asked me to bail him out. Anyway, his pride wouldn't let him do it."

"Ok, but remember, everything has to be on the table or I can't help you. Is there anything else you haven't told me?"

She lowered her head so that her hair fell across her face. Finally she looked up.

"I just don't see how this has anything to do with Thorpe's death."

"What happened?" I asked.

"Somebody, I don't know who, broke into my account at the Sparhafen Bank in Zurich. They couldn't transfer money unless I myself, or someone representing me, could do it in person with my full approval. I have several numbered accounts not only in Zurich but also in Wintertur and Bern, but the one at the Sparhafen Bank has the most."

"How much?"

"Forty-seven million."

Meredith whistled, but remembered to keep the decibel level in check.

"Whoever it was knew he couldn't get any further than just information on what I had, there are other fail-safe mechanisms in place. The bank notified me that someone had compromised the account but didn't expect any further problems after they recoded it. To make sure, the other banks were notified and the same thing was done. I thought everything was ok until..." she broke off.

"Until what?"

Her eyes glistened as she held back tears.

"Until I got a call from Jonathan. He has been in Nicaragua for a few months and he is very happy there. He had been looking for something that made his life meaningful and he found it. Jon grew up having anything he wanted. Maybe I spoiled him but he is an only son. I am so proud of him because he went to Nicaragua to teach and he literally found himself. I could see it in his emails and hear it in his voice when he called, but then we didn't hear from him for several days. He had emailed almost every day and then nothing. We didn't react right away, assuming he was busy and maybe found a girl friend. And then the call came..." Chloe stopped and rubbed her palms together.

Meredith wanted to put his arms around her but held back. If she wanted contact she would initiate the move.

"It was Jon. He is being held by some guerilla group, they have a funny name, El Grupo Cero."

"The Zero Group," Merrie said.

"You know Spanish?"

"I told you I got a good education."

She smiled wanly. "I'll drink to that." She lifted her glass in a toast.

They sipped a moment and then she picked up the narrative again. "Jon said he was being treated well. Most of those holding him are his age. There are young women in the group too. Very idealistic and dedicated. They want my money to support their cause."

"How much?"

"The amount in my Sparhafen account, forty-seven million."

"You can buy a whole army with that kind of money, including tanks."

"I know. It's completely irrational. We offered them immediate cash, using the money Buddy was hoping to get from Jim Thorpe."

"The money he needed to pay for his houses?"

"Yes. My funds are in a trust. You can't just write a check payable to El Grupo Cero. We told them we could get together half a million in cash if they would release Jon. That's why Buddy went down, to talk to them, reason with them."

"And?"

"They wouldn't listen. They want all or nothing."

"What about Jon?"

"They won't let Buddy see him. Jon is hidden somewhere outside of Managua. He could be anywhere. They only let us talk to him on his cell phone."

"Buddy should contact the Embassy down there."

"No!" she said too loudly. She stopped and listened until she was satisfied she hadn't awakened anyone, and lowered her voice again. "They said we were not to contact anyone. That's why I haven't talked to the police. I can't take any chances, even here."

"How can they bother you here?"

"Merrie, those guerillas could not possibly have hacked into my Zurich account by themselves. Buddy is convinced someone locally is helping the guerillas, someone who knows that I have money and believes in their mission. Buddy figured he could handle this himself, plan his disappearance, fly down to see the guerillas and bring Jon back."

Meredith was beginning to put two and two together. "Did he fake the whole thing with the canoe?"

Chloe nodded. "He cut his finger purposely and dripped it on the canoe and set it adrift."

Meredith interrupted, "expecting someone would spot it and call the police." He had to smile at the way he was used. "Did you have any idea what I was planning when I came to your house the next day?"

"Not at first but when you went upstairs and asked to use the bathroom..."

"You really wanted me to get a sample of Buddy's DNA because you wanted his blood identified, to make it look like foul play while all the time he was in Nicaragua."

"That's right, and I didn't have to involve the police to make it happen."

"Chloe, I have to hand it to you."

She ignored his compliment. "Everything was going according to plan, but then Jim Thorpe's body was recovered from Lake Harriet." Chloe reached out and gripped his hand. "When I saw you on TV with the recovery team, I knew I needed you to help me. I couldn't do it alone any longer."

"You need a lawyer."

"I have a lawyer, a whole firm of lawyers, but I can't involve them. I wasn't even planning to tell you."

"Maybe it no longer matters. Whoever is involved already suspects you've told me because of the warning on my car. You said you didn't think Thorpe's murder had anything to do with Buddy's disappearance, but now I'm beginning to wonder if Thorpe wasn't involved in getting access to your account and was killed because of it."

"Oh God, I never thought of that."

"After what you've told me, Chloe, it hangs together. Breaking into a Swiss account takes special skills, the kind you'd find in someone who works at a bank."

"Why would Thorpe have anything to do with that guerilla group?"

"I don't know. Maybe there was to be a payoff, get access to Chloe Boynton's fortune and we'll cut you in, say, five per cent, a nice tidy sum of two and a half million."

"There would have to be some connection. How could they have met in the first place?"

"A third party? An intermediary?"

Chloe suddenly sagged as if the weight she was carrying was more than she could bear. "They can have it all. I just want Jonathan home."

She leaned forward and put her head on his shoulder. "I'm scared. Please hold me," she whispered in his ear.

He put his arms around her and rubbed her back. He could feel her trembling through the terrycloth. Was she clinging to him as a plea for help or was she clinging to him because she wanted something else? He didn't bother with empirical analysis, he just let it happen.

17

The only light came from the table lamp in the living room far enough away so that Chloe and Meredith were like silhouettes on the white bed sheet. Nothing covered them on this warm night. At the window, a soft breeze fluttered the sheer curtains inward.

They were lying on their backs staring at the ceiling.

"Better go," he said, illuminating his Timex. "It's nearly four."

"The owners told me they get up at five to make breakfast."

'Wish I could stay for it."

"Me too." She squeezed his hand.

"Can't risk it."

She laughed. "Imagine their reaction if we came downstairs together."

He rolled on his side and stared at her profile, wanting to trace it with his finger.

"Don't tempt me."

He had never before felt so close to a woman. There were many in his life, some steady for a year or two like Vicki, others on a winter break at a resort, what he referred to as a poolside pickup. His was an empty life, admittedly. Here he was nearly fifty-five and nobody cared if he lived or died. Better if he died in a fire as a hero, but a hero to whom?

"What are you thinking about?"

He sat on the edge of the bed and turned to look at

her. "You are the first woman I've met I really give a damn about."

"Very romantically stated."

"You know what I mean. I care for you. I worry about you."

She stared at him a long time as if taking his measure. "This doesn't make matters any easier for us."

He sighed. "I know. How do you feel? About me I mean?"

She moved closer so she could touch his arm. "You have more going for you than you give yourself credit for. You are a real man, Meredith Gilbert, courageous, tender, intelligent."

"I appreciate the compliment."

"And," she said, sitting up, her breasts filling out, "that's all I will tell you."

"I can live with that." He got up and used the bathroom to dress. When he came out Chloe had her robe on again.

"Where do we go from here?" he asked. He meant their relationship.

"Managua."

He didn't think he heard her right.

"What?"

"While you were dressing an idea came to me, crazy maybe, but at least it gives us a plan, a direction. Everything here has come to a standstill. I have to sneak around, afraid of being followed. The police want to question me."

Merrie walked to the window and looked out on a slowly gathering dawn. "If you run away the cops will consider it an act of guilt, and you'll be a fugitive like Buddy."

"I'm not running away. I'm going to Managua to find my son."

"If Buddy hasn't been able to do that, what makes you think you can?"

"I have options Buddy doesn't have."

"Like what?"

"The ones you possess, Merrie, what I told you just now, strength, courage, intelligence."

He turned and looked at her quizzically. "What do you have in mind? You want me to go with you? Is that it?"

"Isn't that what you do for a living, help people?"

"You were thinking this all along."

She shook her head. "I would go even if you turned me down."

Merrie mused for a while. "I guess I could take some time off. I've got 75 vacation days piled up."

Chloe brightened. "And you speak Spanish."

"You should see how often I use it on fire calls."

Relief spread through her body like a warm glow. "Speaking of calls I have to let Buddy know that we're coming."

Merrie was beginning to have misgivings.

"Have you told him anything about me? Does he even know I exist?"

"He knows that you found the canoe and worked with the police to retrieve Thorpe's body."

"That explains who I am but not why I'm coming to Nicaragua with you."

"To take over negotiations. You can act as a neutral third party, something Buddy can't do. He's family, too close to be effective," Chloe spoke as if she had rehearsed her lines.

"I've never been to Managua. Buddy knows his way around." Like a reluctant buyer listening to a sales pitch, he wanted his objections overcome. "He might not like having me there."

"Negotiations are at an impasse. Buddy will welcome you."

Welcome his wife's lover? he wondered.

She seemed to read his mind. "You wouldn't be jealous would you?"

"Jealous of Buddy?" he said defensively. "He's your

husband."

"But you're sleeping with me."

Meredith took a deep breath and exhaled slowly. He looked past Chloe at the bed they had just made love on, questioning his motives. Was he really trying to help her or was he so obsessed that he would do anything, anything, to be with her, even agreeing to a cockamamie idea to travel to a foreign country with what were probably false expectations. And what would happen with the three of them together, a triangle of two men loving the same woman?

"Ok, call him. Might as well bring him up to date on everything..."

"Everything?" she asked coquettishly

"Well, not quite everything," Meredith replied, grinning.

"Got your passport?"

He nodded. "One thing concerns me though," he said. "The police have probably contacted airport security. You might get picked out."

"We're not flying commercially. We're going on a private jet. We'll fly out of Holman Field in St. Paul, the airport celebrities use. Pack lightly. We can get everything we need down there."

"When do you want to leave?"

"Right away, tomorrow. Can you call the station and tell them you'll be away for awhile?"

Merrie had a sinking feeling in the bottom of his gut. Chloe had the trip to Managua already planned. This was not a sudden inspiration. It was simply her way of manipulating him into agreeing to go with her. Well she succeeded, and look how easily she did it.

Chloe came to him and threw her arms around his neck. "Oh, Merrie, I adore you!" She pressed her mouth against his and her words were nearly smothered, but he heard them as if they were being shouted inside his head, echoing and re-echoing countless times, and he did not want the sound ever to stop.

18

Meredith had a taste of how the privileged live when he climbed into the compact cabin of the Lear Jet 25D, bending over to accommodate his height. There were six seats--no not seats, easy chairs of Cordwain leather that swiveled next to porthole-shaped windows. Designed to carry eight passengers, this long-range model was reconfigured to six for extra fuel tanks.

Chloe had arrived ahead of him, in her seat with the lap belt fastened. Merrie sat across from her. She was dressed in a pants suit styled for comfort, in light mauve that complemented the cabin's earth tones, as though she had consulted with the Lear's interior designer before selecting her travel wardrobe.

She was all business; none of the playful, girlish qualities that defined her persona at the Inn in Osceola were evident. She barely acknowledged him and he wondered whether she approved of the way he was dressed: an aloha shirt with what he considered a subdued hibiscus floral pattern, tan lightweight chino urban slim-fits, ankle crew socks and loafers. Before deciding what to pack in his dull-green Dakota carryon he had checked Managua's five-day forecast on his iPhone: 97, 97, 97, 97, 97. Well, at least it was consistent.

He buckled up and leaned back in the supple leather waiting for takeoff, recalling how he had covered his bases before leaving town. Getting time off at the station was no problem; he had so much vacation time everyone was glad to see him go. Except for the golf course, brother Tad didn't give a fart where Meredith went. Meredith figured a call to Ben would be his most problematic but fortunately he got Ben's voicemail, and so he left an innocuous message that he would be out of town for a few days and would get in touch when he got back. If Ben needed to call he had Merrie's cell number. The only suspicion came from Vicki who insinuated that he was having a rendezvous with another woman. She was right but for the wrong reasons.

Holman had three runways primarily used by corporate aircraft, and it was busy enough so that the jet had to wait twenty minutes for clearance. Merrie had always flown commercially in the cattle-car section and was familiar only with the lumbering, bumpy take offs of 727s and A320s. The Lear seemed to float even before it was airborne; he detected little difference between being on the ground and in the air until the pilot put the spear-shaped aircraft almost vertically skyward. He wouldn't mention it to Chloe but he was having the time of his life living like a millionaire.

Their heading was nearly due south, no time zone changes, just time, five hours and twenty-two minutes to be exact. They spent the hours looking out the window immersed in their own thoughts. At one in the afternoon the copilot delivered gourmet box lunches and tenths of wine. As they dined, Chloe brought Meredith up to date. She had talked to Buddy who was going to meet them at the airport. He had arranged for Meredith to stay at the Intercontinental Hotel in Managua's relatively new MetroCentre shopping center, where, not coincidentally, Buddy had a suite. The three would have a late dinner in the five-star hotel's Voltes Restaurant after check-in and a rest—as long as Buddy and Chloe were paying it was fine with Meredith—and plan a rendezvous with the leader of El Grupo Cero. Buddy had a rented car and driver. It all seemed as simple as a walk in the sun.

The jet touched down at Managua's Augusto C. Sandino Airport a little after four p.m. central standard time, having lost an hour because Nicaragua was not on daylight saving. The Lear taxied to a gate away from the main terminal, a building which had an interesting architectural style, slightly reminiscent of Eero Saarinen's TWA terminal in New York. The small jet engines whined down to silent. The copilot came out and unlatched the door. As it swung up and the stairway swung down, a rush of hot moist air entered the cabin like an unwelcome party crasher.

Chloe was the first to climb out. Merrie maintained a discrete distance, crouching in the jet's doorway as Chloe walked toward a tall, broad-shouldered man in shorts, a collared golf shirt and an Olympic Hills Golf Club cap. How he managed to look unperturbed in this tropical sweatbox, Merrie could only speculate because the heat and humidity were almost unbearable. But then Buddy had been down here long enough to get acclimated while Merrie had just arrived.

Meredith waited patiently for the obligatory embrace between husband and wife, which to him seemed a bit cool, given the temperature. Chloe then turned as if to signal that it was ok for him to leave the aircraft and join them. Heat radiating off the asphalt came through the soles of his shoes as he walked over. The two men shook hands as Chloe made introductions. Buddy's hand would take an extra large golf glove, Merrie noted, and he had a certain roughness, as though he had been cut out with crimping shears rather than regular scissors.

"Let's get out of the sun before we burn up," he said. His voice was gruff and authoritative, a man used to giving orders. He was tall enough to look down on the top of Meredith's skull. "The first thing we've got to do is get you a cap. Don't worry about your luggage. It will be delivered to the hotel."

They walked to a nearby parking area to a waiting car. It was a late-model, dark-blue Buick, its engine working overtime to provide cold air inside. They climbed in; Chloe and Buddy in back and Merrie in front with the driver, more like a gofer than an equal.

Chloe and Buddy spoke in low voices, having a private conversation muffled by the whine of the struggling air conditioner. The driver was a thin Nicaraguan man who spoke halting English, and so Merrie addressed him in Spanish. The driver smiled and relaxed, and began showing off points of interest as he drove down the wide main boulevard called Calle Terra Norte to the center of the city.

They climbed out of the Buick under a two-story portico at the hotel's entrance. The hotel was traditional in design with three finials on the flat roof some 15 stories above their heads. Inside, the lush lobby had flattened arches and large sconces throwing light upward. All in all it was typical corporate hotel design. They parted on the seventh floor where Merrie got off the elevator. They ciao-ed one another and planned to meet in the restaurant at 9 pm, tropical dinnertime. Merrie walked on plush hallway carpet to 707 and carded himself in to a pleasantly large room with a pair of queens, the requisite dresser, night tables and writing desk, a large flat screen television and a view of the MetroCentre, a large urban retail/office/condo development that the hotel was a part of. Managua was a modern growing city, Meredith could see as he surveyed the scene from his window, a city not unlike Minneapolis in size, pulse and vitality. So how could a group of revolutionaries exist in such a seemingly innocuous, conventional metropolis?

But Nicaragua's history told another story, a Central American tragi-comedy of US involvement and intrigue, revolutions and scandals like the Nicaraguan-Contra Affair in the 1980s that involved the Reagan Administration. Merrie turned away from the window and lay on the bed to rest, his mind awhirl with new experiences and old dilemmas. He nodded off for an hour, got up, turned on the local television and tried to follow the news in Spanish. Nothing about El Grupo Cero but he would have been surprised if there were. He showered and hung his clothes up, storing the empty Dakota in the closet, and dressed for dinner, putting on a fresh shirt and the same pants he wore on the plane.

He came downstairs early and headed for the Scenario Bar overlooking the swimming pool. He walked through tall wrought-iron gates into subdued lighting from iron chandeliers. Lots of metal, he thought, as he took a leather stool at the bar. What do people drink down here: Peña Coladas, Margaritas, Rum and Coke? On the recommendation of the bartender with whom he conversed in Spanish, Meredith ordered the Macua made with Nicaraguan rum. He sipped his drink in the nearly empty bar and when the bartender began rearranging napkins and putting glasses away Merrie motioned him over.

"Si Senor?"

Merrie knew his Spanish was too spotty for the questions he wanted to ask and so he said, "Usted habla Englis por favor?"

He nodded with a ready smile. His black hair was slicked back with pomade. "I wouldn't have this job if I didn't."

"I was wondering if you ever heard of a group calling themselves El Grupo Cero?"

He didn't expect this. "I thought you wanted me to arrange for a girl for the night."

"Some other time."

He shrugged. "Well, senor, since such groups shun publicity, there is not much to tell. They don't want to make lines in the paper, you know?"

"Headlines," Merrie confirmed.

He nodded and turned to go back to stacking glasses.

Merrie reached in his pocket and held up a twenty so the bartender could see it in the mirror behind the bar. He looked about before reaching for the bill and pocketing it.

"Well, senor, you hear talk."

"Like what?"

"Young people with big ambitions, true believers, but what they believe in I am not sure. They call themselves El Grupo Cero because they want to go back to zero, to start over."

"Start what over?"

"Everything. A new world order, I've heard." He pulled the corners of his mouth down. "I don't know what they have to complain about. They come from respectable families, rich fathers."

Merrie was surprised. He expected that they would be a ragtag bunch hiding deep in the jungle dressed in surplus camouflage uniforms.

"How would I contact them?"

"Why, at their homes I suppose."

"Homes?"

"As far as I know, several live in the Villa Fontana, an exclusive area west of the city."

"How many?

"Altogether? I suppose half a dozen."

"Do you know any of them?"

He shook his head. "I am a bartender. They are upper class." he wiped the bar with his towel, not because the bar needed it but because he wanted to make a transition. "May I ask you a question, senor?"

"Go ahead."

"Why are you interested in Grupo Cero?"

"They are holding a family friend for ransom."

The bartender shook his head, a puzzled expression on his face. "No, senor. These are peaceful persons, college educated. If they kidnap someone, especially an American citizen, it would be all over the news, on the Internet. We would know about it. Besides why would they? For money? They have plenty of it. For publicity? Exactly what they don't want. No, senor, your information is faulty."

A party of four came in and sat at the bar for pre-dinner cocktails. "'Excuse me, senor."

"Wait," Merrie touched his forearm. "Give me a

name, please. Someone in the group I can contact."

He reached in his pocket for another bill. The bartender moved his palm downward.

"No need, senor, you have been generous enough. A name that would surprise you is Abelardo Esperidon."

"Why would that surprise me?"

"His father, Ernesto," the bartender said, spreading his arms out in both directions, "owns Metro Centre."

Meredith was surprised all right. He sipped his Macua and memorized the name, repeating it over and over until it was lodged in the synapses of his brain. Meanwhile the bartender mixed drinks with skill developed from years of experience. Every move was orchestrated to impress the customers so they would leave a big tip.

Was the story Chloe told him about El Grupo Cero kidnapping her son also orchestrated? Rich, non-violent, idealistic kids out to change the world, including the son of the guy who owns MetroCentre. So why in hell would they kidnap a schoolteacher from Minnesota?

19

Meredith waited in the lobby until Chloe and Buddy came out of the elevator a little after nine. Now hatless, Buddy displayed a comb-over of sandy-colored hair covering his male-pattern baldness.

"Did you get some rest?" Buddy wanted to know. His tan slacks were so sharply creased you could slit an envelope with them.

"Enough."

"Hungry?"

"I could eat."

Chloe gave Merrie a half smile, as much as he could hope for. She was dressed in an ankle length outfit with a richly crocheted shawl to keep her shoulders covered in the artificially cool air. They crossed the lobby to the Voltes Restaurant where the trio was escorted by an overly erect maître de to a linen-covered table under an enormous chandelier. The dining room had the quietness of a library as waiters speaking in low tones took patrons' orders. The patrons themselves, an international set of mostly businessmen whose companions were beautifully coiffed, leaned toward one other as though exchanging corporate secrets. The table setting of fine crystal and china also had what seemed to Meredith an arsenal of forks, knives and spoons. He was not familiar with this kind of high-society overkill, and hoped he wasn't revealing his bourgeois background by choosing the wrong utensil.

When the waiter came they all decided on the Catch of the Day. Buddy ordered a bottle of Torii Mor Dundee

Hills Select Pinot Grigio 1997 to go with it. They commented idly until the wine steward brought the bottle. He cradled it so Buddy could see the label, uncorked it with a slight pop, poured a small amount in Buddy's glass and waited expectantly for Buddy to wave it under his nose, sniff, and sip a dainty amount, rolling his tongue before swallowing, an elaborate show of ostentation, Merrie thought. At home he would have drunk half the bottle by now.

After the steward poured wine for all, Buddy lifted his glass and said, "Here's to success." A few seconds elapsed before Merrie was asked the inevitable question: "So you are a fireman?"

"We're not an endangered species."

Chloe laughed which made Merrie feel appreciated, but it seemed to irritate Buddy.

"I didn't suggest you were, Mr. Gilbert. However, I want to thank you for flying all the way down here to help us." He smiled ironically. "This has become more complicated than we were led to believe."

Merrie didn't think that was possible. "How so?" he asked.

"El Grupo has done a real number on my son."

"Has he been tortured?"

Buddy shook his head. "Not tortured, brainwashed."

"How did that happen?" Merrie asked.

"My son...our son has always been..."

Chloe interrupted. "Jon was an impressionable child, Merrie. I admit that I sheltered him. He resented me for it. He rebelled against me." She looked into Merrie's eyes. "That isn't so unusual is it?"

He thought about his own youthful rebellion when he chose to be a fireman rather than what his mother had wanted him to be: a priest. "Not at all," he said.

Buddy took over again: "Jon's messages became radical, militant, as if someone else were speaking for him."

"That's not untypical in a hostage situation. The

prisoner becomes emotionally involved with his captors."

"Yes, but we didn't expect him to embrace their cause. He has joined them. He even helped them write a manifesto, 'Levantmiento a Partir de la Cero a un Nuevo Principio.'"

Merrie said, "'Rising from Zero to a New Principle."

"It seems noble and worthwhile, young people unhappy with the world as they see it and wanting change. But instead of changing the world they have changed Jon. And here's the twist. Jon is the one demanding Chloe's trust money. He wants Chloe to turn over forty-seven million to them. He says she has so much money she won't miss it. Are those the words of a son, or the words of someone brainwashed against his mother?"

"Do you have any idea where he is?"

Buddy shrugged helplessly. "This country is mostly rain forest. We'll never find him."

"You can find him where there's a signal."

"Signal? What do you mean?"

"A cellphone signal. It would be much more likely that Jon is holed up in a rich man's house than a hut in the jungle. Maybe not far from where we're sitting."

"What if they move him around?"

"Cell phones store location files. You just need to tap into the technology. I'll bet the American Embassy has people who know how to do that."

"I still haven't given up hope that we can do this ourselves. We have to find Jon and bring him home whether he wants to or not."

"You're talking about an intervention."

"If that's what it takes. Jon doesn't trust me, he trusts only the people who hold him."

Chloe looked pleadingly at Merrie. "You are all we have. They won't let Buddy see Jon."

"If Jon has changed as radically as you say, then it's Jon who doesn't want to see his dad."

"That's why Chloe asked you here." Buddy said.

"This is my plan in a nutshell: I will notify Jon that we are ready to talk business and you are our representative. No money unless he meets with you. And when you do, I'll take over."

"Take over? How?"

"I've hired men trained like a S.W.A.T. team. They will follow you, overpower the members of El Grupo, grab Jon and get him the hell back where he belongs."

On that note of bravado, the entree was served, a huge mound of salt which the waiter broke open to reveal succulent filets of some kind of ocean fish, Merrie didn't know what nor did he care, it was delicious. They ended the meal with sorbet and a rich Nicaraguan coffee.

Afterward, as they walked into the lobby, Buddy said, "Managua comes to life now. Chloe and I are going out for stroll. Let's meet tomorrow and go over details." It was clear that Merrie wasn't invited to join them. He wouldn't have anyway.

"I'll stop at the gift shop for that cap you said I needed."

He bought one in navy blue with a white-stitched hotel logo for thirty dollars, an exorbitant sum but, as he studied his reflection in the elevator mirror, he decided that it looked fine on his head. Once in his room he relieved himself and sat on the edge of the bed with his iPhone. There would be roaming charges but this was a useful call.

Al answered. "How are you enjoying your Managua vacation?"

"Great. All quiet on the Western Front?"

"If you mean Station 28, no calls so far. What's up?"

"Got a question. Remember a few years ago when we joined some other fire departments and contributed a surplus pumper to the Managua Volunteer Fire Department?"

"Yeah, I remember. A Pierce Dash Pumper, right?"

"That's the one. Can you look up the Agenda Report

on it?"

"What for?"

"Since I'm here, I want to say hello to the guys we gave it to."

"That's nice, but if I were you I'd hang out on the beach and watch the bikinis."

"If I have time."

"You better. All of us here are enjoying your break vicariously."

"Call me at any hour. Consider me 24-on."

When Al called back it was past two in the morning. Merrie had his window open and was lying on the bed listening to the sounds of street life wafting up and into his room. It was soothing, the movement of traffic, the sounds of voices and laughter. Being a fireman had conditioned him to a nocturnal existence. He was truly a night person.

"Here's the info on the pumper you asked for."

Merrie grabbed the hotel's complimentary note pad and ballpoint on the nightstand. "Go ahead."

"We donated a 1999 Pierce, apparatus number 503, made in Appleton, Wisconsin, to Benemerito--B, e..."

"Just read it off, Al."

"The Benemerito Cuerpo de Bomberos de Managua. What does that mean?"

"The city's volunteer fire department."

"Oh, yeah, says so right here. The Managua fire department has two fire stations serving a population of 1.6 million people. Shit, that's not near enough."

"I know."

"They have 24 permanent firefighters and 350 volunteers working 48 hour shifts. They could use a union."

"Maybe I should try to organize them. Any local names, addresses?"

Merrie could hear paper rustling. "Can't find any."

"Never mind. What you gave me is a big help."

"So, you're going to see them?"

"Yup, pay a courtesy call in the morning."

He lay down but couldn't fall asleep. He dressed and went outside for a walk. The air was balmy, comfortable, small wonder people were out promenading, including elderly couples and mothers with baby strollers. He strolled up the avenue people watching. He found Managua a pleasant city, and it made him question the motives of rich kids who wanted to use zero as a starting point, as though all the advantages they had growing up didn't amount to anything. Maybe that was the answer. Their lives were too easy, boring; without challenge, risk, even danger. He wondered if the tropical climate with its manana attitude didn't have something to do with it as well. Who was it that said youth is wasted on the young? Was it Shaw? Whomever, the saying was a good fit for the Zero Group. Perhaps when they reach Merrie's age they might think differently. He was quite happy, even smug, that he was not twenty again. He was looking forward to meeting the puerile members of the Zero Group to see if age and experience would best youth and idealism.

20

The next morning Merrie got up at nine, early for Managua, and went down to the poolside buffet, which was sparsely attended. In this climate where people go to bed late, they get up late. He had finished breakfast when Chloe showed up, leisurely dressed, but the stares she got from the waiters were far from leisurely. He felt like preening when she sat down next to him.

"Where's Buddy?" he asked.

"His body clock is adjusted to the night life here. He'll probably sleep until noon. I wanted to talk to you alone anyway." A waiter brought her coffee. "Now that I'm with him again, I feel more helpless than ever."

Interesting, Merrie thought, Chloe referring to Buddy as a pronoun. "Why?" he asked.

"He seems trapped in some kind of time warp, as if we were living on parallel planes. He's there, I'm here, and we don't connect."

"Maybe it's always been like that, but you just noticed."

She stared at him over her raised coffee cup. "Because you're here too?"

"Could be."

"We both want to get Jon back."

"Of course, but you are looking for me to do it, not him. If I were in his shoes, I'd be jealous, too. Sometimes I wonder if you really know how much presence you have, the power that you exude."

"You're the first man who's ever told me that. Maybe that's what I've always needed, someone strong like you." She reached over and pulled her fingernails through his thick tangle of arm hair as though she were combing it. The touch sent an electric charge through him. He could not believe the incredible effect she had on his psyche.

"Chloe," he said, needing to change the subject, "I want to tell you something."

"What is it?"

"I asked the bartender in the Scenario last night if he'd heard of El Grupo Cero. They are not front page news, but he did give me the name of a member."

"Who?"

"Abelardo Esperidon."

She pulled her hand away. "Why would you believe the word of a bartender?" she asked, her voice had a nervous edge.

Merrie shrugged. "Bartenders hear a lot. It's the nature of their business."

She suddenly turned cold. "I'm disappointed that you did this without telling me."

"Why are you upset?"

"People talk, this is a nosy society. That bartender could just as easily tell someone that an American was asking questions about El Grupo. It could spoil Buddy's plan."

"You call bringing in a S.W.A.T. team a plan?"

"He likes to talk big."

"What about contacting Abelardo? Maybe he can help us."

"That is impossible. Please don't bring him up again, especially in front of Buddy."

Merrie felt cornered. This could be an opportunity lost. "What is it about this kid that makes him too hot to handle?"

"It's a personal matter," Chloe said emphatically. She crossed her legs and all the male wait staff paid attention. Under the table the toe of her shoe hit his shin. It was not accidental, more like a message. "I'm hungry, let's order breakfast."

Frustrated, Merrie rose from his chair. "I've already eaten. I think I'll pay a courtesy call on my counterparts in Managua."

"Counterparts? You mean firemen?"

"We're a band of brothers no matter what country we come from."

The look on her face told him what she thought of his idea. "I brought you here for one reason and one reason only: find Jon."

"I'll be back soon." He could feel her steely gaze follow him all the way to the exit. He didn't look back, recalling what happened to Lot's wife in Genesis.

Meredith caught a taxi outside the hotel and told the driver in Spanish to take him to the main fire station. They drove on a confusing array of boulevarded streets and angled secondary roads packed with parked cars. Looking out the window, he wondered why Chloe reacted so negatively when he mentioned Abelardo's name. The taxi pulled up in front of the fire station that looked for all the world like a large residence, the same concept as Station 28 in Minneapolis, intended to blend in with the neighborhood. The fire station was set diagonally in a triangular park with access to two major thoroughfares. Meredith had totally forgotten to exchange dollars into córdobas but the driver beamed when Merrie held up a ten.

"Merica dollah no problem, senor." he said.

Merrie told him to keep the change, which made the driver even happier. He walked up the wide concrete drive, the sun fiercely baking his head. He was happy to be wearing his new golf hat. At left, next to the large metal folding doors was a small entry door. He opened it and walked into a familiar scene: a spacious garage with two red trucks facing front, a wall of metal lockers and firemen's hats on hooks, fluorescent fixtures hanging up high with several tubes burned out. One of the fire engines was the gifted Pierce Pumper, its equipment polished to a high gloss. They were taking good care of it. He looked around for someone to talk to. He saw no one about, and so he walked to the back of the building where the living quarters were. He came upon a common room—monkish-plain with a table, folding chairs, a counter, cookstove and refrigerator. Two men were sitting at the table drinking coffee and playing cribbage. He watched the two men counting 15s and runs—except for the Spanish it was just like home.

"Buenos dias, camaradas."

They turned, attentive to being called comrades.

He told them in Spanish that he was a visitor from America. "Mi nombres Meredith Gilbert." He added that he was one of the firefighters who helped donate the Pierce Pumper

They put down their cards, stood up, embraced Merrie with kisses on both cheeks and introduced themselves as Pablo and Juan Carlos. Juan Carlos appeared to be the boss, at least he was dressed as if he were, a white shirt that had cloth bars on the shoulders.

"Es usted el capitan?"

"Si, si, senor."

Merrie explained that he, too, was a captain.

Juan Carlos unfolded a chair and set it by the table. "Por favor, sientese."

Merrie joined them and they talked shop for a while which morphed into personal histories about family and children. They were surprised that Merrie was not married and had no children, at least none that he knew of, which evoked laughter.

Small talk, he knew, was the custom in countries like Nicaragua, a necessary prologue to serious business. When he felt it was comfortable to change the subject he asked if either had ever heard the name Ernesto Esperidon.

Both men nodded. "El viene de un familia bien conocida."

The bartender was correct: Ernesto was the developer responsible for the hotel Merrie was staying at as well as the attendant shopping complex, MetroCentre. Esperidon made a good front, Merrie was told, an elegant mansion and a collection of classic cars, but the rumor was that he had overreached when he built MetroCentre, and investors were concerned that the parent company, Empresa Constructruccion Imperio, ECI, was having problems making good on its notes.

Merrie now knew of two developers on the ropes: ECI and Boa Constructors. Could there be a connection? Too preposterous Merrie wanted to think but it nagged him.

"Usted tiene un computer?" he asked.

"Ordenardo?" Juan Carlos responded. "Si, si." He stood and ushered Merrie to an office adjacent to the common room with an oak desk and chair that looked as if it had once been part of a film noir set. There was a large cork board on the wall that was dotted with pushpins holding dozens of sheets of paper for assignments, addresses, maps, engine maintenance records, vacation schedules and, who knew, maybe even Spanish Conquistadores guard-watch assignments. He sat in front of a sturdy Dell Optiplex 780 monitor with Juan Carlos looking over his shoulder to help him get on the internet.

Merrie entered ECI and found its official website with glowing accounts of success, nothing but boilerplate. He punched in Ernesto Espiridon and got pages of Ernesto Espiridons all over Latin and South America, even the USA. Seeing USA on the screen gave him an idea. He typed in R&S Bank, Bloomington MN USA, and played around with various links until he found an entry for the bank's Annual Report and downloaded it. He could have walked around the block but it was worth the wait. In the Bank's balance sheet he discovered that the financials were categorized into residential and commercial, and Boa Constructors was halfway down the list of commercial accounts, not too big not too small, a Goldilocks Corporation, he thought, priding himself for his clever simile. He was about to close the site when he noticed an asterisk on Boa's line. He almost missed it. He looked for the connecting asterisk, finding it at the bottom of the page in very small type, like the disclaimers one sees in car-lease ads. He squinted to read the line: Empresa Constructruccion Imperio (ECI) of Managua Nicaragua, doing business as BOA Constructors, Minneapolis, MN USA, $45,500,000.

He rolled the chair away from the desk, staring at the monitor. What in hell is going on? R&S is a regional bank, prevented from doing business abroad. And, yet, there is ECI on R&S's balance sheet, money funneled through Boa to ECI. He wondered if the deal with the Montreal Bank had been a desperate, last-ditch effort to be in compliance before bank regulators found out that R&S had lent a Managuan corporation more than forty mil using Boa Constructors as a front.

And what about El Grupo? Jon Boynton was trying to wring millions out of his mother's trust to fund their quixotic cause, a huge amount of money that begged the question, why would a renegade group of young kids from affluent families need that kind of swag? It didn't hit Merrie at first but then he realized that the 47 million El Grupo demanded from Chloe was nearly the same as R&S's loan to ECI: $45,500,000. That was no coincidence.

His face must have revealed his confusion. Juan Carlos stared curiously with his ink-dark eyes.

"Es algo incorrecto?"

Merrie shook his head. He wondered if these guys knew anything about the Zero Group. "Usted ha oido hablas El Grupo Cero?"

Juan Carlo called out to his partner still in the common room. "Hey, Pablo, eschucho esto. El Grupo Cero!" He began laughing.

Pablo joined them in the office, laughing as well.

Merrie stared uncomprehendingly. "What is so funny?" he asked.

"El arranque de cinta el grupo cerro es bombero

voluntario!"

Merrie couldn't believe what he was hearing and it was evident that the two firemen were having a great time watching Merrie's jaw drop as they explained how the heir to one of the richest families in Nicaragua and founder of the Zero Group became a volunteer fireman: Abelardo Esperidon. He attended private schools in Europe, they weren't sure where. He returned home after graduation, went to work at ECI but hated sitting behind a desk in a business suit, and craved adventure. The gift of the Pierce Pumper was big news in Managua and it gave Abelardo an idea: why not join the volunteer fire fighters, become one of the 350 in the Benemerito Cuerpo de Bomberos de Managua?

As he listened in wonderment at this unfolding story, Merrie was also transfixed by the energetic moves--hands waving, shoulders shifting, torsos swinging--and he speculated that the firemen were either reacting to the sheer pleasure of telling the story or this was simply a part of their expressive culture.

"El nino era bueno!" Juan Carlos said, slapping his thigh and laughing along with Pablo.

Now Meredith understood that they were laughing not to make fun of the young man, they were laughing in praise of him. And Meredith laughed, too, for the same reason.

The story continued: When Abelardo showed up to volunteer, no one took him seriously. He was just a rich kid out having fun. But he worked hard, learned how to handle a pulsating fire hose, climb a ladder and, most important, respect equipment. He knew cars from his father's collection and studied the Pierce maintenance manuals, which he downloaded off the Internet. He taught himself to become a master mechanic and was eventually put in charge of maintaining the Pierce Pumper, not just the engine but also the compressors and hydraulics that ran the high-pressure pumps and extension ladders. He was even given a certificate of accomplishment from the Pierce

Company in Oshkosh, Wisconsin.

And being a fireman so affected Abelardo, Juan Carlos continued, that the young volunteer founded El Grupo Cero. Having lived a life of privilege, he had never before been exposed to the poverty and the wretchedness he saw in tugurios where he helped put out fires. As Abelardo became disenchanted with the way the rich lived in gated compounds with swimming pools, tennis courts and six-car garages, his father, Ernesto, became disenchanted with his own son. An ultimatum was delivered, typical of a patriarch of old South American families: quit the volunteer fire brigade and the quixotic El Grupo or be disowned. In a fit of pique and stubbornness, Abelardo moved out of his parents' home and into Firehouse Three, bunking permanently but moving to a different bed as shifts changed.

Meredith asked if he could meet him.

"Si, si." They explained that Alberado would enjoy meeting an American fireman. And, Juan Carlos added, "Y el habla Ingles!"

Meredith was glad to hear that. His Spanish was being stretched to the limit.

Juan Carlos called a number on the dispatcher's telephone and spoke such rapid Spanish, Merrie had trouble understanding but a few key words: American, fire captain, visitor.

Juan Carlos handed him the phone. "Hello," he said into it, "this is Meredith Gilbert."

"Good morning, Captain Gilbert, I am Abelardo Esperidon." His voice was smooth, well modulated, his English inflected with the crisp enunciation of those who attended schools of refinement.

"I've heard a great deal about you from Juan Carlos."

"All good, I hope."

"High praise from a fellow fireman. I'd like to meet you."

"I'm sure we can arrange that. When would you

suggest?"

"Today.

"I am a volunteer. My time is my own. How about lunch?"

Merrie knew lunch here would be in the middle of the afternoon. He looked at his watch. Ten after ten. "How about breakfast?"

"May I suggest Grillo's, a cafe near the Station."

While waiting, Merrie was given a detailed examination of the Pierce Pumper that Abelardo so proudly maintained. Juan Carlos cited statistics of the runs and putouts the rig had been involved in. Merrie nodded appreciatively even though he knew the equipment by heart. He acknowledged that the old truck was lovingly cared for. The bright work glistened, the red paint waxed to a bright shine. It was all very impressive. He excused himself to use the toilet which gave him time to check his messages and found a text from Chloe: Meet for lunch 2 pm important.

He texted back: K.

Abelardo drove into the lot in a dusty Ford F150, giving it the appearance of a working man's truck. He jumped out, a dark-featured lad of average height, who moved with the litheness of a panther. He walked fast as if eager to meet the American fireman. The two shook hands, and there was the immediate bond that occurs between persons with shared experiences.

They walked to the Grillo, a bustling cafe with high tables that you stand at to eat. There was a noisy commotion about the place, filled with patrons who seemed always in motion, even while they were eating. Merrie enjoyed the atmosphere, it gave him a lift.

"Juan Carlos tells me you are a master mechanic. That's quite an accomplishment." He almost had to shout to be heard as they were shown to a table.

"Thank you, Captain Gilbert."

"Call me Meredith."

"I was raised to address my superiors formally. I'd prefer to call you Captain."

"That's more respect than I get back home."

Abelardo looked away, not sure how to take Merrie's offbeat humor.

"You are a man of more than singular accomplishment," Merrie added, "I understand that you founded El Grupo Cero."

"Idealism and youth, a heady combination, don't you think? After I became a fireman and made calls to the tugurios, and saw firsthand the conditions so many people lived in, I knew I could not go back to my old life. Others who shared my beliefs banded together, nothing revolutionary mind you, just young people who meet at coffee houses and discuss the inequities in the world. We named ourselves El Grupo Cero. We intended to remain apolitical but it wasn't easy, especially when an American friend, Jonathon Boynton, joined us."

Meredith leaned forward so he could hear over the din. "Whom did you say?"

"Jonathon Boynton, we met in Zurich at school."

Merrie leaned back. Jackpot. "Tell me about him."

"In college he was quiet, introspective. But after he moved to Nicaragua he became quite radical in his thinking, and this surprises me because he comes from a prominent family in Minneapolis..." Abelardo stopped. "Isn't that where you also are from?"

Merrie nodded.

Abelardo furrowed his forehead. "Is this a coincidence?"

"The Boyntons are trying to contact Jon and I've been asked to intercede. His father claims that El Grupo Cero brainwashed him into demanding money from his mother's estate to support their cause."

"El Grupo doesn't need or want money. It is a grass roots organization. How much is he demanding?"

"Forty seven million."

Even with the noise Merrie could hear Abelardo whistle. "That is unbelievable."

"So you don't know anything about it?"

"My involvement with the fire department has taken up much of my time but, even so, someone would have told me."

Merrie thought for awhile. "Maybe it's a made-up story."

"But why?"

"I don't know, but I intend to find out. When was the last time you saw Jon?"

"I haven't seen him for weeks."

"Can you get in touch with him?"

"He has an apartment in the old town, near the school where he teaches English."

Merrie wondered, if he is that easy to get hold of why hasn't Buddy contacted him? "I want to meet Jon as soon as possible, tonight if you can set it up."

"What shall I tell him?"

"Tell him there is a plot to swindle his mother out of her fortune, and if he wants to stop it, he has to see me."

"If he says no?"

"His dad will come after him with a S.W.A.T. team."

Their breakfast arrived, Spanish omelets, thick-cut bacon, dark bread that tasted like molasses, and steaming coffee that also tasted like molasses. They ate without talking. Presently Abelardo, raising his voice several decibels to be heard, said, "Jon confided to me that his father was strict and overly demanding. Jon was expected to go to work for him, eventually taking over the business, which he had no interest in. That is why he came to Nicaragua." Abelardo made a wan smile. "Very like my own circumstance. My father was bitter when I joined the fire department. He considered it a personal affront that I would choose a job that dirtied my fingernails."

"There is nothing more noble than working with

your hands."

"I wish my father thought so."

Merrie smiled sympathetically. "Someday he will."

"You don't know our culture." Abelardo became crestfallen. "My father is stubborn and he will never change his mind. Even on his death bed."

Merrie felt his gorge rise in defense of Abelardo. "You know what I'd tell your father if I saw him? I'd tell him to get off his ass, come down to the firehouse and check out that Pierce Pumper you keep in top shape. Then I'd have him go on a run, preferably to his own house, and watch you save it from burning to the ground."

When Merrie finished his diatribe, Abelardo shouted "Hooray!" so loudly he was heard above the noise. Diners turned to look at him, smiling in support even if they didn't know what he was cheering about.

Merrie looked around, feeling embarrassed that he had gone so overboard, but he wanted to show Abelardo how much he admired him. If he had a son he'd want him to be just like this kid.

Abelardo gripped his arm. "Would you?"

"Would I what?"

"Talk to my father?"

Merrie stared. He had to be more careful how he expressed himself in a country where people take you literally. "I don't think it's my place to..."

Abelardo would not let go of Merrie's arm. "No one has ever told my father off, like you just did."

"Not to his face I trust."

"I'd love to see the look on it if you did."

Abelardo grew serious, "My father is a bully because no one has the courage to tell him what he needs to hear. He would listen to you, he may not like it, but he would listen because he admires cojones and you, dear friend Captain Meredith, have cojones." He let go of Merrie's arm and leaned back, awaiting a reply.

Meredith wanted to help Abelardo. He liked the kid so much he would say yes but he could not forget his mission here: find Jon and bring him back. Merrie didn't have time to take on another assignment; fight one fire at a time was his motto. Then he thought about the link between ECI and Boa and wondered, what the hell, why not kill two birds with one stone. If he had the cojones Abelardo said he had, he could press Esperidon into telling him why his company and Buddy's are mixed together in R&S's balance sheet.

"Abelardo, I'd consider it an honor."

The young fireman finished his breakfast with gusto. "This is a day of good omens," he said exuberantly. "I will arrange two meetings: one with Jon and one with my father."

21

Abelardo gave Meredith a ride back to the hotel in his Ford 150. The souped-up engine with straight pipes had a deep-throated sound as the manifold vibrated the exhaust gases out of the engine and into the air. It was a kid thing to do, making pedestrian's heads turn, mostly in annoyance, as they drove by, something Merrie once did when he was a teenager with the first car he ever owned, what he lovingly nicknamed Plodge, a '36 Plymouth Coupe with a '38 Dodge engine.

Abelardo promised to call Jonathan and set up a time to meet, tonight if that could be arranged. Merrie was to come alone, no parents, or the deal was off. It was up to Merrie to convince Jon's parents they could not be present at the rendezvous. Abelardo would call, give Merrie the time, and pick him up at the hotel.

Meredith was glad to return to the hotel because neither the pickup nor the fire station was air-conditioned. The cold air hit him like a wide-open refrigerator and he shivered briefly as his body became accustomed to the abrupt drop in temperature.

He went to his room to freshen up before contacting Chloe and Buddy. He had big news--meeting Abelardo-- but he wasn't sure how they would take it, especially Chloe who was angry that he even brought up his name. Still, the fact that Abelardo was going to arrange a meeting with Jonathan should please them. He smiled into the mirror. Merrie to the rescue, just the way a fireman should act. Will Buddy's nose be of out of joint over this? Feeling smug, he took a long shower, luxuriating in the pinpricks of water hitting his skin. He toweled off slowly, perhaps sybaritically, as he imagined Chloe looking at him from the doorway taking pleasure in seeing him like this, in the raw, pulling the towel back and forth across his arched back.

As he donned fresh slacks he noticed that his cellphone on the coffee table was vibrating. Probably Chloe calling to see how his morning went. He picked it up and saw that it was Ben. He hadn't been in Nicaragua more than a day and already the Americano Policia were calling, he thought, laughing to himself. He debated for an instant, considering whether he should answer or call Ben back later. In his present state of elation, Minneapolis was so far off his radar screen as to be nonexistent. But he knew Ben was a no-nonsense guy and would not call unless he had a damned good reason for doing so. Maybe there was news about Thorpe's murder.

He answered, "Gilbert."

"Where the living fuck are you?" Ben was in a no-nonsense mood all right.

"Why do you want to know?"

"I've got a summons for your arrest, that's why."

"What in hell are you talking about?"

"There's an APB out for you and we can't find you anywhere, like you disappeared off the face of the earth. That goes double for Mrs. Boynton and triple for her old man. Answer my question, Merrie, where are you?"

No sense beating around the bush. "Managua, Nicaragua."

The silence that followed was long enough to park an 18-wheeler. "You are *where?*" Ben finally asked.

"Managua Nicaragua, southwest off the tip of Mexico, between Costa Rica and..."

"I know where it is, goddammit!" Ben stormed back. "Just tell me what the hell you're doing there!"

"I came to help Chloe Boynton get her son back."

"Her son?"

"His name is Jonathan. He got involved with a

group called El Grupo Cero, a bunch of radical kids who want to change the world. Buddy hasn't had any luck contacting him and she asked me to be a kind of third-party intermediary. So we flew down here yesterday in a private jet. Not a bad way to travel by the way."

"Merrie, if you're bullshitting me..."

"That's why her husband left town. He couldn't advertise that he was coming here to help Jon, and so he faked his disappearance."

"Why didn't you tell me?"

"I'm telling you now. It's possible Thorpe's killing is connected to Nicaragua."

Merrie could sense that Ben was shaking his head in disbelief.

"There's a huge commercial development here that was funded by R&S Bank using Boa Constructors as a money laundry, so big it makes Boynton's business look like a lemonade stand. Jonathan is being held hostage in exchange for bailout money to save that development using Chloe Boynton's trust fund in Zurich, a fortune she'd have to turn over in exchange for the safe return of her son. I talked to the kid whose father is the developer and he's going to set up a meeting. I hope that will lead to some answers..."

"Listen to me, Merrie, before it's too late. You've been dragged into some crazy conspiracy theory with that Boynton woman. She's got you so mixed up, you'd believe anything. Buddy killed Thorpe, and his wife helped him skip the country. If you separate yourself from her I may be able to help you. If you don't, you will go down too. You are involved in a conspiracy to commit murder. Aiding and abetting a capital crime. Book a commercial flight as soon as you can and get your ass back here. You'll be arraigned, but plead not guilty, post bond, and be free in an hour."

"Then what?"

"Hire Meshbesher. He's a good defense lawyer."

"Can't afford him."

"How about Mrs. Moneybags?"

"Who?"

"Mrs. Boynton. You say she's loaded."

"I'm not going to beg money off Chloe. And I'm not coming home until I clear not only my name but hers as well."

"Yeah? And what about her husband? Are you going to clear his name too?"

22

Meredith found Chloe and Buddy in the outdoor pool lounge under an umbrella having a drink. Buddy was sipping a martini and, as Merrie sat down, he ordered another one. Merrie wondered how in hell Buddy could drink martinis in this heat. Chloe was working on a glass of white wine with an ice cube.

Merrie, deciding he needed to keep his head clear, asked for a Diet Coke. He had to tell them about meeting Abelardo and the plan to rendezvous with Jon, effectively bypassing Buddy, and defying Chloe's admonition to shut up about Abelardo. Merrie expected a blow-up and he had to be ready to counterpunch.

The prospect of confrontation caused a sudden, involuntary shudder of anxiety, the same reaction when he entered a burning building, hearing the joists overhead crackle, knowing that everything could come crashing down at any second.

Chloe looked at him. "Are you all right?"

He shrugged. "Still getting used to the climate."

Buddy laughed condescendingly, "Here you sweat, not shiver." He looked at his Rolex. "You're late. Chloe told me you visited a fire station."

"I went to see a pumper donated by American firefighters a few years ago."

Buddy laughed. "I'd be amazed if it's still running."

"It's been well-maintained by the station's master mechanic. I met him today."

Buddy said snidely, "I didn't think Nicaraguans

could master anything, let alone mechanics."

"He was educated in Europe. A bright young kid who happens to be a friend of your son's." Merrie hesitated, waiting to see who would react first. It was Chloe. She nearly spilled her wine.

Buddy was still processing the information when his second martini was served. Fortunately, the waiter's arm came between them or Buddy might have been more physical.

"Someone who knows Jon?" he demanded.

"Abelardo Esperidon."

Buddy swallowed his second martini in two gulps and chewed the olive furiously. "What the fuck are you up to?" he hissed, particles of olive flying through the air.

"Meeting him was pure coincidence. He's a volunteer at the fire station. Small world," Merrie smiled even though he knew there was nothing he could do to ease the tension.

Chloe stared. "I asked you not to interfere."

"Is that what the bump on my leg meant?"

Her face reddened.

"What have you two been hatching?" Buddy glared at his wife. "If you've been fooling around behind my back with this fireman..."

Even though he intensely disliked being patronized by this blowhard, Merrie decided a calm approach was better than going in with guns blazing.

"Abelardo wants to help. He thinks he can arrange a meeting with Jon. It's worth a try. You want to get your son back, don't you?"

"Of course we do," Chloe said, "we all do." She was looking at Buddy but addressing Meredith.

"Are you really buying this bullshit?" Buddy said, still fuming.

"I'm not selling, I'm telling," Merrie decided to fire back. "Abelardo is going to talk to Jon to see if he will meet me."

"What makes you think he will?"

"Abelardo and Jon are friends. I think Jon will listen to him. He's a bright, caring kid and wants to help. And they both have issues with their fathers so that gives them something else in common."

"What issues?" Buddy asked suspiciously.

Meredith explained Abelardo's falling out with his father.

"Dumb kid, he should listen to his old man. He'll never get rich chasing fires, right, fireman?"

"Please," Chloe intervened, "stop carping at each other." The bickering between the two men was clearly wearing on her. "Maybe we should just get help, go to the local police, someone at our embassy..."

"We already talked about that," Buddy snapped. "This is a private matter. No police, no embassy officials nosing around, asking questions."

"Ok, then. What Merrie proposes may be our best chance after all to make contact with Jon, can't you see that, Buddy?"

All Buddy could see right now was another martini but when he raised his arm to signal the waiter Chloe pulled it down and gave him a look that said, you've had enough.

Buddy acquiesced. "All right, all right."

"Like Chloe said," Merrie continued, "this might be our best chance to make contact with Abelardo's intervention..."

"Intervention!" Buddy jumped in. "I saw that on a Dr. Phil show. He helped parents get their teenage son into rehab."

"Jon is not a teenager, he's an adult and if he doesn't want to see you there's not much you can do about it. It will be up to me to convince him."

Buddy looked Merrie in the eye. "And if you can't?"

"Then you can move in with your S.W.A.T. team."

23

Merrie left Buddy and Chloe to simmer in the stew of their mutual and, as far as he was concerned, self-destructive mistrust. If there ever was a marriage in jeopardy, this was it and confirmed his suspicion that marriage was not for him. But then, he speculated, what if he had met Chloe before she had met Buddy. Would he have married her and, instead of being her lover, being the guy she argued with across the table? No, he decided, being a lover no matter how short it lasted is better than being a husband no matter how long it lasted.

Moreover he was pissed at Buddy for referring to him by his job description rather than his name. This mockery made him even more determined to find Jon and expose Buddy for what he was, a gutless wonder. Even so, his rational side knew what really was frustrating him: not being able to get close to Chloe. His mere presence was a constant reminder that it was Buddy, not Merrie, who saw Chloe naked every day during her intimate moments, argued with her, had make-up sex on the floor.

These thoughts caused Merrie to ache with jealousy – his groin was like a war zone and he yearned for Chloe to lick his wounds.

Merrie had long endured the boredom of down time but waiting for the hours to pass in this sultry climate was like waiting for an iguana to move in the hot sun. He figured more than half of his work life was spent waiting, waiting for the claxon horn to blare and, when it did, the inevitable rush of adrenaline spurring him to action, climbing into his setups and then racing to the truck (the fireman's pole now a relic of the past). He could look back on three times he came close to death, and it was a combination of luck, training, experience and, most of all, the competence of his fellow fire fighters that saved him. Overcome by smoke, he was dragged unconscious out of a smoldering building by Al. Another time, the ladder he was on suddenly jerked and knocked him sideways, nearly plunging him to the ground five stories down. And the third time, a suicidal drunk, with half a dozen DUIs who had just totaled his car for number seven, pulled a knife while Merrie was trying to pull the man free, and slashed him right through his canvas jacket and into his chest, leaving a red scar to remind him that he could die bravely or foolishly depending on the circumstances.

Finally, while watching Spanish television, his phone rang. He reacted as he if he had been roused by the firehouse claxon horn. He jumped to his feet, ready for action.

He answered, "Gilbert."

"Mr. Meredith, it is Abelardo calling."

"With good news, I hope."

"I would say so, yes. I spoke with Jon. He agreed, but only to see you. No one else."

"When?"

"Tonight, late."

"How late."

"Midnight. I will pick you up at your hotel at 11:30. It is a fair drive."

"I'll be ready, but I don't want anyone to see me." Merrie still did not trust Buddy to attempt a so-called intervention just to one-up the fireman. "I'd rather meet you somewhere else. How about the hotel parking ramp?"

"Inside?"

Meredith had thought this out in advance. "Yes. Drive up to level five where I'll wait for you by the exit door. Do you have any other vehicle besides that Ford with the straight pipes? It does draw stares."

Abelardo laughed politely. "Those are very sophisticated mufflers. I can shut them off anytime."

And why shouldn't he be able to? Merrie asked himself. The kid's a master mechanic.

"Great. I will see you at 11:30, level five, the hotel ramp."

After dinner alone he went back to his room, and put the charger on his phone even though it was at 90%. He wanted it fully charged at 100%, a number he also hoped would reflect the success of his mission. At eleven o'clock he rode the hotel elevator to the second level balcony and took a stairway down the covered walkway toward the MetroCentre, still alive with late-night shoppers. The route to his rendezvous with Abelardo had to be circuitous in case he was being followed, and so he wandered through the concourse pretending to window shop and looked at reflections in the glass to see if there was anyone who didn't have the honed-in stare of a shopper. He stepped into a gift store and studied the greeting card section where he settled on sympathy cards, figuring that if he needed a card at all it would be one for sympathy. Looking out the window of the shop, he didn't see anything out of the ordinary and yet he was still uneasy. This was the sort of danger he had never faced before: an unseen enemy. Maybe it was his heightened imagination but then all he had to do was remind himself that Jim Thorpe had been murdered. That was Minneapolis and this was Managua, but only a fool would assume there was no connection.

After what he figured was a long enough passage of time, he left the shop without buying anything and walked to the elevators. He hung back until the door closed, making sure he was the only passenger in the car. He rode up to level six, got out and walked the ramp stairway down to level five where he took up a position behind a pillar. The ramp was dimly lit, with few cars parked at this high level, probably those of people working in the complex.

Meredith stayed in the shadows and waited. Presently a pickup came up the ramp, headlights shining ceilingward; no unearthly sound of throbbing pistons, only the normal hum of a well-tuned engine. It was Abelardo with his straight pipes turned off. Merrie came out from the shadows as the pickup came alongside. The young man stopped and Merrie climbed in. Abelardo pulled into a vacant parking spot, adroitly backed the truck out and reversed his path down the ramp and into the street. It was 11:30 p.m.

Abelardo drove purposefully, quietly. Conversation was at a premium as he steered his truck through traffic, which became less congested when they reached the outskirts of the city whose diminishing lights behind them became an afterglow against a dark sky. Soon, the truck's lights were the only illumination in an otherwise empty two-lane road.

Presently Meredith asked, "Why are we going so far?"

"Jon's wish."

"Is he wishing as Jonathon Boynton or as head of El Cero?"

"A little of both, I think. He is wary, suspicious. This is not the carefree playboy I knew in college."

"Why is he willing to see me?"

"To send a message, he told me. He wants a conduit to the outside world. You, Mr. Meredith, have become that conduit."

"He doesn't even know me."

"I wouldn't say that."

"What do you mean?"

"El Cero has allies beyond the shores of our little country. He may have learned a few things about you."

Merrie thought about the warning scratched on his Cadillac. "Even in Minneapolis?"

"It is always possible, inasmuch as Minneapolis was his home. And, of course, the source of the money."

"You mean his mother's inheritance?"

Abelardo did not respond and when Merrie turned he saw him nodding his head.

"How do you know all this?"

"We were friends, compatriots, we confided in one another, at one time we were partners in crime."

"Crime?" Meredith asked. "Like murder?"

"At one time I believed that if it would advance our cause, I would not rule it out."

"Are you aware that a bank officer in Minneapolis was murdered? He's connected to Jon's father, Buddy Boynton."

Abelardo took his eyes off the road and looked briefly at Merrie. "When did this happen?"

"A month ago."

Abelardo did not reply.

Merrie looked out the window at the darkness hugging the road. Where were they going? And, more important, what in hell was he doing here in the first place? It had all started innocently enough, or so it appeared at the time, an empty canoe which initiated a phone call to Chloe Boynton. And now here he was entrusting his very life to a Nicaraguan he had met only today. He had the strange and unnerving sensation that he was in a long dark tunnel with no exit, trapped in a venture that gained him absolutely nothing except the un-promised love of a woman.

Abelardo slowed and turned onto a dirt drive. He stopped, doused the lights and cut the engine. The stingy light of a gibbous moon revealed the silhouette of a farmhouse.

"I will wait here."

Merrie got out of the truck and stood for a moment, taking in the gloomy scene. Then he walked slowly, carefully as though on a treacherous path, to a narrow porch with square posts holding up the roof.

He climbed two steps onto a wood floor that sagged under his weight. He opened the door and entered a dark room. A figure sat by a table.

The figure spoke, "Sit across from me."

Merrie bumped into a chair and sat down. "Did you forget to pay your electric bill?"

There was a condescending laugh. "Only Managua glows at night."

"How do I know you are Jonathon Boynton?"

"Ask me a question. Ask me about Minneapolis."

"Ok. Where did you go to high school?"

"Breck," he responded quickly, "at the intersection of Highway 100 and Golden Valley Road a mile west of Theodore Wirth Lake."

"Good enough," Merrie said, satisfied. "It's a far cry from Breck to a Nicaraguan farmhouse isn't it?"

"Not far enough to escape the stupidity of governments, churches, corporations."

"Can you be more specific?"

Jon angrily struck a match and lighted a cigarette. "Don't mock me." The brief light exposed a delicate nose and drawn cheeks with acne scars. His fingers were trembling. "We can no longer sit idly by and watch the collapse of our planet. We are on the verge of mass extinction. The earth will become uninhabitable. Is that the legacy you want to leave your children?"

Jon was either high or programmed. Were they alone in the dark or was there a figure hidden in the shadows listening?

"You sound like someone who has memorized his lines."

"No one is telling me what to do."

"I want us to be honest with each other."

"How can you be honest if you are speaking for my parents?"

"I am speaking for myself. I want to find out if you are really being held by El Grupo or you are a pawn in a conspiracy to get access to your mother's money."

Jon was silent for a moment drawing on his cigarette, the glow blinking like a tiny red warning light.

"Why should I confide in you?"

"Have you got anyone else?"

"Do you trust my parents?"

"I came here to help them get their son back, but I learned a few things since arriving that makes me wonder if I *can* trust them."

"Were you offered a reward?" Exhaled smoke punctuated his words.

"To bring you back? No."

"You were bought one way or another, Mr. Gilbert."

Merrie smiled wryly in the dark. Jon was correct. Merrie had been bought, with his mother's guile. "I want to help you, not them."

"You underestimate the situation. You could be killed."

"Like Jim Thorpe?" This was a stab in the dark, figuratively and literally.

"Who is he?" Jon asked, almost defiantly, and dropped his cigarette on the wood floor, grinding it with the tip of his shoe as though it were a scorpion.

"Your dad's banker in Minneapolis. He was fished out of Lake Harriet a month ago."

"What has that to do with me?"

"There is a Managua connection. The dead man's bank was involved in financing the MetroCentre."

Jon shifted in his chair. The legs strained. "You are well-informed."

"I do my homework. What's the connection, Jon?"

"My mother, it all hinges on that..." he began and suddenly the door behind Merrie burst open and in a split second, before he had a chance to react, to protect himself, a large sack was thrown over his head, trapping him in filthy air. He squirmed to free himself but powerful arms pulled the sack down over his body. A rope secured the sack firmly to his torso. He heard Jon yelling amid a confusion of chairs crashing and the table falling over. Merrie lunged blindly sending someone into the wall with a heavy grunt and Spanish curses. He hurled himself back and forth, seeking another body to collide with when he was hit over the head. Whatever hit him was not hard, but yielded like a bag of onions. It was enough to daze him and drop him to his knees. A heavy boot pushed him over and he was on his back with someone sitting on his stomach.

A panting voice said in Spanish, "Lie quietly or you will suffocate."

The gunnysack was loosely woven and he could breathe if he didn't struggle. But he could talk.

In Spanish he said, "What have you done to Jon Boynton?"

For an answer, two men smelling of sweat and tequila pulled Merrie to his feet. They dragged him outside and, using the loose ends of the rope, tied him to a nearby tree. In the distance he heard a starter grind and a rough engine come to life. The vehicle came closer, doors opened and closed, and wheels spun sending pebbles slamming against his body. The sound of the engine receded and in a few seconds Merrie was alone in utter silence.

"Abelardo!" he called out. "Are you there?"

Nothing.

Merrie strained against the rope and shouted again, "Abelardo!" Still nothing. Where the hell is he? He said he would wait.

Sweat poured from Merrie's body as he struggled and the foul air in the sack labored his breathing. He wouldn't last long if he didn't get the sack off his head. His sweat was mingling with the dirt turning it into a muckiness that covered his cheeks and oozed down his neck. He forced his face against the sack to see if he could chew a hole to breathe through but he couldn't get enough tension. He cursed in outrage at being bushwhacked, furious with himself for not being more cautious, for not sitting facing the door, for not insisting that there be light so he could see better--not, not, not! How could he be so stupid! Thoughts tumbled one over the other looking for answers. Who knew he was here other than Abelardo? Did El Grupo hire the attackers? If so, were they concerned that Jon might choose his parents over their ideology and go back with Merrie? Or maybe they were Buddy's henchmen, his S.W.A.T. team. But how did they find him, he was so goddamned careful not to be followed.

Jon was ready to tell Merrie about his mother's wealth when the goons attacked him. "It all hinges on that," Jon had said, and then all hell broke loose. Maybe the thugs were waiting outside listening and, when Jon decided to talk, they rushed in. How come Merrie didn't hear anything?

He had to clear his mind, stop thinking about anything other than getting out of this fucking sack! He relaxed his muscles, going into survival mode. He'd been in tight places before and lived to tell about it. Would he live to tell about it this time? And if he did who would be around to listen? He turned his hands up as far as he could and gripped the gunny sack and pulled it down under the rope, then he gathered more material, pulling down again several times until the material was taut over his head. He was now able to push his mouth against the rough weaving, almost gagging at the awful taste, and began to chew a hole. Little by little, spitting out pieces of material he chewed off, he was able make an opening allowing him to breathe fresh air. This revived his sapping energy and he continued chewing like a mantis devouring a leaf until he made a hole big enough to push his head through. He looked down at the rope around his waist. He spotted the knot and worked his fingers until he was able to loosen it. Hours seemed to pass before he was free of his bondage. He pulled the sack off, fell over and lay on the dirt looking up at the sky, taking in deep gulps of air.

Gazing at the stars he thought about the guy sitting on his stomach, telling him to stop struggling or he would suffocate, as if he were concerned about his welfare. The attackers could have killed him right then instead of tying him to a tree. Maybe the attackers figured he would free himself. How many were there? Merrie remembered fighting two men. That meant there had to be at least one other to grab Jon and carry him off. One person could easily have done that. The kid didn't appear very strong. Where did they take Jon and, more important, why?

Merrie felt the cell phone in his trouser pocket; the attackers didn't bother to take it because they knew there was no signal out here in the country. He got up feeling greasy from the combination of sweat and dirt on his face and body. He walked around to the back of the farmhouse and found what he was looking for: a hand pump with a washtub under it. He pulled up water. It was cool and refreshing. He bent over letting the water pour over his face, he opened his mouth and let the cool water wash down his throat. He rinsed his shirt, wrung it out and put it back on. The damp material against his skin felt good. He walked back to the front of the house, sat down on the steps and waited.

24

Merrie checked the time on his iPhone. It was after one, several hours until dawn. He decided to stay put and not try to find his way in the dark. He remembered that Abelardo had turned onto the dirt road a mile or two back. With morning light, he would follow it until he reached the main highway and hail a car. Maybe he could use his cell phone by then. He would not call Chloe or Buddy. No, he would call Juan Carlos. In an emergency, call a fireman.

A half hour went by. Patience was not one of his virtues--perhaps he had none--but he forced himself to stay calm to preserve his waning energy. He was getting hungry. At least he had water to drink of which he availed himself several times, walking around the house to the pump and drawing up the fresh well water. It was fortifying.

Around one forty-five he heard a vehicle coming toward him. He was ready to run into the woods as the headlights came closer. Then he stopped and listened carefully. The engine was not rough and out of tune like the car the attackers drove away in. The cylinders in this engine were in perfect harmony; a subdued but eager rumble came out of the exhaust. Had to be Abelardo in his souped-up Ford 150. Merrie walked toward the road as the pickup approached. Abelardo called through the open window. "Are you all right?"

"I have been better," Merrie said.

"Get in."

He climbed into the passenger seat. "Where did you go?"

"The men who took Jon away told to me leave or I would end up like you. I drove about a mile down the road and parked behind some bushes. After they drove by, I waited to make sure they weren't coming back and returned to get you."

"How come I didn't hear them until it was too late?"

"You are no doubt familiar with the stereotype of the Indian in American cowboy movies, able to sneak up on the white man and surprise him? Well, we are Indian, too."

Merrie did not laugh. "Who were those guys?"

"Hired thugs, I suppose."

"Who hired them?"

"I do not know."

When Abelardo reached the main highway he turned in the opposite direction from the one he took on the way to the farm.

"Where are we going?"

"Back to Managua but in a roundabout way. I don't want to run into anyone coming back to the house."

"You think they will?"

"You might be a piece of unfinished business."

Merrie was convinced Abelardo knew more than he was admitting. "How do you know I might be a piece of unfinished business?"

Abelardo turned and looked at him.

"Suspicions."

Merrie was not satisfied. "Did you know about it? In advance, I mean, when you were driving me out here."

"No."

"Shit," Merrie said, "I could have died." He recounted his struggle in the filthy gunnysack.

Abelardo said, "I am sorry, Captain Gilbert, I was told to mind my own business, forget I was ever there. But I did not abandon my new friend."

"I was certain we were not followed here. How did they know about the meeting?"

"My guess is that Jon staged his own abduction."

146

Merrie stared at Abelardo. "But why?"

"To be seen as a martyr. El Grupo is foundering. No one is interested in a radical group any more. Revolutions are passé. Look at the Metro Centre my father built, does that suggest Nicaragua has any further interest in revolutionary upheaval?"

This did not occur to Merrie. Did Jon fake his abduction the same way Buddy faked his disappearance with the empty canoe? Like father, like son? Merrie had a sudden wash of goose bumps on his arm, the way you feel when you have a flash of insight. If Jon staged his own kidnapping, he needed Merrie to be his witness, to spread the word that he had been kidnapped. If Merrie had died in the melee, it would be like the falling tree making no sound because no one heard it. The assignment was to make it look real enough to convince Merrie his life was in danger but not real enough to let him die. It nearly backfired.

And now a qualm of guilt coursed through him for assuming, even for a moment, that Abelardo had something to do with the attack.

They drove silently until Merrie saw the glow of city lights on the horizon. "Will you drop me off at my hotel?"

"Are you hungry?"

"Famished."

"Let us have something to eat first."

"I'm a mess," Merrie said, even though his shirt had dried.

"You look a bit wrinkled, that's all. Besides where we are going it will not matter."

Abelardo stopped at a roadside tavern. Even at this hour of the morning, the lot was full of cars. They entered to noisy conversation, a calypso band performing on a small stage and, best of all, air conditioning. They found a booth in back and ordered tacos and beer.

Merrie was dejected. "Now I'll have to admit to the Boyntons that I was outwitted by their son." When the beer came, he lifted the foamy glass. "Here's to failure."

Abelardo put his hand on Merrie's arm. "I would not use that word, my friend. Unsuccessful perhaps but not failure. If you want to speak of failure, all you need to do is consider my situation. Remember when I told you my father disowned me when I joined the fire brigade?"

Merrie nodded.

"It bothers me night and day that he thinks I failed him."

"No, Abelardo, he failed you. You are everything a father could expect in a son."

He nodded his appreciation. "I wish he could hear those words."

"You should tell him."

"I told you he won't even talk to me, but he would hear it from you."

Merrie was too exhausted even to think about the casual, even innocent, remark he made only yesterday that he would come to Abelardo's defense. He drank some beer.

"Why not tonight?"

"Do what tonight?"

"Talk to my father. It is an opportunity to redeem the night, from an unsuccessful endeavor to a successful one."

Merrie had just been through hell and didn't have the energy to consider another cause. "You are overstating my ability to sway your father, Abelardo, a man I have never even met. Besides, it's late."

"Not late for Nicaragua, Captain Gilbert. This may be my only opportunity. I may never see you again after tonight."

What Abelardo said could be true, given not only his unsuccessful attempt to contact Jon, and Chloe and Buddy's clear hostility toward this young fireman, what was left for Merrie but to express his regrets, pack his bag and leave town? As he pondered these negatives, a sudden thought re-occurred to him—Abelardo's father, Enrico

Esperidon, owned the development company deeply involved in R&S's debt conspiracy. Meeting him would be an opportunity to ask about Esperidon's huge loan from R&S Bank, a loan that inevitably tied him, Buddy and the late Jim Thorpe together. This might be a productive night after all.

"All right," Merrie said, "I will talk to your father."

Abelardo raised his beer glass. "If you succeed in getting through to my father, I will be your friend for life. Salud!"

25

The now cooler night air coming through the open windows of the Ford 150 helped clear Merrie's head. They were somewhere in the suburbs on a boulevard of elegant homes with high stone walls and wrought iron gates shielding expansive lawns and turnaround driveways. Security lights turned night into day. It was after two a.m.

"When do people go to bed?" he asked, more to himself than to Abelardo. "So... what's the plan?"

"The security gate has a call button. A guard will answer. Do not reveal that I am in the area. Make the case why you want to see my father."

"Shall I speak Spanish?"

"No, your Spanish is too crude and will arouse suspicion."

"Thanks."

"No insult, amigo," said Abelardo, the first time the young Nicaraguan addressed Merrie as a friend. "The guards speak English."

They smiled at each other, mano-a-mano, fireman-to-fireman.

Merrie got out and approached the gate as the pickup disappeared into the darkness. It made him shiver with apprehension. He pushed the bell and waited. Presently a guard came up to him. He was uniformed in khaki and wore a side arm that he was fingering just in case.

"Who goes there?" he asked in Spanish.

"An American wishing to see Enrico Esperidon on a

private matter."

"State your business if you please," the guard said, switching to clear but heavily accented English.

"As I said, it is private."

The guard shook his head. "It is late and he is not seeing anyone tonight." He turned as if to go.

"Tell Mr. Esperidon I am a friend of his son, Abelardo."

The guard turned back. "One moment." He had an earbud headset with a mike clipped to his lapel. He bent his head and spoke softly into it. He looked at Merrie. "How do you know him?"

"I am a fireman. I met him at the fire station. He asked me to speak to his father on his behalf."

The guard spoke again into the mike. After a brief conversation he said to Merrie, "Mr. Esperidon has retired."

The guard began to walk away.

"Hold on," Merrie called after him. "Tell him I also have important information on the default of Metro Centre's loan from R&S Bank in Minneapolis, Minnesota, USA."

The guard stopped but did not turn around. He bent his head and spoke into the mike. A moment passed and Merrie heard a click and the gate slowly swung open. An electric motor whirred, interrupting the otherwise surreal stillness.

Merrie entered a world he had never seen before, a world of opulence almost beyond description. Outdoor floodlights illuminated sculpted shrubbery, banks of terraced flowering shrubs, huge palms, an endless lawn that looked woven like a fine rug and, rising from the rich landscape, an even richer edifice, a Spanish style home with a colonnaded verandah running its full length. Behind it was a bank of arched windows at least ten feet tall.

Following the guard, Merrie stepped off the wide driveway onto a flagstone walk to a pair of carved wood doors as wide and high as a Multiplex movie screen.

A houseman opened them, and the guard motioned Merrie to enter a vast hall with a grand staircase and a chandelier the size of a head on Mount Rushmore. The doors closed leaving the guard to his duties outside. The houseman, wearing a black vest and trousers, eyed Merrie as if he were looking at road kill.

"I was in a sack race but it was no picnic," he said in Spanish.

The houseman continued to show his disgust as he ushered Merrie across the wide expanse of oak flooring toward a door to the left. The artificial light was almost blinding in its intensity. It seemed to come from everywhere: in recesses and sconces, hanging from tracks --all intended to turn night into day, if you can afford the electric bill.

Merrie was ushered into an office of paneled wood and black leather furniture. The door closed behind him and he was alone. He looked about, turning slowly in a 360-degree circle, taking everything in. There was a lot to look at--paintings, tapestries, bronzes on pedestals; brocade drapes gracing the tall windows, a parquet floor with elaborate diamond shaped design. He was staring down at it when a section of wall paneling opened. A small, elegant man entered, wearing a velvet smoking jacket over a lace nightshirt. His jet-black hair was pomaded flat to his skull, the part down the middle like a saber cut. He walked behind an ornately carved desk about the length of an airplane landing strip.

"I see you are admiring my floor. It is from a rococo palace in Austria built in 1732, the year your first president, George Washington, was born."

The reference to America's early history was not lost on Merrie. Esperidon wanted to make his superiority and sophistication crystal clear before the conversation even began.

"What happened to the palace?" Merrie asked, staring across the broad desktop. He could have used binoculars.

"It is not of my concern."

Of course not, Merrie thought. Why worry about raiding the past to decorate the present.

Esperidon sank into a large leather desk chair that seemed to envelop him fondly. He motioned to Merrie to sit across from him. He put his fingertips together and stared at Merrie as though he was looking at something distasteful.

"You are a man who knows no bounds. You are a housebreaker. You invade my privacy..."

"You let me in," Merrie corrected him. "Maybe it was something I said."

"You are also impertinent."

Merrie leaned forward. "I was attacked by a gang of thugs who tied me up with a sack over my head. I nearly suffocated. Nothing you can say to me will top that."

"Then you had a big enough night without coming here."

"I was rescued by your son. I thought you would like to know this. "

Esperidon shrugged. "That is his new vocation, rescuing people."

"What's wrong with that?"

"It is his father he should rescue," Esperidon said with bitterness, "not an American with an acid tongue."

Merrie ignored the barb. "He is parked nearby waiting to see you."

"And you are here to tell me I should?"

"You're his father aren't you?"

"In name only. He abandoned me when I needed him most."

Merrie wasn't going to let him wallow in self pity. "You abandoned him."

Esperidon pulled himself up and the leather under him exhaled. "How did you get yourself mixed up in a private family affair?"

"I met Abelardo at the fire station. He helped me arrange a meeting with the same motive as this one, an attempt to reunite a son with his parents."

"And, from what you just told me, it ended in failure. Why do you feel this one will succeed?"

"I see a man who listens to reason. I also think you miss your son. And I promised I would help him. I don't want to fail twice in one night."

Esperidon leaned back, less tense, less on guard. "You are a man of contrasts, Mr. Gilbert. On the one hand you have a callous manner and on the other you speak with compassion. Which of these are you?"

"A little of both. Like your son I am a fireman. Every time we go on a run we face injury and death, perhaps our own, and when we go home we are expected to act normally. The worst question a fireman can be asked is, "How was your day today?" How do you talk about a child dying in your arms, or a body burned beyond recognition? You become cynical in order to hide your real emotions." Merrie stopped. "My apologies for getting preachy."

"No apologies needed, Mr. Gilbert. Tell me about what happened to you earlier tonight, when you were attacked."

"I had a rendezvous with Jonathon Boynton, the son of someone you may know, a business partner perhaps-- Buddy Boynton." Merrie watched for a reaction. His host acted bored.

He continued: "His parents hoped that I could convince him to come home. Abelardo drove me to an isolated farmhouse to meet Jonathan. After Abelardo left, men burst in on us. Jonathon was kidnapped and I was tied to a tree with a sack over my head."

Esperidon looked at Merrie's wrinkled shirt. "You said that, as a fireman, you are used to danger."

"Usually I am backed by my crew. This time I was alone."

"But my son rescued you," he said, almost wistfully.

Merrie nodded. "If he were my son, I'd be immensely proud of him."

Esperidon stared. "Did he offer you a monetary reward? If so you will be very disappointed as he has no money of his own."

Merrie laughed. "I was asked the same question by Jonathan Boynton. I'll give you the same answer: I'm not for hire."

"So--you are a man of principle."

"I try to be."

Esperidon shifted ever so slightly on his leather throne. "Tell me, Mr. Gilbert, why did you say that you had information on a Metro Centre loan from R&S Bank?"

"To get your attention."

He smiled grudgingly. "You succeeded. A sad commentary, is it not, that appealing on behalf of my son did not get my attention but a reference to my business dealings did."

"How about trading favors?" Merrie pushed on. "I'll tell you what I know if you agree to see your son."

"You want to bargain with me?" he asked, his ego arching.

"Take it or leave it." Merrie figured curiosity would win out. He was right.

"You drive a hard bargain, but a fair one," Esperidon replied.

Merrie settled back in his chair and began his tale, starting with the discovery of Buddy's empty canoe, his meeting Chloe, helping in the search for Buddy's body but finding instead Jim Thorpe's, agreeing to fly with Chloe to Managua to meet with Jonathon.

"And there you have it."

Espiridon listened intently and then said, "This information is of little use to me."

"I'm not through yet." Merrie looked into Esperidon's dark, implacable eyes. "Now I'm moving from fact to theory, listen to this: Buddy is desperate because he asks for an extension of his loan through his friend Hank Riker, but his boss, Jim Thorpe, turns it down. Buddy is angry and desperate. He kills Thorpe and runs away. He flies to Managua where his son, Jon, lives. Jon is a friend of Abelardo whose father has borrowed money from the same bank as Buddy's. Through Hank Riker, Buddy finds out that Metro Centre is also in financial trouble. Buddy sees a way to use his son's relationship with Abelardo to meet you. Buddy is thinking big. To hell with McMansions in Minneapolis. Here is a ripe shopping center, a huge commercial business, waiting to be plucked. If he can get his hands on his wife's fortune, he buys up the loan, and takes control of Metro Centre, your baby, Mr. Esperidon, your pride and joy."

"You have a vivid imagination, perhaps too vivid."

"I think I'm on to something. Buddy offers you a deal--his wife's money for a major interest in your company. How does this sound?"

"Inventive I must say, but there are serious flaws in your theory. For example, you said that the banker Hank Riker is mixed up in this. Why would he risk his reputation, his very job, on such an enterprise?"

"Get even with his nemesis, Jim Thorpe, for one reason, and get a piece of the action for another."

"But do you seriously believe that Mrs. Boynton would turn over her wealth for such a risky venture?"

"Not willingly. Buddy asks her to be his business partner, but she turns him down. Then he thinks up an elaborate scheme to kidnap his own son, hiring local guys to abduct Jon and hide him in a farmhouse outside of town. They demand a ransom, Chloe's millions tucked away in Zurich. She couldn't possibly turn her back on her son. Buddy's plan is to keep Jon hidden until Chloe transfers the money to an account he can access. But I show up and, with Abelardo's help, I visit Jon at his hideout. Somehow Buddy knows where I am, and sends his hired hooligans to grab Jon in a desperate move to keep his plan alive."

Esperidon was thoughtful for awhile, then said, "Some of your assumptions have been shrewdly accurate, for that I give you credit. But allow me tell you where your story goes astray. First some background. I have been to Minneapolis, the City of Lakes, as you call it. I have traveled there twice in my quest for funding. Like Buddy Boynton Mr. Thorpe turned me down, but Mr. Riker was more helpful. He suggested I contact someone who might be able to help me. It was not Buddy Boynton."

Merrie straightened, tensing up. "Who then?"

Esperidon smiled like the Cheshire cat. "His wife."

"Chloe?" Merrie was confused, stunned even. "I don't understand."

"Her millions and my Metro Centre. A perfect combination."

Merrie tried to assimilate this information, make sense of it. Here he was, wildly speculating, hoping to get Esperidon to admit to something, anything, but not this. Not Chloe.

"You mean you're dealing directly with Chloe?"

"I met her at her home, a beautifully modern house in one of your suburbs, Edina, I believe, on a day when Buddy was out of town on business. She has an exquisite art collection. The Maxfield Parrish is exceptional."

Merrie sank back in his chair, defeated.

"I discovered that she and I have much in common, good taste among them, a predilection for the better things in life. Moreover, our sons are friends, the reason that initially brought us together."

"Where does Buddy fit in?"

"He doesn't."

Merrie now understood he didn't fit in either, except as Chloe's Lover of the Month, a plaything, a toy; her sycophant, her toady, her lapdog. He felt betrayed, but what right did he have to feel this way? Who was he but a common fireman and she, a phenomenally rich, socially prominent woman. She pretended to love him while at the same time she was casting her lot with an elegantly refined, European-educated Nicaraguan. He laughed aloud, derisively.

"Is there a joke?"

"Yes, and it's on me."

Esperidon looked intently at Merrie as if he were trying to read his mind. "May I ask you a question, a personal question?"

"Go ahead."

"Are you in love with her?"

"No," he forced himself to say. "Just friends."

"You intrigue me, Mr. Gilbert," he said, not believing a word of Merrie's denial. "You found a way to enter my inner sanctum, sit across my desk reserved only for persons of high rank and privilege, and come up with a story you hoped would provoke me into telling you more than I should. You are competitive and imaginative, a man of substance I can match wits with. I'd like to hire you."

Merrie was surprised, but then this was a night of surprises. "Doing what?"

"For the time being let me say that your skills would be of extreme value to me." He opened the top drawer of his desk and brought out an embossed business card. He slid it across the shiny surface to Merrie. "Few people have my card. Think it over. Call me if you decide to come to work for me. Otherwise I trust you to destroy the card."

Merrie put the card into his pants pocket. "I'll give your offer serious consideration, especially if you agree to talk to Abelardo."

Esperidon smiled. "Perhaps if you joined the team, it would provide the incentive my son needs to come back to Metro Centre."

Merrie smiled back. "Then you'd have two firemen on your payroll."

26

The reunion between father and son was not teary-eyed as Merrie expected, but all business as the two mediated their differences. After a few minutes, Merrie, so exhausted he could barely keep his eyes open, asked to be excused. Two grown men could sort out their issues and resolve them without any further help from a dreary-eyed Americano.

He was delivered back to the hotel not in Abelardo's full-throated Ford 150 but in a whisper-quiet Mercedes 450 SEL driven by the guard who had earlier questioned him at the gate. All was lighthearted now as the burly watchman and Merrie made light banter back and forth in Spanish and English.

Merrie walked into the hotel at 3:07 a.m. according to the large clock over the desk. He expected the lobby to be quiet but this was South America and music came from the bar and sounds of splashing from the pool. He walked across the lobby with a few stares following him. The night clerk was wary of his disheveled appearance until he realized that Merrie was a guest.

"I fell in the pool," Merrie told him as he walked to the elevator. As he rode up he debated whether he should wake the Boyntons or get some sleep and talk to them in the morning when he was refreshed and, he hoped, coherent. He'd tell them everything except his session with Esperidon. All they needed to know was that he was not able to rescue Jon. He'd also be in better shape to cope with their disappointment and just as likely their recriminations. The flight back to Minneapolis in the cramped jet with Chloe and Buddy will be wordless purgatory.

He let himself into his room with his key card, stripped down and languished under a hot shower. He left a wake up call for 9 and fell on his bed into a deep sleep within seconds.

The morning call was worse than waking up to a fire alarm at the station. He forced himself into a sitting position, yawned, stretched; and then did 30 pushups to jar him awake. He shaved, dressed and went downstairs to the coffee bar, downing two quick cups before placing his call to the Boynton's' room.

There was no answer. He checked the restaurant, the bar and the pool looking for them. He scanned the lobby. Not seeing them, he went to the desk. "Can you tell me if the Boyntons have gone out?"

The day clerk looked at his guest ledger, running his retracted ballpoint down the list of names.

"Mr. and Mrs. Boynton checked out earlier this morning."

Merrie leaned forward and looked at the book, not believing the man. "Checked out? What time?"

"Six a.m."

"Did they leave a message? Anything for me, Gilbert?"

"No, sir. Nothing."

Puzzled, Merrie looked around expecting to find answers in the plush leather furniture, the derivative designer paintings, the Doric columns, the people walking about...

He turned back to the clerk. "Do you know where they might have gone?"

"As far as I know, they left the country to return to America. There were three."

"Three?"

"Yes, three in the party when they checked out."

"Who was the third person?"

"Their son. Jonathon Boynton, according to his passport."

The impact of what Merrie just heard needed a second or two to sink in and when it did, the monstrous, stunning import of what Chloe had done to him, he shouted, "That double-crossing bitch!"

She had sucked him into her vortex of deceit, her grand plan to rescue Jon. Everything he committed himself to, sleeping with her, agreeing to come to Nicaragua, was all part of a ruse. And he was a willing participant, blinded by his passion for her. And now that she had her son back, Merrie was no longer needed, dumped like a piece of trash.

"Senor, senor," a voice broke through his turmoil of anguish.

"What?" he asked, realizing finally the attention he was drawing to himself. Disapproving stares were glaring him down.

"Are you all right?"

"No," Merrie replied, making an effort to recompose himself. "Tell me, how was he?"

"Who, senor?"

"The son, Jonathan. Did he appear anxious or nervous? Was he restrained?"

"Restrained?" the clerk asked incredulously. "No. He was calm."

Probably sedated, Merrie thought. He had to get back home and blow things up, right in Chloe's face. "I'm leaving. Will you arrange a flight for me to Minneapolis?"

The clerk motioned with his head. "In the concourse. There is a travel agent who can arrange something for you."

"Thanks." Merrie began to walk away.

"You will be checking out?"

"As soon as I can arrange a flight."

The clerk ahem-ed politely. "There is the matter of your bill."

"Bill?"

"Two nights, senor."

"I am a guest of the Boyntons."

The clerk shook his head. "They paid only for their room. The amount you owe is nine hundred and sixty dollars, American, that is if you check out before noon."

Merrie felt his cheeks flush. "This is bullshit."

The clerk looked around. "Please, senor, your language."

Merrie held out his hands in surrender. "Ok, ok." He walked over to the travel office, a small space filled with colorful posters, a metal file cabinet, a pair of tan leather chairs and a showy brunette sitting behind a desk. She wore a flared skirt with a floral print and a white lace blouse tied spinster-like high on her throat with a red ribbon. She was able to book Merrie on an American Airlines 12:30 flight and a connecting flight on Delta at 5:30 for four hundred sixty dollars.

He gave her his Visa card, which she swiped. Nothing happened. She swiped it again. After the third attempt she said to Merrie: "Senor, your card will not accept the charge."

He felt goose bumps crawl up his neck. He always lived on the edge including his credit. "I must have maxed it."

"Do you have another card?"

Merrie shook his head.

"Cash?"

He opened his wallet. Six twenties and some ones. "Not enough. I have a hotel bill to pay as well."

Tucked next to the bills was Esperidon's business card and for a while Merrie debated if he should accept the mogul's job offer and ask for an advance on his salary. It pleased him to think that if he did some of the money might come from Chloe's stash.

The agent was waiting with an expression of helpless sympathy.

"Let me make a call," he told her and stepped into the concourse. He thumbed Ben's number.

"Where the fuck are you?" the voice said when Merrie's call got connected.

"Trapped in Managua."

"Trapped, like you're in trouble?"

"Sort of."

"Call 911."

"I'm coming home. But I need airfare."

"Did you say welfare or airfare?"

"Actually both. My Visa card is maxed. Will you pay for my ticket?"

"How much?"

"Four hundred sixty."

"Jesus."

"Plus my hotel bill."

"And that is...?

"Not quite a thousand."

"Fifteen hundred dollars in all?" Ben hollered.

"I'm good for it, you know that. I'll go to the Credit Union as soon as I get back. Give the gal your card number, will you? I gotta get outa here."

Merrie waited for an answer long enough, it seemed, to sing 99 Bottles of Beer on the Wall. He finally filled the void with, "You are famous for your protracted silences."

"That's because words cannot express how I feel."

"I'll explain everything."

"Including your screwed-up life?"

27

Merrie landed at MSP just before 10 pm, having suffered three hours and twenty minutes in a center seat between an overweight wheezer and a middle-aged woman who kept nodding off on his shoulder. He took an Airport Cab driven by a turbaned Indian whose sentences ended higher than where they began.

He walked into his apartment. It smelled as if he had been gone a month. He opened the slider to let in fresh air and dumped his dirty clothes on the floor, bile climbing his throat as he looked down at the pile of laundry, an appropriate symbol of the mess he had made of his life. He took a shower, the second time in twenty-four hours, the other in Managua after being bushwhacked. He wished the hot water could cleanse not only his skin but his broken spirit as well. He stood in the tub until the hot water ran out, and then toweled off harshly, wanting to rub himself into oblivion. He fell on his bed naked and went into a deep, almost comatose sleep.

He awoke alert but not refreshed. He didn't want to make breakfast, so he drove to Starbucks on Excelsior and Monterey for a scone and a trenta. He was back in Minneapolis earlier than expected, and had three days more before he was expected back at work. He wished to hell he had never spotted that canoe. How much simpler his life would be now. But not nearly as exciting, he rationalized.

His first order of business was to visit the Credit Union on Douglas and Highway 55 in Golden Valley, draw out the fifteen hundred he owed Ben, plus another five hundred in cash for himself, and drive over to the Park Police office on Dupont. He passed the backside of Lakewood cemetery, the polished granite tombstones in heavy shade from the arching elm branches overhead.

Ben ushered him into his office after Merrie announced himself at the front counter.

"Here's your money," Merrie said, turning over the check from the Credit Union. He stood opposite Ben's spartan oak desk, chipped and worn from a century of use.

Ben stared. "You look exhausted. You need a vacation."

"I was on vacation."

Ben smiled. "Sit down."

Merrie stayed on his feet.

Ben rocked in his oak office chair, a creaky relative of the desk. "Tell me about Nicaragua."

"It was hot."

"In more ways than one?"

Merrie nodded. "I'll fill you in later, promise, but I have a score to settle first."

Ben stopped rocking. "Does the score you want to settle have anything to do with Buddy Boynton? Where is he?"

"I wish I knew."

Ben stood so he was on the same eye-level as Merrie. "You have a death wish?"

"All I'm sure of is that he is no longer in Nicaragua."

"Boynton remains a fugitive and if you get between us and him, you will be arrested as well."

"I'm ok."

"Merrie, you're close to retirement. Are you willing to risk your pension?"

"What are you driving at?"

"Do you think the fire department will send your retirement checks to the St. Cloud Correctional Facility?"

Merrie smiled inwardly. He had a backup: a job in

Nicaragua. "I'll chance it."

Ben sighed with frustration. "Am I blue in the face? I should be. I've warned you for the last time. We've got Boynton's house under 24-hour surveillance. Sooner or later we'll find him. And you better not be caught in the net." Ben put Merrie's check in his wallet, sat down and began looking at a file on his desk.

Merrie waited a few seconds. "Is that it?"

"That's it."

Merrie drove his Caddie home, parked and sat behind the wheel, thinking. The Boyntons wouldn't be dumb enough to go straight home, nor would they check in at a motel, too risky. That left the farm in Scandia. Odds were that the police didn't know about it or Ben would have said something. Would Buddy, Chloe and Jon hole up there? Maybe they aren't even in town. They had access to a private jet and unlimited funds, for all he knew there could be other hideaways, a chateau in Province, a chalet in Wintertur, a lodge in Aspen, a hale in Hilo.

Since he was sitting in the car already, he mused, at least he could drive out to Scandia and see if anyone was there. He stopped at a Subway and ate on the way. It was late afternoon when he reached the farm. His plan was to park some distance away from the farm and sneak up on foot but he decided this was too much like Hawaii 5-0, so he drove right up the lane to the house, parked and got out. The classic tractors were still lined up in front of the tool shed. Everything was the way it had been on his last visit except that the curtains were drawn on the windows. He tried the door. It was locked of course. He stood on the small porch wondering if he should break the lock and go in to see if there were signs of habitation--food in the Fridge, an unmade bed, clothes hanging in the closet.

"Hey! You! Who are you?"

The sharp voice cut the air like a jet breaking the sound barrier. Merrie jumped from surprise and spun around assuming his instinctive attack mode. A man was approaching him from the barn in gray-striped overalls that had seen many harvests. He carried a shotgun, which Merrie recognized as a Remington 870, Model 12, a real old-timer just like the farmer. He had his finger on the trigger and the muzzle crooked over his extended arm. He meant business.

Merrie walked carefully down the steps to the ground. "A friend of the Boyntons."

He pointed the twin barrels at Merrie's heart. "How do you know this place?"

"I was here once before."

"Who with?"

"Mrs. Boynton."

"Describe her."

"Ah...blonde, slender, a knockout, gray-green eyes, tilted nose, great body..."

"All right, all right, don't get smart with me." He advanced another step, an old guy at least in his seventies, but he was wiry underneath the baggy overalls. "What do you want here?"

"I'm looking for the Boyntons."

"They ain't here."

"You the caretaker?"

"I watch the place for them. I come over three times a week, like today."

"Have you seen them?"

"They're in Nicaragua."

"No they're not. They left yesterday. Have they been in touch with you? The police want to talk to them."

"You the law?"

"Plain clothes," Merrie ventured, "Minneapolis Homicide."

The old man's eyes narrowed as he digested Merrie's bald-faced lie. Apparently it went down ok.

"You wearing a gun?"

"Didn't think I'd need one." He glanced down at the old man's shotgun. "Now I'm not so sure."

"Just protecting the farm. How'd I know you was

the law?"

"It's ok. Put it down."

The shotgun fell to his side. "Why you driving that old clunker?"

The word stung Merrie but he had a ready answer. "I use my own vehicle. Like I said, plain clothes."

That seemed to satisfy him. "Well, if you wanted to see the Boyntons you just missed them."

Damn! Merrie thought. "What were they doing here?"

"They was already here when I come over to check things out. I was surprised to find a strange car in the yard and them in the house, and they was as surprised to see me. They packed up in a hurry and left, like they was running away from something."

"Did they say anything? Tell you where they were going?"

"They was nervous, that's for sure, but they didn't say nothing special."

"Was their son with them?"

"There was a young kid which I presumed was their son. I never seen him before. There was another guy, too. I didn't like the looks of him, nervous. He kept really close to the boy."

"What did he look like?"

"Parted his hair down the middle, you don't see that much no more. Had a mustache, too, a little one."

That sounded like the architect, Karl Mittelstadt.

"Can you tell me what's going on?"

"There is a warrant for Mr. Boynton on suspicion of murder."

The old man whistled. "Is there a reward?"

"There's talk of one."

The mention of a reward, however suspect, warmed him up. He was an easy mark. "Well, I sure want to help." The farmer reached into the top pocket of his overalls and drew out a wrinkled piece of paper. "Things just didn't seem right, so I wrote down the license on the car when they drove out."

A break after all. "What kind of car?"

"Fancy car of some kind, German make maybe. Dark blue."

"If Boynton is apprehended, I'll make sure you get the reward."

The old man beamed at the prospect of a windfall. He cradled his gun, pulled out a carpenter's pencil he kept in his pocket and wrote down his name and address on the paper. "Here's how to reach me." He handed it over.

Merrie shook hands and walked back to his car. He had to figure out what to do with the license number. He could turn it over to Ben but Ben was so pissed he would not allow Merrie the pleasure of seeing Chloe in handcuffs. No, Merrie wanted his own sweet revenge in private, face to face with Chloe. Afterward let the cops take her in, he wouldn't give a damn. He headed for Marine on St. Croix and parked in the lot across from the General Store where he and Chloe met for their rendezvous. He rolled down the window, shut off the engine, and picked up his phone. It was bitter irony to him that he chose this place to call her from. As he expected, he got her voice mail.

"Chloe," he said, "call me. I was at the farm and I know you were there with Buddy, Jon and somebody resembling Karl Mittelstadt who was paying a lot of attention to Jon. I have the license number of the car. If I don't hear from you in half an hour I'm calling the police. They will nail your husband, and you and Jon too as accessories. Would you rather deal with them or me?" He hung up, his heart pounding.

He people-watched as he waited, tourists and townspeople. They were easy to tell apart. The half hour inched by like a house being moved. His deadline came and went. Two things were at play: either she hadn't checked her calls or she thought he was bluffing. He decided on option one and gave her another half hour, not a second more. He drummed his fingers on the steering wheel.

Finally his phone binged. He took a deep breath and answered, "Gilbert."

"This is Chloe."

"I said a half hour. Apparently you still don't take me seriously."

"This was the first chance I've had to call you." Her words came in short bursts as if she were short of breath.

"Where are you?"

"Hinckley. We stopped at a McDonald's because I told them I had to go to the bathroom. That's how I was able to call you."

"Where are you heading?"

"Canada, Thunder Bay."

"What's up there?"

"An airsrtrip. We're flying to Zurich."

"Zurich?" Merrie said, surprised and baffled at the same time.

"We came back long enough for me to get documents so I can turn my money over. I'm being forced against my will. Buddy is demanding access to my money or he'll never let me see Jon again. He's carrying a gun and he won't let Jon out of his sight. I'm scared, Merrie. We have to do something to stop him."

"What about Karl?"

"Karl? He'll do anything Buddy tells him. He's more afraid of him than I am. Please help me!"

Merrie went into an emotional tailspin. He planned to get even with Chloe for dumping him and now she wanted him to help her again. "There is nothing I can do. Get off your phone and dial 911."

"Merrie, listen to me. I don't have much time before Buddy gets suspicious. He has a gun and if he sees so much as a squad car he'll start firing."

"What about Nicaragua."

"What about it?"

"You dumped me, left me without so much as a goodbye."

"It wasn't my doing, you have to understand that. I didn't know where you were. You never came back to the hotel."

"I wonder why."

"What do you mean?"

"Didn't Jon tell you what happened?"

"The extraction was very hard on him. He hasn't talked about what happened."

Merrie looked out the window of the Cad. A breeze rustled the sun-sprinkled leaves of the boulevard elms. It was truly a beautiful day. All he had to do to enjoy it was hang up, get out of the car and sit on a park bench. That's all, nothing to it, just hang up, open the door and get out. Get out, the phrase kept repeating over and over in his head but he wasn't paying enough attention.

"I'm in Marine. By the time I catch up, you'll be in Thunder Bay. I don't have my passport."

"We won't cross the border until tomorrow. We're staying overnight in Karl Mittelstadt's cabin on Lake Vermilion."

"What can I do?"

"I'll tell you how to find it. Be there by midnight. Park on the road away from the cabin. I'll wait until Buddy and Karl are asleep, and then come out with Jon. You can take us away."

"You said Jon was not cooperating."

"No, I said he is not communicating. He is just as terrified of Buddy as I am."

Merrie was skeptical. "You really think we can get away with this?"

"You're my one and only hope, Merrie. Please."

He wrote down the directions she gave him.

As he drove north on I35 he thought about other questions he should have asked Chloe. Where will they go? Where will they stay? What about her relationship with Esperidon? What about Buddy's gun? If he uses it against the police, will he hesitate using it on me? Merrie never carried a gun.

His glumness intensified as the sun set to his left and he had to turn his lights on to see. He exited the freeway at Cloquet, headed due north on State 33 until he met up with 53 to Virginia. Once there he stopped for gas at a Seven Eleven, used the toilet, and bought a ham and turkey sandwich, a large Classic Coke and a Twinkie. Back in the car, he ate his dinner, and waited for the desired sugar rush to lift his energy level, however briefly, before he continued on.

Feeling somewhat buoyed, he took County 169 to Tower, a small town that willingly had never shaken its past. He drove slowly down the historic main street of 19th century storefronts, hardly longer than the driveway of one of Buddy's McMansions. He knew a little about the town and the nearby Soudan iron ore mine which had a neutrino detector 2300 feet below the surface.

He decided to park on a side street and sit there until it was time to drive to the cabin. It was northwest of Tower, on a narrow jut of land called Hoodoo Point, a name that really spooked him. Vermilion was a large, spread-out glacial lake with many channels and islands, where it is easy to get lost if you don't know the territory. He found a local radio station, KELY, and listened to fishing reports, a polka by Whoopee John Wilfhart, a commercial for Thursday Night Karaoke at the Landing, and an endless reading of stuff for sale, from a 32-foot Kennedy houseboat to an Ashley wood stove, but it provided background noise for his dark thoughts. The complexity of this midnight escape began to sink in. The police after Buddy, Buddy after his wife's fortune, and Meredith the middleman. If this turns out to be a foolhardy mission, then he will be the fool.

At 11:00 he made his move. He needed to locate the cabin and find a secluded but accessible place to leave the car. Hoodoo Point had a narrow road with mailboxes on either side. He drove slowly, scanning each until he saw the address Chloe had given him, 324. He passed it, doused his lights and turned into a driveway, backed out and drove by the house some fifty feet down the road and parked where, he figured, he could make a fast exit once Chloe and Jon showed up. He got out and walked back to 324. A night-light illuminated a modern structure, not a cabin in the traditional sense but a house with a rustic look, what an architect would design when he wanted to combine woodsiness with modernism. A tree trunk skinned of its bark supported the roof over the entryway. From where he stood, the house appeared to have two levels, the lower one opening up to the lakeshore. He hoped the sleeping quarters were on that level, down one from the main entrance. A four-door BMW, parked in the gravel driveway, matched the license number the farmer had given him.

Merrie stood behind a high shrub that separated the property from the road and waited. This was the worst, waiting. He put his hands in his pockets to control their trembling. He inhaled deeply but could not fill his lungs. His chest throbbed from a pronounced heartbeat. His body was geared for flight—release his mental brakes, throw out the clutch and burn rubber. There was still time to save himself but he remained where he was, a prisoner of Chloe. She held the key to everything that was important to him. If he called Ben and told him where to find Buddy he would make points with Ben but lose them with Chloe. If he gave her up he gave up any chance of finding out who killed Thorpe, who scratched STOP on his car, who abducted Jon. All he'd been through in the past month would be for nothing. Besides, he didn't want to go back to his old life just yet, three days on, two off, dinner with Vicki and golf with Tad. He'd rather risk his life than die of boredom.

He had to develop a plan. There will be no time to think when Chloe and Jon come out of the house, just run to the car and drive like hell. But to where? The only place that he could think of was his apartment. Buddy didn't know where he lived and so, at least for the time being, they would be safe. He smiled at the prospect of Chloe seeing his dump, wrinkling her nose as she took in his untidy lifestyle. Regardless, she would have to accept staying there until a permanent solution was found. The only one that came to him was to return to Nicaragua and hide out with Esperidon. Merrie had the telephone number, his own version of 911. Esperidon would not hesitate to protect them in his walled-in fortress. After all Merrie had Mrs. Moneybags with him. And if they did fly to Nicaragua, Merrie had to have his passport, and so a stop at his apartment to get it was mandatory.

His thought process was interrupted by a latch click. He peered around the shrub at the porch. The front door opened and under the porch light two figures emerged, Chloe and Jon. He came forward to greet them.

Chloe saw him and she shook her head to warn him off. Perplexed he stepped back into the darkness, and then froze. Behind Chloe and Jon were Buddy and Mittelstadt hauling suitcases. Jesus! They were all coming out. Merrie pushed himself into the shrubs and held his breath. Chloe was talking, loudly he realized, to let him know what was going on.

"It's the middle of the night, Buddy. I thought we were leaving in the morning."

Buddy said something Merrie could not hear.

"Who would be looking for us?" Chloe said. "No one knows we're here."

As they loaded the trunk of the BMW he heard Buddy say, "Never mind. We've been here long enough."

"But we need a good night's sleep. The plane doesn't pick us up until noon. We'll be sitting in the car for hours. And then sitting another ten hours to Zurich."

"We can't risk sticking around here any longer," Buddy said. "How do I know that fucking fireman isn't on our trail?"

Buddy's uncanny accuracy clutched Merrie's chest like a vice.

"You're paranoid, Buddy." Chloe said. "How could he possibly know where we are?" Her voice transmitted a coolness that was meant for Merrie, keep calm, she was telling him.

The four climbed into the car, Buddy behind the wheel; next to him was Mittelstadt, Chloe and Jon got in the back. Doors slammed shut.

Buddy started the engine and the lights came on. As he turned onto the road, the BMW's beams swept the Caddie. Merrie now cursed what he had assumed was a strategically good decision to park past the cabin.

Brake lights suddenly illuminated the area in an eerie red as the BMW slammed to a stop past Merrie's Cad.

Buddy rolled down the window to get a better look. "Who's car is that?" he yelled, looking at it over his shoulder.

"You'll wake everybody up, Buddy," Merrie heard Chloe from the back seat. "Is that what you want to do, attract attention?"

"That car wasn't there when we drove in," he said, his mind overcome with suspicion.

"Someone is visiting a neighbor, probably staying overnight. Come on, let's go."

Meredith had to hand it to Chloe. She was as icy as a Siberian sled dog.

The brake lights went off and they drove away. Merrie could just make out Chloe looking back at him from the rear window mouthing a message, like an actress in a silent film: follow us.

He waited a few seconds, got in the Caddie and drove down the road with his headlights off, well behind Buddy's taillights. The old Caddie and the new BMW were the only cars on the road and if Merrie kept a respectful distance he could keep an eye on Buddy without him getting suspicious. They drove through Tower, now a ghost town in the middle of the night, and headed southeast on Highway 1. Fortunately it was a rural road devoid of traffic this late at night, pitch-black except for the BMW's bright crimson horizontal strips of LEDs which, for Merrie, served as a pair of beacons. Buddy kept well below the speed limit, apparently not wanting to attract attention. A state trooper can come out of nowhere. Buddy probably was not in a hurry anyway, plenty of time to get to Thunder Bay. There were only 40 miles to Lake Superior and another 75 or so to the Canadian border. All Merrie could do was follow behind, impotent and helpless.

He had to depend on Chloe to make the move, to alert him when it was time to try a rescue. Fortunately, Merrie had plenty of gas and he guessed Buddy would stop at an all-night gas station before crossing the border. Chloe could then go to the john, as she did before, and contact him on her cell phone. She had the perfect hideout from the men, the women's toilet. It was her call, in more ways than one. She better have a plan because he didn't.

And if he couldn't help her, what tangible difference would it make for either one of them? All she needs to do is cut a deal with Buddy, settle down in Managua and have a pretty good life. And Merrie could get back to what he did best, lead a platitudinous existence.

Turn around, he told himself, life ain't so bad, predictable maybe but secure. Head for home and sleep till noon. That's what you ought to do. Nothing could be simpler. And because nothing could be simpler he drove on, watching Buddy's taillights ahead, still vainly hoping against all hope that somehow, someway, he and Chloe could make a life together while Buddy spent the rest of his in prison.

At least there was one thing Merrie could appreciate about Buddy. He was easy to follow, except for the occasional hill when the BMW disappeared over the crest. But Merrie was able to pick it up again when he came down the other side. On a long flat stretch, a lone car passed the other way, the first one since leaving the cabin on Lake Vermilion. The driver, seeing that Merrie was driving without lights, flashed his brights in warning. It startled Merrie out of his complacency, and he dropped further behind the BMW, concerned that Buddy might have noticed the signal out of his rearview mirror.

Another hill loomed ahead and the taillights disappeared once again. As Merrie came down the other side he expected to see the red orbs in the distance but there was only darkness ahead. Maybe there was a curve in the road where a stand of tamarack blocked Merrie's view of the highway. Without the BMW to light the way, it was harder to sense the road. He slowed down, feeling his way along, staring at the white center lines to guide him. He drove like this for a minute but saw nothing. He wished there was traffic so he could turn on his lights and blend in, but the rural road was as empty as a turkey's brain. He decided to turn on his lights. This silly game of hide and seek was not getting him anywhere. Take charge, he decided, catch up with Buddy and force him off the road. So he had a gun, so what? That could simply be the phallic symbol of an inadequate manhood. All bluff and bluster. And the architect; Merrie had already talked to him. The guy was a pushover.

He turned on his lights and drove to the junction of Highways 1 and 61, without seeing the BMW. Buddy must have turned off somewhere and doused his lights. He must have figured out he was being followed. Merrie made a left in the direction of the Canadian border and came upon Illgen City, a town that reminded him of Marine on St. Croix because of its quaintness, smallness and the fact that the buildings were all on one side of the street, in this case facing Lake Superior across the highway. He pulled into what looked like an inn dating back to the thirties. A sign said Cabinola Bed and Breakfast. He turned and parked facing the street, cut his lights and engine, and waited. Sooner or later Buddy would have to drive by and, when he did, Merrie was going to have it out right here in Illgen City, rescue Chloe and Jon and take them back to Minneapolis.

Ten minutes later the BMW came down the street

and passed him. Merrie started the Caddie and burned out of the lot, nearly spinning out of control as he jerked the car a hard left into the lane right behind Buddy. He pulled ahead of the BMW and cut into it so that Buddy would either have to slam on his brakes or hit him. Buddy chose the former. Merrie threw his transmission into park, jumped out and approached the driver's side of the BMW, fully expecting to face Buddy's gun but instead Buddy rolled down the window and looked up at Merrie as if he had been pulled over for a violation.

"Do you want to see my driver's license?" Buddy chided him.

Merrie ignored him and peered into the back seat.

"Are you ok?" It was a stupid question but he couldn't think of anything better to say.

Chloe stared straight ahead ignoring Merrie, as were Jon and Karl.

Buddy said, "I had a feeling I was being tailed, so I pulled into a farmyard and waited for you to pass. And the car that came by with its headlights turned off was the same car parked in front of Karl's cabin. And now I see that this phantom car turns out to be yours. I thought we dumped you in Managua. I have to give you credit, you are one tenacious sonofabitch."

"I never give up," Merrie said.

"This time you will, fireman. Move your fucking car. It's in my way."

"And if I don't? Are you going to shoot me?"

Buddy was perplexed. "Shoot you? What are you talking about?"

"Like bang-bang," Merrie said, pointing his index finger at Buddy.

Buddy laughed. "Who says I'm carrying a gun?"

"Chloe."

"Chloe?" Buddy turned to look at her. "You told the fireman I was packing a gun?"

She stared down at her lap.

"Did you talk to him?" he demanded.

"At that McDonald's in Hinckley. While I was in the bathroom. I called him."

"You called him?" Buddy asked incredulously.

"I had to. Merrie left a message threatening to turn us in if I didn't tell him where we were."

Merrie stared at Chloe in wonder. Was she distancing herself from Merrie, or was this a strategy to mollify Buddy?

"Why didn't you tell me?" Buddy demanded

"I didn't want to get you excited the way you are now."

Her saying that did not make Buddy any calmer. "You tipped him off and I wasn't supposed to know about it?"

"She's afraid of you, Buddy," Merrie interrupted. "You're forcing her to leave the country against her will. That's kidnapping in case you didn't know."

Buddy opened the car door, pushing Merrie back. "So she called her knight in shining armor to come and rescue her, is that it?"

"She doesn't want to go with you."

Buddy got out of the BMW and stood in front of Merrie, his anger getting the best of him. "What's going on between you and my wife, fireman?"

Mittelstadt, who up until now had sat immobile, reached out the window and put his hand on Buddy's arm. "Let's go, Buddy. Don't make a scene."

He shook off Karl's grip and stood before Merrie like a towering inferno. "How come she thought it was ok to call you?"

"She knows she can depend on me, which is more than she can say about you."

That did it. Buddy lunged and caught Merrie in his mid-section sending them both sprawling to the pavement with Buddy on top. He outweighed Merrie by 30 pounds and it felt as though someone had dropped a cement block on Merrie's stomach. He heaved his chest for air and struggled to push Buddy away. He stretched his legs over

Buddy's ass and twisted. He managed to ease the weight from his torso but Buddy tenaciously hung on, and started using his fists as battering rams on either side of Merrie's head. Merrie heard screams and shouts mingled with the buzzing in his ears from the beating. He got a hand under Buddy's chin and pushed with all his might. Buddy stopped hitting Merrie on the head in order to break Merrie's hold, which was beginning to take effect. Merrie knew that if he jerked his hand up as hard as he could he could break Buddy's extended neck and for a moment it seemed the right thing to do, simply a matter of survival. Merrie eased off his leg grip so that Buddy could roll over and when he did, Merrie brought his knee up and got Buddy in the groin. A direct hit that forced him into a ball of pain. Merrie jumped to his feet.

Chloe, Jon and Karl were standing in a circle, watching in a kind of abject horror as though wondering, how did it come to this?

"Chloe, take Jon and get in my car!" Merrie rubbed his ears, trying to stop the sound of pounding waves inside his head.

Chloe stared at Buddy who was roiling on the pavement holding his genitals. "I can't just leave him lying there."

"Karl will take care of him. Come on, let's go."

She seemed in a catatonic state, unable to move, or to make a decision.

"Mom?" Jon asked tentatively. "What are we going to do?"

"You were afraid of him a minute ago," Merrie said. "Do you think he's going to be any easier to deal with now?"

Chloe was anguished. Merrie had convinced himself that she was a hard-hearted woman, but this was an unfamiliar side of her that he wished he could preserve and keep only for himself.

"We better leave before someone calls the police. You don't want to be picked up too do you?"

She shook her head. Reluctantly, she took Jon by the hand and walked over to the Cad. As they climbed in, Buddy pushed up on one elbow and shouted, "You won't get away with this, you bastard!"

In his nervous state Merrie forgot he had left his engine idling, and turned the ignition to the starter position, grinding the solenoid against the spinning flywheel, and the sudden high-pitched, metal-on-metal noise had the rattling effect of fingernails on a blackboard.

He shifted the lever to drive, now concerned that he might have damaged the transmission, and made a u-turn south. From the front seat Chloe was craning her neck to look out the rear window. From the back seat, Jon was doing the same while Merrie looked in his rearview mirror. They shared the same scene: Karl helping Buddy to his feet the latter shaking his fist in the air.

"What if the police come after that loud noise you made?" Chloe asked. "Buddy will be arrested all because of me."

"Isn't that what you wanted?" Merrie asked in desperation.

She felt in her pockets for a Kleenex. She wiped her eyes and blew her nose. "My luggage is in the BMW. Even my handbag. Passport, credit cards, cash. I have nothing with me, Merrie."

"Shit" he said angrily. Why didn't he think of that? "You can get them replaced."

"Go through that mess? We have to go back."

"Chloe, do you understand how dangerous that is? Buddy is in a wild state."

"Everything is in my bag. The papers I need to sign over my trust, the safe deposit key. Buddy could throw all that away. God, what a mess this is."

"You want to go back?"

She looked at Merrie imploringly. "Maybe I can reason with him."

Merrie was not aware of headlights bearing down on them from behind. Suddenly the BMW pulled abreast in the passing lane, cruising easily alongside the struggling Caddie. Karl was driving and Buddy had the window down on his side pointing a gun.

"Jesus! There he is!"

Buddy fired twice at Merrie. One bullet ricocheted off the pillar and sparks flew. The other bullet hit the windshield at an angle and bounced off, the glass crinkling.

"Get down!" Merrie shouted. Chloe ducked while Jon in the back seat yelled at his father even though Buddy couldn't hear him. "Dad! Dad! What are you doing? You're shooting at mom and me!"

Buddy had gone berserk. And Karl had as well because he was maneuvering the car to help Buddy hit his target. Whenever Merrie speeded up so did the BMW and when he braked, the BMW braked too. Another shot was fired. This one did not miss. Merrie felt a searing pain run down his left arm and into his hand, which was gripping the steering wheel. His arm went numb and dropped like a lead weight.

Merrie began to feel lightheaded. There was nothing to do but pull over to the side of the road. The BMW fell back and parked behind them. Merrie opened the door and held up his good arm in surrender.

Buddy got out of the BMW and walked toward the parked Caddie. The way his knees came together indicated that his crotch was still giving him pain. He held the gun casually at his side, in charge now, grinning with victory.

"I told you you wouldn't get away with it."

Merrie leaned against the Caddie. He began to feel light-headed. He reached over and gingerly felt his shoulder with his good hand. Blood was flowing all the way down to his fingertips.

"Got you did I?"

Merrie nodded. "Shoulder."

Chloe and Jon were standing behind Merrie, holding on to one another.

Buddy looked over at them. "Get in the car."

"What about Merrie? We have to call an ambulance."

"I'm not going to use my phone and risk having the call traced."

"We can't just abandon him."

"Yeah? Like you weren't going to abandon me just now?"

Merrie's eyes drooped. He was barely conscious.

"If you leave him here he'll bleed to death. You want to get stuck with another murder?"

Merrie fluttered his eyes open. "What other murder?" he asked.

"Shut up!" Buddy yelled to Chloe. "Get in the car, like I said."

Merrie heard doors slamming as in a dream. Rubber squealed on the pavement but the sound barely registered. He sagged to the ground, his back against the side of the Cadillac. He struggled to make sense of what had happened but he was getting woozy. All he could do was sit on the ground and wait, wondering whether he was waiting for deliverance or death.

Part II

28

"Stop it!"

The stern, authoritative voice startled Merrie out of a dream world in which he was floating like a bubble on warm air only to have it burst suddenly. He looked up from a hospital bed. He was in a curtained cubicle in the ER of some hospital; he didn't know where or even care. Standing over him and cutting off his aloha shirt was a female doctor with so short a bob that for a moment he thought she was male. Apparently Merrie was pulling at her hand not wanting his shirt to go in the waste bin.

"It's so bloody, you wouldn't want it anyway," she said and kept on cutting.

"I won't have anything to wear."

"An orderly brought in your bag from the car."

"Where is the car?"

"Impounded, in the parking lot behind city hall. I was told it has a couple of bullet holes in it. You're luckier, you only have one."

Merrie managed a smile. She was not only smart but also smart-alecky, and he liked that. Under the starched white jacket and pants she had on, he imagined a good figure which, he guessed, was in its mid-forties. He read the name on her badge: Harriet Spenser, MD.

Harriet, he thought, just like the lake back home. "How long was I lying out there?"

"Long enough to lose a lot of blood. Another ten minutes and you would have been on a gurney in the morgue, and the medical examiner would be looking down on you instead of me."

It was then Merrie noticed the IV tube leading to his right arm and the stand with a bag of dark crimson suspended from a hook.

"Who found me?"

"A driver who thought you were a passed-out drunk. Your windshield was smashed like you hit a deer. He called 911."

It was ironic to Merrie that he was now the rescuee rather than the rescuer.

"Were they firemen or EMTs?"

"EMTs. Why?"

"Just wondering."

"No need to be coy. We went through your wallet. You ID'd as Meredith Gilbert, Fire Captain, Station 28, MFD. How in hell did a fireman from Minneapolis end up getting shot on the North Shore Drive?"

She was nosy, too, but Merrie supposed it was par for the course when you work in ER.

"Drive-by," he said.

"In Illgen City?" She shook her head.

"By the way where am I?"

"Lake View Memorial Hospital, Two Harbors, about ten miles from where you were found."

Now that his shirtsleeve had been cut away, he was able to see the damage to his shoulder. Blood oozed out of a fleshy tear.

"What's the damage?" he asked, looking up at the doctor who, from this angle, had interesting nostrils.

"You must have turned instinctively before you were shot because the bullet, which is a small caliber by the way, most likely a .32, hit the fleshy part of your shoulder, and tore the capsular ligament. You're lucky no bones were hit. I'll stitch you up. You'll have to wear a sling for awhile but you'll be as good as new."

"I was afraid of that."

"Wearing a sling?"

"No, being as good as new."

She eyed him curiously. "You know, you are much too cynical for someone who damned near died. You should be on your knees thanking god. And you know what else? Where I practice medicine, gunshot wounds come in two categories, one, accidental like deer hunting, and the other, with intent to do bodily harm, like a shooting during a domestic argument or in a bar or parking lot after too much booze. But if the gunshot victim is lying by his car in the middle of an empty highway, it's an entirely different category, more like big city crime, so my guess is you are in trouble of some kind, big trouble to be left for dead. Someone really wants you out of the way. What are you mixed up in? Drugs? Organized crime?"

Merrie was enjoying himself so much he had to laugh.

"Did I say something funny?"

"Well, not funny so much as intriguing."

"Was I getting close?"

"No."

"Why were you shot, then? I know damned well it wasn't a drive by like you said, or a random attack. So who shot you?"

"You're getting personal."

"If you had died it would have been even more personal, like contacting your next of kin."

Merrie thought about Tad's reaction if Tad were notified that his brother had died from a gunshot. He would be confused before expressing grief. A fire maybe, but a gunshot?

"Look, Doctor, I appreciate you following the Hippocratic Oath to take care of me, but I don't think I have to answer any questions unless I'm under another kind of oath, like the kind you take in court."

"All right, no more third degree. Lie still now, I'm giving you a shot so I can stitch up your wound."

Merrie came to in the recovery room. His arm was bandaged with long strips of tape across the hair on his chest.

"I hope the tape doesn't sting when I have to take it off," he said to the doctor when she showed up to check on him.

"I should have used duct tape," she said, smiling at him.

"When can I get out of here?"

"Noon. My replacement, Doctor Miller, will release you."

"How do I get back to Minneapolis? My car has a smashed windshield."

"Take a bus."

"Greyhound still running?"

"Jefferson, out of Duluth."

"I'll rent a car."

"No car rental around here, but even if you could rent one I wouldn't advise driving by yourself all the way to Minneapolis."

Merrie shrugged. "Ok, bus it is."

"You'll need a lift to Duluth." She reached into her pocket and handed him a card. "Call me after you make a statement to the police."

"Do you have time to take me?"

"Sure," she replied offhandedly, as if helping him out was no big deal.

He looked into her hazel eyes, softening now, less professional. He could relate to what she did: taking care of people in an emergency, a profession where you have to be detached because if you aren't, sooner or later the emotional seams will come apart to expose a lonely vulnerability.

He didn't see a ring on her finger and so he had the impertinence to ask, "But don't you have someone to go home to?"

"Yes, but Melvin can wait."

"Who's Melvin?"

"The cat."

Merrie turned down hospital food for a hamburger and fries down the street at a diner called Boyd's. Afterward, before reporting to the police, he went to look at his car. The tow truck had backed it into a corner of the City Hall parking lot. The Caddie was a sorry sight, its windshield a spider web of tiny cracks, as well as a dent in the pillar.

He went inside the court house, a nondescript cinderblock building with narrow windows, to talk to the duty officer, a young kid in a black uniform who looked at the sling on his arm sympathetically. Merrie was questioned across a table with a tape recorder. He was vague: Didn't know who shot at him, an accidental discharge of a firearm maybe, or a case of mistaken identity, which was absurd on the face of it considering how many 1990 Cad Devilles there are on the road at two in the morning. But the youthful cop played along. It was clear he wasn't interested in making a major issue out of a minor incident since there were no corroborating witnesses. Most important, Merrie was a public servant, same as the cop, and there was professional compassion if not kinship between them. Case closed.

"Sorry, Captain Gilbert, I'll have to charge you for storage and the tow of your car," the young cop said. "But you need to replace your windshield, so I'll throw in a tow to Danny's."

"Who's that?"

"A body shop. Danny is my brother-in-law."

"Good," Merrie said, "And have him repair the scratches on the driver's door."

He called Dr. Spenser for the ride to Duluth. She picked him up just after two in front of City Hall in a Prius, medium-dark blue to match her jeans and chambray shirt. He liked the way she leaned over to help him fasten his seat belt. She smelled interesting – no lingering antiseptic odor, just a faint hint of jasmine.

"Did you get some rest?" he asked as the car moved

them in utter silence.

"Four hours. Hard to sleep in daylight."

"Do you have the graveyard shift often?"

"We split it up, the other doctor and I, four on three off."

Sounded familiar. "Do you get to sleep on duty?"

"There's a cot. We don't get many bullet wounds. You're my first since deer hunting season last fall."

"I didn't mean to mess up your record."

"Just what *are* you messing up?"

He looked at her. "Does there have to be something?"

"Someone is out to get you, and not because you are a nice guy who goes around doing people favors."

He didn't say anything. Not that he wouldn't have wanted to but this was no time to drag someone he barely knew into his vortex. He looked past her at Lake Superior stretching to the horizon. "One helluva big lake," he said.

The doctor swallowed a sigh. "That's why I live here."

"You sail?"

"The love of my life," she said as though this excluded a man. "I have a Mermaid."

"Mermaid?" Merrie asked. It didn't sound like much.

"A 32-foot sloop made in Denmark. Big enough for blue water sailing which means I can go anywhere in the world with her."

"But she's on Lake Superior."

The doctor smiled at him. "Someday I'll put out to sea."

"Don't you need a crew?"

"One can always use a mate. Do you like sailing?" she asked.

"I've never tried it, but I do like adventure."

"Then sailing is for you."

29

Merrie was miserable for the entire bus ride to Minneapolis. His shoulder throbbed and the air conditioning was on too high which made him shiver. There were stops in Moose Lake, Sandstone, Hinkley and Pine City before hitting Minneapolis, four hours in a smelly, noisy, rocking bus. He took a taxi home and collapsed on the bed without undressing. Tomorrow he would call in sick. No one at the station needed to know why. He could hear their derision if they knew that one of their own took a bullet rather than rescuing someone who did. The one bright spot in his otherwise gloomy mood was the prospect of seeing Dr. Spenser again to remove the stitches. He would also pick up the Cad with the new windshield. Allstate covered the whole thing. These thoughts relaxed him and he fell into a deep sleep. It lasted until midnight when his cell rang.

He answered angrily at being woken up, "I'm not on duty!"

"Thank god, you're alive!" It was Chloe.

"Alive but barely awake," he said, favoring his shoulder as he sat up. "Where are you?"

"Zurich."

"Are you staying there?"

"Only long enough to wrap up business."

"Then what?"

"We fly to Managua."

"Managua?"

"Our new home."

So that's where they are going to end up.

"What time is it in Zurich?"

"A little after seven in the morning. I'm in a coffee shop."

"Buddy with you?"

"He's asleep."

"Jon?"

"He's here with me."

"So you can't talk."

"Why not?"

"Privately, I mean."

"It's fine. Tell me how you are."

He decided to play it down. "I'm ok. Just a flesh wound. A few stitches, that's all."

"You took an awful chance stopping us. You should have aborted when you saw all of us coming out of the cabin together."

"I had nothing to go on but your SOS, Chloe. And so I tried to be the hero."

She sighed deeply. "I'm sorry."

He wondered if she really meant it. "Well, it's over now. I'm back home with my arm in a sling. I had to give a statement to the police."

"What did you tell them?" She seemed anxious.

"The interviewing officer, a young kid, didn't want his small-town existence disturbed, and so I made up a story about mistaken identity. What if I had told him the truth, that a rich business man and a prominent architect tried to kill me?"

"No one would have believed you," she said and attempted a conciliatory laugh.

The sheer absurdity of it all reached him and he too laughed, easing the tension between them.

"Speaking of the prominent architect, was that his BMW?"

"Yes."

"He left it behind?"

"Karl didn't come with us."

"He didn't?" Merrie asked, surprised. "Where did he go?"

"Back to Minneapolis, taking care of what's left of Boa Constructors. Karl is an acting partner and Buddy gave him power of attorney. He's liquidating assets, paying off creditors, trying to avoid bankruptcy."

So Karl was cleaning up the mess Buddy left behind. Merrie began to wonder if Karl was also involved in Buddy's disappearance. The empty canoe, the murder of Thorpe. Buddy could not have acted alone. And Karl drove the car Buddy used to shoot him. That alone makes him a person of interest, as the cops like to say.

"I feel like liquidating him," Merrie said.

"Don't blame Karl. He wanted to turn around and take you to the hospital, but Buddy wouldn't let him." She was silent for a moment. "I had plenty of time to think on the plane. I'm through, Merrie; I'm getting a divorce. Buddy is jealous, of me, my net worth. All he has is a failing construction company, and I'll be damned if I'll bail him out. The developer who built MetroCentre, Enrico Esperidon, approached me. He found out about me, probably through Jim Thorpe, and offered me a business proposition. It's impossible to explain what it's like to have a fortune and be afraid to touch it. My dad made it, with a little luck maybe, but it was his accomplishment, not mine. I simply inherited it. And I've been a prisoner of it ever since. Then when I had a chance to do something with my inheritance, Buddy interfered. Let him play the big shot, if that's what he wants. He can be Esperidon's partner, and in return I get a generous annuity plus the house and the art collection, which is worth millions."

"Don't do it, Chloe, don't give him a divorce."

"Why shouldn't I?" He sensed tears falling between her words.

"It's a trap. Buddy *wants* you to divorce him."

"What are you talking about?"

"MetroCentre got a big loan from R&S, but R&S is a regional bank and cannot legally lend money outside the country."

"That has nothing to do with Buddy."

"It does because Boa Constructors was involved in the scheme."

"Boa Constructors and MetroCentre? You have to be joking."

"Your husband's business was the instrument through which forty-seven-and-a-half million dollars were illegally funneled to MetroCentre. Does that amount ring a bell?"

There was a moment's hesitation and then a gasp. "That's what is in my Sparhafen account."

"Yes, what El Grupo demanded for Jon's return. It fits together, Chloe. R&S Bank was negotiating a merger with a Canadian Bank to legitimize the MetroCentre loan. It fell through when Jim Thorpe, the chief negotiator in the deal, was killed. The loan could no longer be covered so R&S had to call it in. Esperidon needed the money or he'd go under. He knew Buddy through the bank's scheme to hide the transaction. Buddy tried to convince you to invest in MetroCentre but you turned him down. So he developed a plan to get your fortune anyway. He faked his disappearance with the empty canoe, flew to Managua and, using Esperidon's network, hired people to kidnap Jon and hold him for ransom."

"Buddy went there to rescue Jon, not kidnap him."

"That's what he wanted you to believe. But the kidnapping plot fell apart because of my meddling. No wonder Buddy wanted me dead. But here's the ironic twist, he didn't have to go through any of this. Buddy would get what he wanted simply by divorcing you."

There was a protracted silence. "You mean I can throw a monkey wrench into his plan by not giving him a divorce?"

"There's more if you're interested," he said.

"Isn't that enough?" she asked.

"Enrico Esperidon wants me to go to work for him."

"You don't even know him," she scoffed.

"I talked to him, in his office."

"His place is guarded like an embassy. Besides you didn't have time," she said, still in her disbelieving tone of voice.

"It was a busy night." Merrie went on to tell her how busy it was. "He gave me his business card." He read it to her. "Now do you believe me?"

She made a soft whewing sound.

"If I accept his job offer, I call the number on this card. If not, I tear up the card and throw it away."

There was another protracted silence while she thought this over. "Have you made a decision?"

"When Esperidon told me that you were going to be his business partner, I was ready to say yes. But now that Buddy is taking over, I'll tear up the card."

"Do you still love me?"

"Yes," he responded quickly. The question was unexpected and, if he had taken a moment to reflect on it, his better nature might have answered otherwise.

"Then don't tear up the card."

"There's no point in my working in Managua if you're not there."

"I'll make Managua my home if you go to work for Esperidon, we would live together, you and I, live grandly. Travel the world. Don't you want to share this with me?"

His rapid-thought process slowed, taking the offer in. He wondered whether this was her way of getting back at Buddy.

"You're talking to a fireman Chloe. I would fit your lifestyle like a mis-matched glove."

"But you have so much more to offer than putting out a blaze. You're smart, educated, solid. And very capable or Enrico would never have offered you a job. You'd be on the inside, part of his inner circle."

"That would give me status?"

"Why wouldn't it?"

"What about Buddy?"

"It won't be easy, at least at first," she continued,

"but life moves on, and it will for Buddy, too. He'll find someone else and it wouldn't surprise me if, in time, we would all be friends."

Merrie couldn't believe what he was hearing. "You really think we can sweep everything that's happened under the rug?"

"As I said, life goes on."

"It didn't for Jim Thorpe."

"Can't we just forget about him?"

"How can you and I build a new life together with Buddy literally getting away with murder?"

"We have to think of ourselves, Merrie. We can't let anything else interfere with that, not even the past."

"Buddy doesn't deserve to walk around a free man. He belongs behind bars."

"He will settle in Managua and realize his dream of being a big-time developer and there is nothing you can do about it."

Merrie felt his blood surge and it made his shoulder ache. He was tired of getting beat up, shot at, left for dead. And it was all Buddy's fault, beginning on that fateful morning when he found the empty canoe.

"I might accept Esperidon's offer just so I can sneer in Buddy's face. He would love that wouldn't he? The guy he thought he got rid of becomes a thorn in his side."

"Merrie," she cried, alarmed, "this is not a fire you pump water on to put out. Buddy is ruthless and Esperidon even more so. You really don't know him. Together they would destroy you, can't you see that? Your stubborn idealism of right and wrong won't be enough to save you. I don't want to see you get hurt or even killed."

"I almost did, remember? I have a vested interest now, Chloe. I'm going to nail Buddy and bring him back in handcuffs."

"Please, Merrie, don't be bitter. I'll make it up to you, I promise. Buddy didn't say a word on the whole flight. He just sat there seething. But after we got to our hotel he tried to make up to me."

Merrie wondered how far that went. "Did you let him?"

She laughed. "Do you even need to ask? I told you, it's you I love."

30

Before returning to Two Harbors to have Dr. Spenser remove his stitches and pick up the Cad, Merrie decided to play private eye and do a stakeout. It seemed easy enough, sit in a car and wait for his tail to make a move, the way Humphrey Bogart did in "The Big Sleep." Merrie had nothing better to do while his shoulder was healing anyway, and so he could sit in a car as easily as sit on his sofa watching a movie on Netflix. He rented a Volkswagen Beetle and drove over to the offices of Mittelstadt Associates where he parked on University Avenue, across from the lot where his Cad had been marked up a month ago. All he had to do was sit in the VW and wait.

He had a view of the second floor window where Mittelstadt had his office and could make out the shirt-sleeved presence of Buddy's driver. It was four in the afternoon and Merrie figured Karl would come out around five and head to his car in the lot across the street. Merrie planned to intercept him and force him back to the rental where he would grill the architect, just like Bogart but without the cigarette dangling from his lips. Even though he didn't quite know what this would accomplish except getting rid of some of the pent-up anger he felt for Karl the Kriminal.

He sat quietly, listening to jazz on KBEM while watching the front entrance. In the boredom of waiting, Bogart would have burned through a pack of Luckies. Finally, around six, Mittelstadt came out but he didn't cross the street to the parking lot as Merrie had expected, he walked instead toward East Hennepin. Merrie jumped out of the car and followed him as he crossed Hennepin with the green light and entered a corner bar, Whitey's Saloon.

Merrie stood across the street wondering whether he should confront him in the bar or wait until he left. As he hesitated a Volvo S80 drove up and parked on his side of the street. Merrie instinctively stepped into the nearby entryway of Gardens of Salonika and watched as a well-dressed executive got out and trotted across the street to Whitey's. It took a few seconds for it to register but Merrie realized finally that this was Hank Riker, the R&S bank executive who informed Merrie that Jim Thorpe's death had put a monkey wrench in the merger with the Bank of Montreal. Good, he thought. What had been Merrie's plan to confront Mittelstadt may have added dividends with Riker present.

Whitey's was a Northeast Minneapolis institution. Merrie knew about it but this was the first time he'd been inside, a busy neighborhood watering hole, long bar on one side with stools below and mirrors above, and on the other a long line of wood booths set upon a floor of 19th century white and black hexagon tiles. The joint was full of suits enjoying Happy Hour, patrons who probably didn't look forward to going home to a grumpy spouse and unruly kids.

He went to the bar and ordered a Long Board. He spotted Mittelstadt and Riker in a back booth and headed for it.

"Well if it isn't Tweedledum and Tweedledee," he said, holding up the bottle in greeting.

Karl made as if to jump up but Merrie slid into the booth, trapping him. He was wild-eyed, almost spilling what looked like Schnapps.

"Take it easy, Karl. I just want to join the conversation."

Riker stared snidely at Merrie's sling. "Did you fall

off a ladder?"

"Didn't Karl tell you what happened?" Merrie asked.

"I wanted to keep going to Thunder Bay," Karl said defensively, "but Buddy made me turn around."

"So Buddy could shoot at me," Merrie said to Riker. "Three times. One hit my shoulder. Karl's an accomplice with intent to kill, a felony."

"You can't prove it." Riker said.

"There were witnesses."

"Who?"

"Chloe for one, Jon for another."

Riker snorted. "You think you can get a wife to testify against her husband or a son against his father? And for whom? Some fireman having an affair with the wife of the guy who shot you? Sounds like he had a good reason. Didn't you also have a fight with Buddy and force his wife and kid inside your car? You are out of your league, Gilbert, so why don't you climb on your little red truck and fuck off."

Merrie worked to keep his rising anger under control. He had walked into Whitey's thinking Karl was the guy he was going to confront but it turned out to be Riker. He reached over with his good hand and Riker tensed, expecting Merrie to be physical, but all Merrie did was smooth Riker's expensive silk tie.

"Why don't we just calm down and have a little chat."

"We," Riker emphasized the word, "have nothing to chat about."

"Oh, but we do. Like the forty-five-million dollar loan from R&S Bank to Empresa Constructruccion Imperio that went south in more ways than one, a loan hidden in the assets of Boa Constructors that bank examiners would find highly unethical if not illegal, a loan that Jim Thorpe was trying to cover up when he was killed."

"Where have you been nosing around?"

"You didn't know Chloe invited me to fly to Managua with her?"

Riker arched his eyebrows. "So the rumor is true, you are screwing around with the rich bitch."

The name-calling stung Merrie. Now he really wanted to slug him. "Speaking of rumors there's one going around that you were screwing with R&S assets."

Riker became defensive. "That was Jim Thorpe's doing. I was trying to contain the mess, not add to it."

"Is that why you aren't wearing the black armband anymore? Is the time for mourning Jim over?"

Riker briefly looked down at his arm. "Over and done with. I'm now the senior VP for commercial loans."

Karl leaned forward like a referee. "Please, you're talking too loud."

"Why shouldn't I?" Riker shot back. "You could have told me Gilbert was in Managua with Chloe. What else do you think he's dug up?"

"So Karl didn't tell you?" Merrie asked, feeling that he was now getting the upper hand.

"Karl doesn't tell me a fucking thing."

"Too many things happened too quickly," Karl said. "I was going to tell you." He straightened, reasserting himself. "Gilbert knows everything anyway, so why don't we just tell him?"

"Shut up, Karl." Riker said. "This is between you and me."

"Not if I can get Gilbert's help."

"Help?" Merrie asked. "What kind of help?"

"Boa Constructors is filing for bankruptcy. Most of my business has come from Boa, and until I can build a new client base I'll need a bridge loan."

Merrie pointed to Riker. "Your banker is sitting right there."

Riker shrugged. "All right, Karl, have it your way, I'll tell Gilbert. Money is tight and he," Riker pointed an accusing finger at Karl, "is a risk."

"What kind of risk?"

"Bad enough to need a co-signer on a loan from R&S."

"How big a loan?"

"Two and a half million," Riker said.

Merrie stared at Karl. "You think a fireman can raise that kind of money?"

"Not you personally, but you have influence over someone who can—Chloe."

"Well, then, you should talk to her." This conversation was getting surreal.

"She wouldn't listen to me but she would to you."

"What gave you that idea?"

"Do I have to spell it out? She's in love with you."

Merrie had to smile. Everyone seemed to be convinced but him. He asked Riker, "You'll give him the loan if Chloe signs the note?"

Riker threw up his hands. "That's what I was going to explain to Karl when we were so rudely interrupted. Even Chloe can't help him."

"Why not?"

"Her credit is no good."

"How can that be? She told me her art collection alone is worth millions."

"In a divorce proceeding all assets are frozen until a settlement is reached. She can't touch any of it now."

"What about the fortune sitting in Zurich?" Merrie asked.

"She has turned that over to Buddy. He has made sure that his wife can live only on his kindness, and we all know how kind Buddy is."

Merrie leaned against the back of the booth and stared at his Long Board, not touched since he sat down. Well, he thought wryly, Chloe and I finally have something in common: we're both poor. He wondered if she yet knew about her financial straits or had chosen not to tell him. Regardless, it would be unconscionable to abandon her now.

"There has to be a way to keep Buddy from locking

up her assets."

"How? Buddy spent years setting this up. You think you can come up with something over a beer?"

"He's wanted for murder."

Riker laughed. "Don't look now but he's in Nicaragua thumbing his nose at you."

"I know it sounds impossible, but if we could find a way to lure him back."

"Then what?"

"Face trial. If he's convicted, Chloe has grounds to recover her assets."

"You dream big, Gilbert, I can say that for you."

"Well, it's a big problem." Merrie fell into deep thought, ideas whirling inside his head. Finally he spoke. "What does Buddy value more than anything?"

"He's got it, money and power," Riker said.

Merrie shook his head. "He'd give it all up for his son."

31

"I'm sure Hank thinks your crazy," Karl said as he watched the banker drive off in his Volvo.

"Do you?"

"As a German I admire your determination but you are also a hopeless romantic, and that is a dangerous combination."

They walked in contemplative silence, the animosity Merrie had for Karl gone now.

Presently, Karl said, "I have something to tell you."

"You already have."

"There's more, but I didn't want to talk in front of Hank. Want to stop by my office?"

"Sure."

They settled in Karl's spacious office that had once been a freight elevator for cars. Out the window, across the street, was the lot where Merrie had parked his Cadillac the last time he was here.

"You seem to be fixated on that parking lot," Karl said as though he were reading Merrie's thoughts.

"It was in that lot that some asshole keyed my car." He looked at Karl. "The day I came to see you. And it wasn't simple vandalism. Someone was warning me to stop. Stop what I don't know, but it must have had to do with Buddy's disappearance."

"In a way it did.'

Merrie stared suspiciously. "You know something about this?"

Karl took a small razor-sharp knife from a jar of

pencils on his credenza and held it up.

Merrie was puzzled. "What's that?"

"An Exacto-Knife, the tool of the model builder. What every architect has by his drawing board."

Realization of what Karl was driving at began to dawn on Merrie. "Are you saying you scratched my car?"

"With this very knife." He smiled. "I ruined a perfectly good blade doing it."

"Not to mention my door."

"I'll have it repaired."

"Taken care of when I had my windshield replaced," Merrie replied. "But why did you do it? Was it something I said?"

"Not so much what you said as your tenacity. I was afraid you would keep digging until you uncovered something unpleasant. I wish now I had been more, well, Prussian, and had not given way to my panic, but when I saw you walk around the corner to the co-op instead of going straight to your car, I grabbed the knife, ran outside and scratched your door hoping that it would scare you off."

"It pissed me off instead."

"I have learned the hard way, Freund, that you are not easily intimidated."

The German reference to friend did not escape Merrie. "Now that we're no longer beating up on each other, maybe we can join forces to help Chloe."

"That thought also crossed my mind. At Whitey's, you talked about luring Buddy back. How do you propose doing that?"

"A shot from the hip before aiming, but I had this wild idea that the way to light Buddy's fire is to grab Jon and bring him back to Minneapolis."

"In other words, kidnap him?"

Merrie smiled. "There's a nice symmetry, don't you think? Buddy kidnapped Jon and I return the favor."

"He'll be furious."

"Exactly. A crazed man never thinks straight. You

told me once that I was Buddy's nemesis. Knowing I had his son would bring him straight to Minneapolis. And then we'll have him."

"I don't know who is crazier, you or Buddy, but if you plan to go through with this there is something else I should tell you."

"What's that?"

Karl lowered his gaze. "I told you just now that I was afraid you would dig into my past—well, the time has come to tell you. Buddy is not Jon's real father."

Merrie raised an eyebrow. "Is Jon adopted?"

"In a way he is."

"Do you know who his real father is?"

"You're looking at him."

Merrie stared, slowly taking in the stunning revelation. "Are you saying that you and Chloe..." He paused to clear his throat; it was too much to swallow. Chloe had done it to him again, turned things upside down, inside out. Only a day ago she told him she hoped they could spend the rest of their lives together and now, with the news that Karl fathered her son, she had compromised the most important thing a relationship needed, openness. Merrie's bliss had crashed and burned, not a cinder left, nothing but ashes, cold and blowing away.

And yet, when he should be furious, he was feeling sorry for her. Talk about topsy-turvy emotions. He recalled when she first involved him in her life, asking him to be her "investigator," talk to people who knew Buddy, and the person she directed him to first, the key contact according to her, was Karl Mittelstadt. Did she hope he would reveal his relationship with her, to have him tell Merrie rather than Chloe herself because she couldn't, or didn't know how, or lacked the courage, but still wanted him to know? Lay it all out so that she could be honest with him, that she really cared for him, and this was the only way she knew how to reveal her past? He desperately wanted to think so.

"Does Jon know?"

"Chloe and I had a tacit agreement from the beginning that Jon would grow up as Buddy's son. I always resented this but I kept my mouth shut until the fake kidnapping changed my mind. The way Buddy used Jon as a pawn angered me, and I planned to tell him when they got back from Nicaragua but I never had the chance. Things got wild after that, as you well know. You can take credit for forcing the issue. If it weren't for your pressing Buddy, nothing would have changed."

"How did this happen, you and Chloe I mean." Merrie had difficulty asking the question.

"With Chloe's huge nest egg hanging like the apple of Eden over Buddy's head, it was easy for Buddy to become paranoid. Chloe would not help him in what she considered crass development, and that's what really ate at him. She wasn't a miser about her wealth; she just didn't let Buddy touch it. She gave millions to non-profits, Walker Art Center, the Guthrie Theatre, the Art Institute. He became abusive, even threatening. She was more scornful than afraid, and she turned to me for companionship--lunch, going to a modern show at the Walker, we share a similar taste in art. Inevitably it turned to sex. Not often, mind you, but often enough to let our guard down and she became pregnant. Maybe she really wanted it to happen, have a family and get back at Buddy at the same time.

"Buddy pretended Jon was his child and the 'Let's Pretend' show began its long run. I have often wondered if the reason Buddy continued having me as his partner was so that he could keep an eye on me. He is paranoid about anyone finding out that he has a bastard son."

"And now you've told me." Merrie said, "the one man Buddy hates most."

"If he found out he would kill me."

"You don't have to get involved if you don't want to."

"I'm Jon's father. It's about time I start acting like one."

32

Merrie decided to save money and avail himself of bus transportation back to Two Harbors rather than rent a car. The cost of a car was exorbitant, not only because it was a one-way rental but also because there was seventy-five-dollar surcharge to drop it off in a small-market town rather than in Duluth. The decision to save money had one drawback: he had to change bus lines in Duluth, from Jefferson to Arrowhead Transit, a wait of two-and-a-half hours in a dismal bus terminal.

But not having to drive did have one advantage: time for total concentration. Staring out the window at a freeway landscape he barely heeded, Merrie wrestled with a scenario to trap Buddy with the working title, Mission Impossible. At least he had an unexpected ally: Karl Mittelstadt.

A positive outcome of his newfound friendship with Karl was his offer to let Merrie stay in his cabin on Lake Vermilion while up north, even entrusting Merrie with the key.

He got off the bus in Two Harbors at 2:30 in the afternoon. The first order of business was to pick up the Caddie, and he walked to Danny's Auto Body, leaning into the Lake Superior wind blowing across the North Shore highway, the same stretch of pavement where Buddy had shot him two weeks ago.

The Caddie bore no evidence of the damage that had brought it to Danny's in the first place. Allstate covered the windshield and a check for $176.50 took care of the door. For Merrie the Cad was an extension of himself, he felt a lot better now that the car was fixed.

He waited forty-five minutes to see the doctor and when she finally knocked on the examination room door and entered, he was pleased to see that his memory of her did not disappoint, hazel eyes, strong cheekbones and bobbed hair which was not his favorite style but on her looked appropriate. He wondered if she was a lesbian.

Following her directions he sat on the edge of the examining table and took off his shirt. "Lift your arm." He did. "Does it hurt?" He shook his head. "Now swing it in an arc as if you were winding up for a pitch." He did. "Does that hurt?" He tried to cover a wince. "Ok, put your shirt on."

"So, what's the verdict?"

"You need physical therapy to regain full motion. I assume you still want to be a fireman."

"That's what I do."

"Don't expect to be dragging any fire hoses for awhile."

Good news to Merrie. He promised himself he wouldn't go back to work until he had Buddy behind bars.

She consulted her computer screen. "Our clinic has a partnership with Minneapolis Orthopedics at Fairview Southdale."

"Why not here?"

"The best therapists are in Minneapolis. Besides, what would you do here for a month? You'd have at the most two, maybe three, sessions a week."

"Sail," he said.

"What?" she asked in surprise.

"I thought you might teach me. It could also be part of my therapy, learn to sail and strengthen my shoulder at the same time."

"Where are you going to stay? B&Bs rent for the summer and you won't find anything available till after Labor Day."

She clearly wasn't going to offer putting him up but

he didn't expect that, Melvin or no Melvin. "I've got the use of an architect's cabin on the east shore of Lake Vermilion, only an hour from here."

"Looks like you have all the answers."

"Except one."

She looked at him quizzically. "Which is?"

"Will you teach me how to sail?"

Merrie was standing next to Dr. Spenser on a boat dock, looking at a sea-going boat with sails furled, a canvas secured over the cockpit, and piles of rope neatly coiled on polished teak decking.

"It's nearly 15 years old."

"Looks new."

"I take good care of it."

More than two dozen boats were tied up on either side of the dock. Extending into the harbor at least a hundred yards, it moved up and down with the water's undulations. The Doctor had shed her white jacket and wore a hoodie over shorts. Inevitably he compared her to Chloe. Chloe was statuesque, Harriet athletic, Chloe was stunning, Dr. Spenser handsome, Chloe was blonde, Harriet brunette.

"What's her name, Doctor?" He asked about the boat.

"Sally, and mine is Harriet."

Being invited by the Doctor to go by first names made him feel gratified. He was no longer the patient.

"Sally was built in Denmark. She was at a marina in Wisconsin where I bought her three years ago. Thirty-two feet with a 40 horsepower Volvo diesel, a wheel not a tiller, sleeps four if you crowd yourself."

He didn't think that would be a problem. "What about the other she."

Harriet looked up at him with a direct, unfiltered gaze. "Meaning me? Well, I'm forty-nine, I grew up in Hibbing, married early, divorced early, no kids; I graduated from the U of M Medical School and did my residency at Chicago General. I also spent sixteen weeks in Cuba on the Medical Education Cooperation Program." She waited for him to digest the information.

"Cuba? I didn't think Americans could go to Cuba."

"There was a seven-year window when American students were able to go there and study with a full scholarship in exchange for pledging to practice in a small town."

"And you ended up in Two Harbors."

She nodded. "I picked Two Harbors for a number of reasons. It's a great town and the scenery is magnificent, but mainly I picked Two Harbors because I'd be close to a body of water that let me pretend I was at sea when I went sailing. While I was in Cuba I fell in love with the ocean. I even managed to squeeze in enough time to learn how to sail. I earned a captain's license in addition to a license to practice medicine. "

Meredith was truly impressed. She had packed much more into her years than he had in his, or ever hoped to.

"What about you?"

"What about me?" He shrugged; a bit embarrassed that he couldn't match a personal history equally impressive. "I've been a fireman for twenty-five years."

It was like boot camp, with Sally in the slip, learning the craft of sailing. Careful of his arm, Merrie practiced raising and lowering the sails. He learned to tie knots and move on the sloped, narrow deck without losing his balance. Oddly, it was not unlike working on a fire truck--economy of motion, strength without excess, teamwork, and split-second decision-making.

He was a quick study, the only thing holding him back was his shoulder, and he received high praise and compliments from Harriet. After a few days, they took Sally out. Harriet eased the boat into Lake Superior using the diesel engine. Once in open water they hoisted sail and the stiff breeze was like a turbo charge pulling Sally along at 12 knots. Tacking with the wind was tricky and Harriet showed Merrie how to steer without overcorrecting. Following an afternoon of sailing they dropped anchor offshore and Harriet grilled steaks on a small barbeque attached to the railing of the cockpit with a propane tank the size of a 3.5 liter wine bottle. After washing the dishes in the lake, they settled back on the cushions and watched the stars come out.

"Why are you so interested in sailing?" she asked, looking at the night sky, not at him.

"Something new."

"I have the sense that you are always looking for something new."

Merrie laughed but it sounded insincere.

She turned toward him. "What's eating you?"

"What do you mean?"

"I treated you for a bullet wound, remember? You are a man on a mission. I'll even go further, a man seeking revenge."

"Is this interrogation included in the course on sailing?"

"I think the two go together."

He straightened and faced her. "I appreciate what you're doing for me, taking precious time off to teach me how to sail. But I don't want to talk about myself until I get to know you better."

"Are you concerned about commitment?"

He didn't answer.

"That's tough for you, isn't it." It was an observation, not a question.

If he agreed with her, it was an admission of failed relationships, an entire life down the drain. What the hell, he thought, what difference does it make now anyway? Everything is on the line. He couldn't return to early summer when he was just a fireman running around Lake Harriet without a concern in the world except his sanity. And then he spotted the empty canoe...

"I have a story to tell," he said. "Care to listen?"

She nodded and Merrie began, slowly at first as he gathered his thoughts about this complicated chain of events, then speeding up as they flashed through his mind in increasingly rapid succession, and ending with his quixotic idea that he could bring the man who shot him to justice. He told her everything except his affair with Chloe. After he finished he leaned against the cushion and looked up at the stars again.

"Where do I start?" Harriet asked.

"Start with my plan to put Buddy behind bars."

She became pensive.

"Not simple, is it?" he said.

"I don't question your motives which are admirable, but do you really think there is a chance in hell you can succeed in arresting this guy? I see nothing but insurmountable odds. You have to set things up in a foreign country, convince his son to join you, spirit him out of Nicaragua, and return to Minneapolis with Buddy in hot pursuit. You can't do this alone. You need an army."

"I have an army, my friends at the Managua firehouse, but I also need a navy."

"A navy?"

"To provide a means of escape. It finally dawned on me. I can't get Jon out of Nicaragua using conventional channels like a commercial flight. That would be the most obvious way, what Buddy and his goon squad would assume. That's why I want to learn how to sail, Buddy would never expect me to sail to America."

"Why would he? It's the dumbest idea I've ever heard. Sailing on Lake Superior is not the same as sailing on the ocean. You have to know everything about currents and tides, navigation and radio communication, weather patterns and storms."

"I'll hire a crew that knows all of that," he said doggedly.

"You can't charter a boat without a certified captain, and I doubt you could find one who would participate in what amounts to an abduction."

Merrie lowered his head in disappointment.

"Did I throw cold water on your idea, which is what the ocean really is, you know, cold water."

He lifted his head and looked at the doctor straight in the eye. "What about you?" he asked. "You have a captain's license."

"Me?"

"Sure." he said, his enthusiasm on the upswing. "You can be my captain. You learned to sail in Cuba, you know the gulf which is where I plan to sail, and I'd be willing to bet the waters are warmer there."

She smiled.

"Am I right?" he asked her.

"About the water being warmer or about my being your captain?"

"Both."

She didn't say anything for a while. She looked out on the opaque water, up at the starry heavens and then upon Merrie's face, his features indistinct in the darkness.

Finally he asked, "What are you thinking about?"

"My dad. I remember asking him what he thought about my going to Cuba to study medicine. It was a difficult decision, not many got to go, especially women and, given our government's policy toward Cuba, a lot of people thought you were a communist sympathizer if you went there. And so when I asked him what I should do, he said to me, do whatever makes your blood run faster. He was telling me, in other words, to do whatever makes life more exciting, more eventful, more memorable, more... unexpected."

Harriet topped off Merrie's training with a daylong cruise, following the southwestern shoreline of Lake Superior, past the Apostle Islands to Bayfield, Wisconsin. They set sail at dawn, having loaded the mini refrigerator with sandwiches and two bottles of pinot noir, and reached their destination in late afternoon, tying up in a rental slip at the marina. They strolled around the small town brimming with summer tourists and ate early dinner at Maggie's, decorated with hundreds of kitschy toy flamingos. The din made small talk a chore, so they people watched. Merrie wondered what other diners might think of him and Harriet. Did they look like a married couple, too long married because they paid little attention to one another?

"Why are you smiling?" Harriet asked.

"Do you think anyone watching us thinks we're married?" he asked

"I hope not."

"Really? So marriage is anathema to you?"

"Like commitment might be to you?" she responded.

They let it ride, finished dinner and went outside to a setting sun. Walking back to the marina, their hands inadvertently touched and, as if by signal, Harriet slid her arm through Merrie's, and they now did appear as a married couple to the casual observer. They came to a park bench and sat down.

"You know what you and I have in common?" she asked.

"I'm not sure we have anything in common."

"The ER. You on the outside, me on the inside."

"You save them, I just bring them in."

"You don't give yourself much credit for the kind of person you are, do you?"

Chloe's words echoed in his brain, the same critique, only coming from another direction. "You're not the only person who's said that to me."

"Another woman perhaps?"

He didn't want to answer her, not directly anyway. "I'm still a work in progress."

She smiled at him, a critical smile not a comforting one. "A work in progress would never imagine so bold a plan that includes sailing a charter across the gulf."

"Are you still interested?" he asked hopefully, then added, "Maybe it's asking too much."

"That's for me to decide. I told you that my great wish is to go to sea, be a real sailor on a real ocean. Like my dad said, make your blood run faster. Your offer could be my one big chance to realize a lifelong dream." She looked at him long and hard.

"I'll be your captain."

They set sail in the dark. It was not only dark but also eerily quiet, the only sound coming from the water swooshing past the hull and an occasional flap of the jib. Harriet's boat was equipped for night sailing with battery-powered running lights, GPS, VHS radio, and radar whose screen emitted a light green glow. The navigation system was easy to follow, not any more complex than following directions in a car's GPS without the female voice.

"This is easier than I thought," Merrie quipped, handling the big wheel.

Harriet, sitting by him in the cockpit, laughed, and in the seaborne stillness, Merrie truly heard her laughter for the first time, feather soft, sincere, disarming. He felt a warmth settle over him, an unfamiliar sense of security he could not remember since he was a child. He made himself think about how he felt in Harriet's company, so different from Chloe's. With Chloe, it was get your pants off as quickly as possible. He mused that with Harriet it would be different. How different, he wondered, glancing at her surreptitiously.

"Anything the matter?" she asked. "You have a funny look on your face."

"Unfamiliar territory," he ventured.

"Sailing at night?"

"In a way."

After the lights from Bayfield grew dim, Harriet took over the helm. "We'll set up watches. Three on, three off. I'll take the first watch. Get some rest."

"I'm not tired," he said, but followed Captain's orders. He used the cramped head and then laid down in the tight bunk on the port side for no better reason than because he was left-handed. The rocking soon settled his mind and he fell into so deep a sleep that he had to go through several layers of wakefulness to realize that Harriet was shaking him by his good shoulder.

"Time to relieve the watch. Wake up, sleepy head."

Merrie opened his eyes and, in the tight confines, her face was inches from his. He lifted up on an elbow and what happened next was so natural, so unplanned that there was no separation between looking at her and kissing her. They remained this way for a length of time as though experimenting with their mouths like teenagers on a first date. It was light, pleasant work.

Finally, Merrie separated himself long enough to ask, "Who's minding the boat?"

"It's on auto pilot."

"Auto pilot?"

"One thing I haven't told you. The boat can steer itself."

"So we don't have to hurry?"

She nodded. "I may need the time. I'm out of practice,"

"Like riding a bicycle," Merrie said, "you never forget how."

He pressed against the bulkhead to make room and Harriet squeezed in beside him. "Tighter than the back seat of a car," he said and burst out laughing.

It was contagious, Harriet began laughing too, and soon they were convulsed in hilarity, hanging on to each other until they were nearly exhausted. They lay still, catching their breaths. Presently, tuned to one another's wavelength, they began removing their clothing. Merrie helped Harriet pull off her shirt and unhook her bra. He climbed atop her and made slow, caressing love.

"You're very practiced," she said in his ear.

He didn't think that about himself. "It's not me, it's you."

"Thanks." She pushed up on his groin.

Merrie pulsated faster and let himself go. The two

were in perfect sync and the result was explosive.

While resting, she said, "I'd rather not have you tell me about yourself after all."

"Why not?"

"I don't want to hear about other women in your life."

After they dressed and climbed into the cockpit, it was business as usual. "At sea you never break for long," Harriet said, shutting off the autopilot. "Take the conn and use the compass to keep your heading, tack when you have to but always bring her back to one-four-zero. If you are uncertain about anything, wake me up." She returned to the cabin and climbed into the bunk on the starboard side, not the one they made love in.

"Wake me up in three."

Behind the wheel, the canvas looming above him, the bow cutting through wavelets and Harriet slumbering, Merrie had plenty of time to think. Uppermost was her comment that she didn't want to hear about other women in his life. He was relieved he hadn't told her about Chloe. As for Vicki and other casual liaisons, these didn't matter.

Only Chloe.

Did he truly love her? As though he had any moral grounds to think so, his first reaction was to be ruthlessly critical when he learned Chloe had had a long-ago affair with Karl. If anyone had reason to be furious it was Buddy, her husband, not Merrie her lover. Most damning was a new question: what business did he have being critical of Chloe's liaison with an architect when Merrie was now having one with a doctor?

Not now, he told himself, don't get bogged down with emotional issues, there are more important things to think about, and he spent the rest of his watch going over his plan to put Buddy behind bars.

The sun, appearing off the stern as they neared Two

Harbors, slowly spread light across the lake, turning the water into a sparkling blue. There was nothing to compare sun rising over water, what he looked forward to on his morning runs around Lake Harriet but, seeing it rise over a huge expanse like Lake Superior, he could only imagine what it looked like over the ocean.

Harriet expertly brought Sally into the marina, the diesel throbbing at low revs, and she moored the boat at the slip – voyage and lesson now over.

"Do I get a diploma?" he asked as he climbed out of the boat, carrying the cooler and canvas bag with their clothes, now laundry.

"With flying colors." She looked at him expectantly. "How about me? Do I get one too?"

He nudged her until she almost lost her footing on the floating dock.

"Magna cum laude," he replied.

They parted with a long embrace, not willing to let go it seemed. The overnight sail had bonded them, Merrie realized, in a way unique to him. He wondered if she felt the same.

They would not see one another again until their rendezvous in Nicaragua.

33

Singleness of purpose was driving Meredith as he pulled into his apartment building's underground parking. He killed the engine and stared through the windshield at the dank cement block wall with the faded number 23b stenciled on the gray paint, taking inventory of his turbulent emotions. Usually he parked in the open lot since he was always on the go, in and out, but this time he was storing the Caddie, putting her away for awhile, how long he did not know, but as long as it took to put Buddy where he belonged, in prison, facing a life sentence for murdering Jim Thorpe.

He didn't bother to unpack before calling Esperidon. He had to know right away if he could put his plan in motion and for that he needed a cash infusion from Enrico. He held the developer's business card with fingers trembling from anticipation as he punched in the Managua number on his cellphone. He expected a callback message but was surprised, even unprepared, when Enrico answered the phone himself.

"Mr. Gilbert, you have not torn up my card after all."

"Did you expect to hear from me?" Merrie replied, hoping to keep his voice noncommittal, his nervousness in check almost to the edge of boredom as though calling him was way down his priorities list. He did not want to reveal to the developer how much he really hoped to go to work for him.

"Given the lie of the land here, I didn't think you would want to return. I told you my new business partner would be Chloe Boynton but, like many expectations, things change."

"It's Buddy Boynton now, right?"

"Yes, and I have heard enough to know that there is no love lost between you."

"None at all."

"Then you still want to be in my employ?"

"Chloe says we can live in harmony."

"I trust that includes me."

The not so subtle remark stopped Merrie. What was he implying, a ménage a trois? Once and for all he had to find out what was going between him and Chloe, and the sooner he got to Managua the better. "When do I start?"

"You haven't even asked me what I want you to do."

"Go ahead."

"Keep an eye on Buddy."

"You want me to spy on your new business partner?"

"I would not put the emphasis on secrecy. Simply follow him around, but don't hide that fact from him."

Merrie began to wonder if Esperidon was not only playing a game but also playing him for a fool.

"Buddy wouldn't stand for that."

"Precisely."

Was Esperidon the kind of man who found release in sadistic pleasure, getting his kicks by pitting one person against the other, hoping the climax is a fight to the death? Well, Chloe had duly warned him. There was still time to pull out, tell Esperidon he didn't like the job description.

Instead, he said, "You'd have to pay me a helluva lot to do that."

"How much, using your words, is a helluva lot?"

"Fifty thousand," Merrie said, "up front."

There was silence on the other end of the line.

Merrie broke the silence, speaking before Esperidon could break it for him. "Let me assume, Mr. Esperidon, that you don't have a lot of lost love for Buddy."

"Not a great deal."

"I also assume that you'd prefer someone else as your business partner?" Merrie did not elaborate as to who that someone might be. Esperidon knew damned well who.

"In a perfect world, perhaps, but I am a realist. The money comes first, one's personal preferences second."

"You would not be immune to my getting Buddy out of your hair?"

"My goal, however it may be accomplished, is to return Chloe's fortune to its rightful owner. If you can do that, Mr. Gilbert, I will give you a bonus that will allow you to live comfortably the rest of your life."

Merrie thought for a moment. He had to be careful; he was stepping into uncharted territory. Esperidon was a ruthless man of power. He could turn on Merrie as easily as he was turning on Buddy, but as long as he delivered he was safe.

"I'm not interested in a bonus. All I want is fifty thousand dollars, in advance."

"And you will take care of Buddy?"

"I will take care of Buddy." Let Esperidon assume what Merrie meant by that. He gave the developer the transfer information needed to deposit the money in Merrie's credit union account.

"I expect results, Mr. Gilbert."

Or else, Merrie thought. "You'll get them."

Merrie never felt more flush but it was money destined to charter a boat, air fares for himself and Harriet and, if there was enough left over, a private jet from Miami to Minneapolis.

The money was secure but he wasn't. He could not allow self-doubt to creep into his thought process, like buyer's remorse when someone selects a BMW instead of a Ford Focus. If he didn't pull it off he'd have two enemies: Buddy and Esperidon. His life would not be worth a bald tire. Well, it wasn't the first time he'd run into a burning building without knowing if he would make it out alive.

34

Merrie did not expect Enrico's Mercedes to be waiting at the curb in front of the Augusto C Sandino airport following his cabin-class trip back to Managua, nor was it. He could have flown first class--he was flush with more money than he could imagine--but decided frugality was the better part of financial valor.

In any case, he taxied to Enrico's elegant compound and the cabbie, noticing Merrie's discount luggage and attire, simply assumed his fare should be dropped off at the servants' entrance and was duly taken aback when Merrie directed him to stop at the main gate with its elaborate wrought iron grillwork. The driver waited and watched in awe as the gate swung open to admit Merrie who was met with a generous hug by the guard.

"Destacado!" he shouted out his window as he drove away.

The first bone of contention was Esperidon's demand that Merrie live inside the walled estate of the developer's residence. Merrie wanted to accept Juan Carlos's invitation to stay at the firehouse as a volunteer firefighter, which meant he could keep his hand in and go on runs in the Pierce Pumper. More important, he needed the freedom to move and plan, neither of which he could readily accomplish under the intrusive eyes of Esperidon and his guards. But the boss won out, for reasons Merrie considered nefarious, and so he took his luggage and followed a stone path to a one-story building for the hired help, behind the mansion, looking for all the world like a minimum-security prison, which it probably was.

His room was monastic, a bed, writing table and lamp, dresser with mirror above, toilet, shower, and a window looking out on a small quadrangle. No air conditioning but there was a fan. The others living here were native Nicaraguans for whom heat was an accepted factor of one's existence but to Merrie it felt like an oven. He turned the fan on high and sorted his clothes in the dresser. Before leaving Minneapolis, Merrie went shopping at Target and loaded up on shorts and collared golf shirts. He figured he could go three weeks without doing a laundry, depending on how much his exertion made him sweat. Although he hadn't yet seen Esperidon, his new employer sent a message through one of the guards that cocktail hour by the swimming pool was at 8:30, in all probability, his first encounter with Buddy since the shooting. It should be interesting.

Merrie spent the afternoon walking around introducing himself to guards and groundskeepers, and discovered some of them were proficient in English, making it easier to communicate. He called Abelardo on his cell but got voicemail so he left a message letting him know he was back in Nicaragua. Abelardo was Merrie's connection to the firehouse, without which his plan, to use a painful metaphor, would go up in flames.

Eight-thirty arrived and Merrie walked over to the pool, not big enough to park a yacht in but close. The tiled deck had several tables with umbrellas, and a complete bar set up in the shadow of the mansion. Merrie looked around for Buddy and saw only Enrico standing with a martini in his hand. He walked over.

"Are you settled in, Mr. Gilbert?" Esperidon asked.

Merrie took a martini from a tray proffered by a servant who looked as cool as a cucumber.

"Settled in except for the heat."

"You Minnesotans are not accustomed to the tropics. In time you will be acclimated."

"The last time, I wasn't here long enough to get acclimated." Merrie looked around. 'Where's Buddy?"

"At the Metro Centre. He will be arriving shortly."

"Does he know I'm here?"

"Yes, maybe that's why he's late." Esperidon laughed. He was enjoying himself.

"And Abelardo. Is he back on your payroll?"

"Not my payroll, his. We are launching a new company that does marketing on behalf of the Metro Centre. Abelardo is president."

"Running his own business. Better than working for dad?"

"Precisely."

"And the firehouse?"

"He continues to volunteer. That was part of our agreement."

"Good. When can I see him?"

"In time," Esperidon said. "We have to get you organized first."

"Ok, how about a job description so it looks as if I'm gainfully employed."

"That is up to Buddy. You will be his assistant."

Merrie whistled. "I thought I reported to you."

"Being his assistant makes it easier for you to keep an eye on him."

"While you keep an eye on me?"

Esperidon didn't reply, peering instead over Merrie's shoulder. Merrie turned, wondering what had taken his attention away from their conversation. It was Chloe making an entrance. His heart almost seized as he watched her approaching him, her effortless gait, her carriage, her beauty, nothing had changed except one thing: her hair. She had cut it short, probably because of the climate; similar to the way Harriet wore hers. That Harriet came into his mind as he was staring at Chloe unexpectedly jarred him, as though her spell over him was being compromised.

She glowed with confidence and a golden tan, smiling at Merrie as if he were an old friend who happened to drop by. He hoped she was masquerading her true feelings. As always, simplicity dictated her fashion, she was wearing a wrap-around skirt patterned with yellow and rose birds of paradise, covering but also revealing the outlines of her elegant figure. He struggled to control his sense of futility as he watched Esperidon embrace her, letting his hand slide down her backside provocatively. Merrie decided that Esperidon was a fucking sadist.

Chloe disengaged and shook Merrie's hand.

"How's your shoulder?" she asked, letting him know she hadn't forgotten.

"I can lift a martini," he said and showed her.

There were fake smiles all around.

"How is Jon?" he ventured.

Chloe arched a brow suggesting this was not the time to ask about Jon. "He's fine."

"I'd like to see him."

This sparked Esperidon's attention. Had Merrie gone too far?

Not until the second martini was started did Buddy turn up, looking fit and relaxed in white trousers and matching golf shirt.

"Well, look who's here," he called expansively. He walked over to join them. He was all smiles, feigning friendliness. Merrie was ready to slug him but instead he had to shake Buddy's extended hand as though they were at a college reunion.

"I understand you're on the team."

"Team?" Merrie asked guardedly.

"Hey," Buddy said, grabbing a martini and quaffing it. "We're all working together now, right?"

Merrie didn't answer, waiting instead for Esperidon to respond but he didn't, leaving it to the two of them.

"I understand I'm going to be your assistant," Merrie finally offered.

"Not my decision, but Enrico is the boss, right Enrico?" Buddy said looking at Esperidon for confirmation. "Where are you staying?" he asked.

"Here," Merrie said.

Buddy raised a quizzical eyebrow.

"Servants' quarters."

Oh," he said smugly. "I hope you're comfortable."

When dinner was finally announced at nine-thirty, Merrie's stomach was churning like an empty blender. They walked from the patio into an air-conditioned room with a high ceiling, dark-paneled walls and a floor made of parquet strips set diagonally like the one in Esperidon's office. Another raided rococo castle? Merrie wondered.

A sideboard held a variety of serving platters with seafood, cold roasted suckling pig, salad, cut-up melon, cheeses and bread. The table was set with silverware and wine glasses. As they helped themselves, a door at the farther end of the room opened and a woman in a wheelchair was pushed in by a nurse. At first Merrie thought it was Esperidon's mother because she appeared worn and haggard, but on closer look she was too young.

"May I introduce my wife, Isabela," he said to Merrie.

"My dear," he said to her, "This is Mr. Gilbert about whom I have already spoken."

She smiled as if on cue but said nothing. Merrie nodded and watched as she was placed at the opposite end of the table from where Esperidon sat. The nurse brought a plate of food and sat next to Isabella, feeding her.

Esperidon had his eye on Merrie. "My wife is suffering from dementia. She was a beautiful woman once."

"I think she still is," Merrie said, feeling empathy toward her, a woman living in the midst of splendor yet unable to enjoy any of it.

"You are very kind to say so."

"I'm sorry she's ill."

"No need to be. She is not suffering."

Behind those seemingly blank eyes Merrie believed she was.

After dinner Esperidon rose from his chair and walked over to his wife. He kissed her lightly on her forehead and then patted her shoulder. The nurse wheeled Mrs. Esperidon back through the same door they had entered through earlier.

"I like a Cuban cigar after dinner," Esperidon said, "but the smoke does not appeal to everyone. I'm going to my office." He looked at Buddy. "Join me will you? I believe Chloe and Mr. Gilbert have things to talk over."

Walking out, Buddy shot a backward glance heavy with angst.

"Does Buddy smoke cigars?" Merrie asked Chloe when the others had left the room.

"Hates them," Chloe answered and motioned with her hand to step outside through French doors leading to the garden. Chloe led him away from the floodlights to a bench by a pond teeming with orange-spotted koi.

"I didn't want to talk in the dining room," she said. "It's probably bugged. Enrico is paranoid about security."

They sat on the bench remaining quiet for a while. "I wished you hadn't come but now that you're here I'm glad to see you," she said, breaking the silence. "You rescue people. That's what you're good at." She looked at him imploringly. "Rescue me."

He was all too familiar with her predilection for the better things in life. "Doesn't look too bad here."

"Enrico won't let me out of his sight. I'm a prisoner." Chloe stared down at one of the expensive fish opening its mouth for a handout. "This isn't what I bargained for."

"You never bargain for anything. Chloe. You just take what you want, including me."

"Please," she said "No lectures."

"I have to know one thing."

"What's that?"

"I need to hear it from you. Who is Jon's real father?"

She looked at him sharply. "What are you talking about?"

"I saw Karl Mittelstadt."

Her eyes widened, either in surprise or relief, perhaps both. "So he told you something he promised never to reveal."

"Why didn't you tell me? If our relationship means anything, you should have said something."

"It's irrelevant."

"Irrelevant? I risked my life to rescue Jon."

"Whoever his father is, Jon is still my son. That's all I meant."

"What else haven't you told me?"

"Do you think I have something more to hide?"

"If you want us to live together you have to be completely open with me."

"I was a different person then. Naive, gullible, stupid."

"Did you love him?"

"Karl? Of course not. Subconsciously I was probably getting back at Buddy. At least I got a son out of it." Chloe was all ice.

"Don't you ever think about how this has affected Karl? Watching some other guy raise his son?"

"Why didn't Karl say something if he was so perturbed? I could have given Jon up for adoption but that would have meant giving up my only chance at being a mother. What is so terrible about that?"

Merrie stared down at his folded hands. "Karl said he's tired of the masquerade."

Chloe sighed. "I guess I am too."

"Then you need to tell Jon. Karl will do it if you don't. Better to learn it from his mother."

"Buddy would never let me."

"You have to get his permission?"

Chloe shivered. "I'm afraid of him."

"You don't need to be with me around."

She looked at him long and hard. "How do I know you will be around?"

They watched the panorama of fish for a while.

"I wonder if they ever sleep?" Chloe asked.

"I think they just rest."

"That's what I need, a rest, a good long rest."

"Do you really believe we can have a life together?"

"When I'm divorced everything will be different."

Merrie wished he could believe her. "Where does Enrico fit in?"

"He thinks he can have it all," Chloe said, her voice rising. "Buddy, his business partner and me, his mistress. But he's not touching me ever. Can you imagine living in the same house with his sick wife in another room?"

"You can tell he still loves her."

"But she can't give him what he wants. Only I can do that." She shifted her body as if someone had pushed her. "Get me out of here, Merrie."

"I thought you wanted to stay, carve out a new life for yourself."

"With you."

"Would you be better off in Minneapolis?"

She sighed heavily. "From one prison to another, is that what you're saying?"

"You are better off here for the time being, at least until Buddy is behind bars." Merrie was still unsure whether he should share his plan with Chloe to lure Buddy back to Minneapolis, using her son as bait. In her state of mind she might panic and say something to Buddy. It would be the equivalent of a death sentence. This time Buddy wouldn't fail to kill him.

"I thought I was better off," Chloe said, "but not anymore. My money is tied up until the divorce is settled and Buddy is in no hurry to finalize anything. It wouldn't surprise me if he and Enrico conspired to keep me penniless and so I'd remain at their mercy."

"Why would they do that?"

She shrugged. "Enrico is power-mad and Buddy is paranoid, and now with you on the scene the combination is volatile."

"Buddy was cordial to me tonight."

"It's a charade. He fills himself with martinis. I have no idea who Buddy is anymore. I'm more afraid of him than ever."

"Enrico wants me to keep an eye on Buddy."

"See, even he doesn't trust Buddy. Oh, Merrie, what are we going to do?"

He finally understood what he had to do. In all conscience, he could not leave Chloe behind. She would become, in effect, Buddy's bargaining chip for Jon. Merrie saw it now, why hadn't he thought of this before? She was more than a bargaining chip. All Buddy had to do was let Merrie know that something terrible would happen to Chloe if Merrie kidnapped Jon. All three of them had to escape together. He decided to tell her.

"I have fifty thousand dollars."

She stared at him. "On a fireman's income?"

"An advance from Enrico."

He could almost hear the wheels moving in Chloe's head. "Maybe we can work something out."

"It's already been worked out." He told her about the chartered boat but did not elaborate about the boat's captain.

"Why wasn't Jon at dinner? I have to talk to him."

"It's impossible. Do you think Buddy will ever let you see him again?"

"Where is he staying?

"In another part of the house. There are dozens of rooms. It's easy to get lost. There are guards to consider as well, and if they saw you talking to Jon they'd report you to Buddy right away. He's been in seclusion since we got here. He doesn't leave the compound."

"Then it's up to you, Chloe. Talk to Jon, tell him we're getting out of here."

Chloe slouched wearily. "I don't see how."

"A fire," Merrie said, "a three-alarmer."

35

It was after one in the morning when Abelardo finally returned Merrie's call. Merrie was lying on his bed naked reading a Lucas Davenport adventure he'd picked up between flights at Miami International. The Prey series of novels were situated in the Twin Cities area and Merrie enjoyed the local flavour, the streets and neighbourhoods he was familiar with.

"I hope you are comfortable staying in my father's house."

"The decision wasn't mine."

"It never is, Captain Gilbert," Abelardo said cryptically.

"But you've made peace with your father."

"Detente is a better word. Please do not think I am unappreciative of what you did for me. My father relented when I told him I would not work for his organization unless I remain a firefighter and, although I no longer have time to polish the Pierce pumper, I make myself available when there is a run."

That was good news to Merrie because he needed not only Abelardo's approval but also his assistance to execute step one of his plan. And he also had to know how far the loyalty of the young man stretched, and in what direction, toward his father or toward Merrie.

"How do you feel about Buddy Boynton becoming your father's partner?" he asked.

"What little I know about it does not appeal to me. I am not part of the inner circle, nor do I wish to be."

"I will tell you that your father hired me to keep an eye on Buddy."

"It would not surprise me if he has someone keeping an eye on you, too."

Only one person was close enough to keep an eye on Merrie the way Abelardo meant, and that was Chloe. Could she be playing him against Esperidon the way Esperidon was playing Merrie against Buddy? She was certainly capable of it if she felt it was to her advantage. His mind doubled back to what they talked about by the fishpond. He told her he was thinking of a fire, a three-alarmer, but he said it so casually that she didn't question him about it. Given his propensity to exaggerate in order to make a point, maybe she just thought of it as hyperbole. He hoped so because the less she knew the better.

"It sounds like an assignment going nowhere," Abelardo was saying while Merrie was deep in thought, as he always was with Chloe on his mind.

"What did you say?"

Abelardo repeated himself.

"Oh, but it does go somewhere, Abelardo," Merrie replied. "Minneapolis. Buddy is going there very soon."

Abelardo expressed surprise. "How can you be so sure? He is a wanted man in Minneapolis. He is no fool."

"He will be when I'm done with him," Merrie said.

Breakfast was a buffet served outdoors by the pool. Living here isn't all bad, Merrie noted, as he helped himself to substantial helpings of braised eggs, bacon, corn bread and coffee, plenty of coffee. He sat alone under an umbrella until Enrico showed up.

"May I join you?" he asked, his plate lightly loaded.

"What's a typical day for you?" Merrie asked after Enrico had settled in. He still hoped to get a fix on what the Nicaraguan expected of him inasmuch as there was no job description, nor did he expect any.

"I take it you assume you should fit into my routine. That is not why I hired you. Just follow Buddy around. You are on your own. I must have total deniability. Understood?"

Merrie nodded.

Enrico smiled. "But to answer your question, much of my day is spent in boring meetings."

"How do you compensate for the boredom?"

Enrico's eyes lit up. "My antique cars."

Merrie did not want to let on that he had heard about Esperidon's love affair with classic cars from the bartender at the hotel watering hole.

"Really?" Merrie said, "You collect cars?"

"Perhaps you'd like to see them sometime?" he replied, obviously proud to show them off.

Merrie was overjoyed. He loved old cars, otherwise how could he justify driving a 1990 Caddie that had gone through three water pumps, two sets of struts, a pair of CV joints, a radiator, not to mention tires, batteries, brakes, and a new windshield courtesy of Buddy Boynton.

After breakfast, Esperidon took calls in his office while Merrie sat waiting with his third cup of coffee. He hoped Chloe would arrive so he could ask her where Jon was holed up but he didn't see her. Maybe she was reporting to Esperidon at this very moment, telling him about their conversation by the fishpond, a troubling thought that did not rest well with him. As he waited with growing anxiety, Buddy turned up for breakfast. Instantly, negative vibes percussed in the still, hot air.

'Well, fireman, how are you feeling?" he said, getting his breakfast.

"I'd feel a lot better if you didn't call me fireman," Merrie replied.

"Sensitive, eh? Well what should I call you? Executive Assistant?"

"Call me Gilbert."

"I know why Enrico hired you, fireman."

Merrie found it impossible to control his irritation. "You don't have any idea why he hired me, Buddy."

Buddy turned from the buffet table, his body like a ramrod. "What did you say?"

"Figure it." Merrie got up and walked into the garden, working to diffuse his anger, knowing how dangerous it was to lose control in front of Buddy. He followed a landscaped path to a long, flat-roofed out-building that he had seen in the distance but could not identify. Along its foundation was a wide tarmac covered by a continuous portico to keep the sun from baking the asphalt. Steel beams supported the roof. Like a mausoleum, there were no windows to look into, but there were garage doors, seven of them, flush with the wall to create a continuous unbroken facade. It was impressive and had to be, Merrie realized, because this must be the garage where Enrico stored his classic cars.

Next to it was a less impressive structure, very like a pole barn, and Merrie wondered what that was for. In any case, his reverie was interrupted by a voice behind him. He turned to see Esperidon emerging from the path Merrie had followed earlier.

"Buddy told me you came this way. Did you have words?" he asked almost hopefully.

"Not many but they were choice."

"I see. Well, bury your differences, if I may use a metaphor, because I told him that you will accompany him to the Centre in an hour."

"So you really are calling the shots."

"I am merely the chef. The ingredients take care of themselves."

Merrie smiled at Enrico's play on words. He was a player all right. "Before I go will you show me your cars?"

"With pleasure," Enrico said and, using a small remote he withdrew from his trouser pocket, he opened one of the garage doors, which lifted whisper quiet. The door closed automatically behind them after they entered presumably to preserve the humidity-controlled atmosphere. The interior of the garage, unbroken by any support posts, was lighted by hundreds of track lights like those seen in museums. The floods were strategically canted to illuminate each car and, more than that, to highlight elements: hood ornaments, bulbous fenders, shaped rear decks, convertible interiors, enormous eight and twelve cylinder in-line engines displayed with their hoods up. This was as fabulous a collection as Merrie had ever seen. Many of the cars he recognized because of their iconic reputations, the kinds illustrated in high-profile magazines but never seen in real life: a Bugatti racer, a Mercedes touring car with silver fenders, an early Porsche with a hand-pounded body, a Rolls phantom with wheels a 747 could use for landing. One stood out that was unfamiliar to him. He pointed to it.

Enrico's smile broadened. "You like that? My pride and joy."

"What is it?"

"A 1921 Hispano-Suiza Torpedo. Only three survive, one of which you see before you. It is made of tulip wood."

Merrie could detect faint traces of grain under the copper stain and hundreds if not thousands of tiny brass rivets holding the lightweight body together. Wide fenders suspended away from the body accented the distinctive torpedo shape. Big round headlights were mounted high in either side of a flat grille.

"I'll be damned," Merrie said. "I know that car."

Enrico arched his dark eyebrows. "Inspiring," he said. "From where?"

"Philo Vance."

Enrico was puzzled.

"A fictional detective from the 1920s. This is the car he drove."

"You are a very literate man for a fire fighter."

"Firemen have a lot of time to read. I like detective novels. Philo Vance solved some pretty complicated cases."

"Did he? Is that why you like him, because he could solve complicated cases?"

Merrie smiled. "And the fact that he drove a car like this one."

Esperidon was obviously pleased that his Hispano-Suiza was not only appreciated by Merrie but also immortalized in fiction.

They went outside. The hot sun kept them under the arcade. "What is the building next door used for?" Merrie asked.

"I'll show you," Enrico said, still beaming with pride over his conspicuous consumption. "This will also interest you." He turned the dial on a combination lock and opened the door. They went into a dark storeroom. Overhead lights came on from a switch by the door. On the concrete floor, parked as if in a showroom display, were a half dozen pieces of commercial lawn equipment, the kind golf courses use: two riding mowers, a utility vehicle with a trailer, two walking mowers, as well as an edger, a blower and a trimmer hanging from the wall. They were all painted in the distinctive orange-red color of the Toro brand.

"Another Minneapolis connection."

"Bloomington," Merrie corrected, but still impressed. "How many people do you employ to run all this stuff?"

"For a while more than I could afford, but things are turning around for me."

I wonder if Chloe's fortune has anything to do with it, Merrie thought.

As they were leaving the building he spotted a workbench in back, behind one of the big riding mowers. Under it, on a storage shelf, were three bright-red plastic gasoline containers.

36

His day watching Buddy was a waste of time
except that Merrie had a chance to reconnoiter the
headquarters of Metro Centre. Buddy had a private office
but he wasn't high enough in the pecking order to have a
private secretary, having to share one with three other
executives. What tickled him even more was that Buddy
began his workday with a Spanish tutor. From what he
could hear outside the door, Buddy was a piss-poor pupil.
The rest of Buddy's time was spent in meetings to which
Merrie was not invited, so he wandered about, using his
Spanish to introduce himself as Buddy's executive
assistant. Most of the personnel he discovered spoke
English anyway but they appreciated his efforts to speak
their language hoping that their English was as good as his
Spanish. One junior VP even dared to say that Merrie's
Spanish was much better than Buddy's ever would be. The
comment caused laughter all around and revealed how
little respect Buddy's co-workers had for him.

This was fine with Merrie and what was also fine
was his relative freedom once he got to the office. Driving
into the city with Buddy was like an armed truce so
delicate that it could blow up at any moment, but at the
office Buddy had to mind his manners and even pretend
that Merrie was a valued colleague.

Exactly what that meant was to be answered later,
maybe tomorrow. Who knew and who cared as far as
Merrie was concerned, he had other things on his agenda.
While Buddy was holed up in a meeting, Merrie took the
elevator to the lobby and walked to the huge atrium that

connected the office wing with the hotel and dozens of retail shops. He sat on the ledge of a water fountain and texted Harriet Spenser that she should call him within the next thirty minutes. He remained where he was and watched the passing parade of shoppers, tourists and businesspersons. One who caught his eye was an elegant woman carrying a Jack Georges brief case. She reminded him of Chloe and his groin involuntarily arched.

His phone vibrated twenty minutes later. "Hot enough for you?" she asked.

"In more ways than one. Have you settled in at your hotel?"

"I'm sure it's not as luxurious as your place, but it will do."

"Have you made progress chartering a boat?"

"I have, but it's going to cost you. We could charter a private jet for that kind of money."

"That's exactly what Buddy would figure, and he'd track us down before we even landed in Minneapolis. The last thing he would think of is an ocean voyage. It's too romantic for him."

"Not to mention risky. I had to put down half when I signed the contract. Ten-thousand-five-hundred. There's also the cost of flying in a crew to bring the boat back to Puerto Cabezas."

Before leaving Minneapolis Merrie gave Harriet power of attorney so his signature would not appear on anything that could tie him to the charter.

"That's fine. What kind of boat are we getting?"

She described it to him. "A Pacific Seacraft Voyager, a 40-foot honey of a boat I've always wanted to sail."

"Do you think the two of us can handle her?"

"With me as your teacher? Of course."

He depended on her confidence. He'd need every bit of it and more, once they set sail for Miami. They had discussed details prior to his leaving but he wanted to go over the checklist again. "Let's review one more time.

Unless it's an emergency, don't contact me any more. Act like a tourist, go shopping, see the sights, and get acclimated to the heat as much as you can. Have you reserved a rental car?"

"National. I'm going to go like a pro."

He joined her laughter, not so much because it was that funny but because they needed something to break the tension.

"Good, you will have to drive like one. Practice dry runs to the fire station to make sure you know your way but do it at different times of the day so you don't arouse suspicion. We can't afford any slip-ups."

"I know," she said, serious again.

"Do you have a place booked in Puerto Cabezas?"

"Hostel Brisas y Olas. It'll cost you twenty dollars a day."

"That's what I like. The cheaper the better. Buddy is so conditioned to the good things in life he wouldn't bother looking for us in a hostel."

"It's about 100 kilometers to Puerto Cabezas and I'll do a practice run there, too, like you asked."

"This is going to go down in the dead of night. As soon as you get my call, park in the street next to the fire station and wait for us there."

"What do I look for?"

"You might hear it before you see it, a Ford 150 pickup with straight pipes."

37

Every morning before breakfast, Merrie walked the grounds of Esperidon's estate to establish a routine that would not raise curious eyebrows when he passed the pole barn where the lawn equipment was stored. If he saw any guards he would wave a Buenos días and move on. Merrie was part of the household now and he was simply out early, enjoying the sunrise and pleasant temperatures.

By making this a daily activity, he was able to observe the routine of the gardeners, who also started their days early. Maybe it was Esperidon's meticulous sense of order, certainly not the manana way of the tropics, that the gardeners maintained a strict schedule, which benefited Merrie because it eliminated randomness. What did not benefit him was that they locked up the storage building after taking the mowers out, probably more of Esperidon's influence, mostly paranoia. Why the hell didn't they leave it open while they mowed? All he wanted was a small quantity of gasoline they'd never miss.

His plan, if he could still call it that because there were variables over which he had little or no control, was to scare the shit out of Esperidon. Merrie had investigated enough arson cases to know that lighting a towel soaked in gasoline was one of the most obvious ways to start a fire but by the time anyone figured that out, he'd be long gone. A diversion was all he wanted, to take people away from their responsibilities and suspicions long enough for him to spirit Jon out of hiding and reach their rendezvous with Dr. Spenser. There would be little damage to the pole barn except for scorched outside walls. Managua's bomberos would see to that.

The unpredictable variable was Jon with whom he had not spoken since the fateful night when they were attacked by Buddy's goons in the farmhouse and without whom his plan would go up in smoke, an appropriate metaphor he thought wryly. He was totally dependent on Chloe coming through and getting Jon ready psychologically as well as physically. He smiled to himself. He was always in Chloe's hands.

After dinner he and Chloe strolled to the fish pond, which had become a part of the after-dinner routine: Esperidon liked a cigar in his office, which left Buddy either enduring clouds of smoke, however expensive, while talking business or sulking by himself at the dinner table over a digestif. Either way, the two had accepted Merrie and Chloe walking off together as a harmless indulgence. Let the pair have a few minutes together to keep them less antagonistic and, therefore, less likely to get into mischief.

"How is Jon?"

"He's anxious to go home."

"Is he ready?"

"Oh, yes. He keeps asking me, "When?""

"Everything is in place except getting my hands on some gas. I have to figure out a way to get in the building. Security around here is tighter than a drum."

"Is there another way you can start a fire?"

He shook his head. "This would be the quickest and most efficient. All I need is access and a small container for the gas. I haven't figured that part out."

"I have a metal travel mug."

Merrie stared in pleasant surprise. "That'll work. My concern has been to store the gas once I got access to it without raising suspicion. It's so damned smelly."

"You can seal it in the mug and carry it around like it was coffee. Just don't drink it."

Merrie laughed. "Bring it to breakfast tomorrow. Remember, Jon has to be ready as soon as I start the fire. Abelardo will follow the fire truck in his pickup. The gates will open to let in the Pumper and that's when we run outside to the pickup. While everyone's attention is on putting out the fire, we'll be well on our way. And don't bring any luggage. Everything you need is on the boat. Ok?"

They were about to separate when Chloe threw herself in his arms. She kissed him deeply and then whispered in his mouth, "Once Buddy is in jail, I'll be able to clear my name and then I'll be free to start my life over again with you."

He pulled back and studied her eyes, shadowy orbs in the faint light. He hadn't told her who the captain of their boat was, the person who would sail them to freedom, the woman with whom he was also in a relationship.

"Is that what you really want?"

"That's what I really want."

38

Thanking Chloe for lending him her metal travel mug at breakfast the next morning, Merrie made an obvious show of filling it with coffee.

"To tide me over," he said to no one in particular and no one in particular took notice.

There were two more days of "drinking coffee" on his morning walk before an opportunity presented itself. On the way to his room to get ready for "work," he noticed that the door to the storage building was open. He walked over and peered inside. A gardener was getting ready to start the Toro Z Master. He stopped when he saw Merrie. He was a short burly man with a face burnt black from countless days in the sun.

"Buenos días," Merrie said, and told him in his broken Spanish that the Toro was manufactured in his hometown.

The gardener was dutifully impressed and took Merrie's comment as an opportunity to expound on his superior knowledge of the mower's features: handle bars instead of a steering wheel which gave the machine zero turning radius around trees and shrubs, a powerful 29-horse Kohler Command Pro engine, a 48-inch mowing deck of 7-gauge steel, ten mph maximum speed, a cutting height from one inch to five-and-a -half, and ROPS, a Rollover Protection System, most of which flew over Merrie's comprehension of technical Spanish like birds in flight.

"What's that?" Merrie asked, pointing to a round depression in the plastic mounting for the seat.

"Ah," the gardener said in Spanish, "a beverage holder."

"Salude," Merrie replied, holding up Chloe's metal mug.

The man nodded, smiling broadly.

Merrie stood back while the gardener started the mower and drove out into the open. He jumped off to lock the door. Merrie yelled that he'd like to look over the rest of the equipment and the gardener told him to take as much time as he wanted and lock it up on his way out.

No problemo, Merrie thought.

He was never more conflicted than the moment when, at two o'clock the following morning, he lit two bath towels rolled together, the inner one soaked in gasoline, the outer one dry, that were tucked against the wall of the pole barn like a stretched-out dead snake. He had spent his adult life putting out fires and now he was starting one, not using rags but rather the towels from his bathroom embroidered with YSL. He debated whether it was burning up expensive designer towels that bothered him more or being an arsonist. Either way, he thought, here goes, all or nothing. The towels smoldered at first and then little flames licked up, scorching the wood. Merrie figured he needed a minute or two to make sure the fire was not going to die out. The building and the equipment inside may be doomed, a reasonable price to pay for getting Buddy out of everyone's hair, but the garage next to it filled with Esperidon's elegant old cars would not come to harm unless of course the Bomberos were tardy. One could not be as confident in Nicaragua as one could in Minnesota but Abelardo, the presumptive heir to the car collection, assured him the pumper would arrive in time, with lights flashing and horn blaring as Merrie had advised: make lots of noise. The flames were now going well enough to assure a larger conflagration, time for Merrie to sneak back to his room and wait in the dark for the fire to be detected.

It didn't take long. Shouts first from guards patrolling the grounds and then the high-pitched, ear-shattering shriek of a smoke alarm. Pandemonium ensued just as Merrie had expected. Esperidon came dashing out the front door of his mansion, his maroon house jacket unbelted and billowing out behind him like Count Dracula's. He joined the guards who were playing a garden hose on the side where Merrie had started the blaze. For a moment, Merrie, so conditioned to fighting fires, wanted to join them. His presence wouldn't have mattered anyway. A dozen garden hoses would not have helped. He ran instead to the security shack next to the gate and shouted to the guard inside in Spanish "Did you call the fire department?"

"Si si!" the guard shouted back and turned the switch to open the gates. The twin wrought iron sections of heavily decorated tropical flowers and leaves began separating away from each other, hinges grinding from the weight. Having opened the gate, the guard ran off to help fight the fire. Merrie shouted after him that he'd wait for the fire truck and direct it in. He was now alone just as he wanted to be. Presently he heard the sound of the pumper's siren and air horn growing in intensity as the rig drew near. The cacophony was music to his ears. So far so good, but where the hell were Chloe and Jon? His pulse was beating rapidly and he gulped air to hold his anxiety at a manageable level. The fire truck came up the road with lights flashing, and the shiny red vehicle turned and screeched to a stop at the entrance. The driver's window was down and Juan Carlos was at the wheel. He waved and yelled to Merrie that Abelardo was right behind him. Merrie looked. Sure enough, the pickup came around behind the pumper and parked next to the wall. Abelardo jumped out, dressed in his canvas and carrying his fireman's hat. He ran over to Merrie.

"Here are the keys, Captain Gilbert. Leave them in the glove box. Good luck!"

Abelardo jumped onto the truck and the rig roared off to fight the fire.

Merrie smiled to himself. Abelardo would now help save his father's car collection. What better way to demonstrate to Esperidon that his son was a capable fire fighter?

There was a hydrant outside the gate but the pumper carried five hundred gallons of water, enough to put out the blaze. From where he stood a hundred yards away Merrie watched the men hook up two hoses and start playing water on the building, the pumper's diesel engine throttled wide open. The fire would be out in a minute, everything on schedule except Chloe and Jon. Where the hell were they? Merrie looked back at the big house, his concern growing exponentially. The fire now under control, the car collection safe, they'd be spotted, their early morning escape up in smoke like the pole barn. As he stewed, two silhouettes separated themselves from the shadows and approached him. He breathed a sigh a relief when he saw them but his irritation reignited when he noticed that Chloe was rolling a Louis Vuitton carry-on bag behind her.

"What are you bringing with you?" he steamed.

She was nearly out of breath. "My jewelry."

"Is that why you're late? You were packing your jewelry?" he asked in disbelief. "I told you not to bring any luggage! Let's get out of here!"

His spate of anger seemed to affect Jon more than Chloe. He had the paralyzed stare of a deer looking into headlights. Merrie led them to the waiting pickup, took the carry on and tossed it into the bed of the truck as though he were handling a bag of fertilizer. He really wanted to throw it into the shrubbery along the wall.

Chloe cried out, "What are you doing?"

"It'll be fine. Come on, let's get going." Jon got into the jump seat in back and Chloe joined Merrie in front. Making a U-turn and heading for the firehouse, Merrie was beginning to feel the weight of what was going to be a long haul to Minneapolis.

Chloe kept looking nervously over her shoulder, not to see if they were being followed but to see if her bag hadn't bounced out of the truck bed.

"Keep an eye on it, Jon," she said to her son.

"It's perfectly safe," Merrie said. "It can't fall out."

"There's expensive jewelry in it, Merrie."

Her priorities did not sit well with him. "You took so much time we could have been seen. Is your jewelry worth more than Jon's life, or yours?"

"Don't give me one of your lessons on morality," she shot back. "I'm broke in case you've forgotten. Those gems are worth a hundred thousands dollars. I'll need the collateral to borrow money when we get home. How else do you propose I pay a lawyer to defend myself?"

She paused to take in the present moment. "Whose truck is this?"

"It belongs to Abelardo. He followed the pumper and got on the rig at the gate."

"So he's in on this too? Why didn't you tell me?"

"The less you knew the better. If it slipped out that he was involved it would not only have spoiled our chances of getting away it would also have ruined his alibi."

"What alibi?"

"That he rode to the fire with the rest of the crew."

"Isn't that just fine," she said irritably. "You don't trust me but you trust the firemen not to say anything."

"Firemen watch out for each other."

"Oh really? Like you watch out for my jewelry?"

"The nice outcome of this," Merrie said, trying to reason with her one more time, "is that Abelardo was able to demonstrate first hand to his father what he does as a fireman, to make his father proud."

They drove on in combative silence.

"You're heading into the city," she said presently. "I thought we were going to the coast."

"I'm dropping off the pick-up at the fire house. We have a car waiting for us to throw off the scent. When Buddy realizes we're gone, he will be looking all over for us."

"You've thought of everything haven't you?"

"I hope so." he replied.

He pulled into the fire station's lot and climbed out. Parked at the curb down the block was the Chevrolet Malibu. The headlights flashed.

"Who is that?"

"Our ride out of here."

As they approached the Chevy, Harriet got out and ran up to Merrie, throwing her arms around his neck. "You made it!"

Over his shoulder she saw Chloe staring at her with the venom of a black widow spider. She pulled away and the two women sized each other up, one dressed for the sea, the other for Nieman-Marcus. Harriet then glanced at Merrie as though asking who the hell is this? She had good reason to be confused; he hadn't told her there would be another passenger.

"Dr. Spenser," he said, deciding a formal introduction was the better part of valor, "I'd like you to meet Jon's mother, Chloe Boynton."

Chloe stared in puzzlement. "Doctor? Why do we need a doctor?"

"Get in the car and I'll explain everything. We don't have any time to waste."

"What's in the bag?" Harriet asked. "I thought we were traveling light."

Chloe stiffened her back in anger. "Just put it in the trunk."

They piled in with Harriet at the wheel. The icy atmosphere failed to thaw, even after Merrie finally explained everything to Chloe. He didn't expect her to be sympathetic, even when he told her that this was the doctor who treated the gunshot wound inflicted by Buddy, and that she was the one with the captain's license, the one who was going to get them out of here. It got worse when they pulled up at the hostel a half-hour later.

Chloe was beside herself. "What's wrong with that hotel down the road we just passed?"

"That's the point," he explained. "Buddy would not expect us to stay in a hostel."

It didn't help her mood any when she discovered they had to sleep in a dormitory, in their clothes, with the bathroom down the hall.

Harriet was alone with Merrie for a few precious minutes when Chloe and Jon went to visit the bathrooms. They were sitting across from each other on cots in the dark. They whispered loud enough to be heard over the snores and snuffling sounds of twenty other travelers sharing the same space. "Tell me about her."

"Who?"

"You know who. The prima donna in the Oscar de la Renta pants outfit who thinks the sun sets behind her butt."

"Doctor..." he began placatingly.

"Don't play doctor with me, Merrie. That night on Lake Superior I asked you not to tell me about your past life because I didn't want to find out about the women you shared it with. I should have included your present life as well. Are you involved with her? I have to know if we're traveling together."

"We have a relationship," he said.

"Is that part of the deal?"

"She is not part of any deal. Chloe is her own woman."

"Looks like she owns you, too." Harriet sighed. "Are you trying to put her husband in jail so you and she can be together?"

The question bothered him because he suspected that subconsciously this was precisely his motive. "It was her husband who left me for dead."

Harriet nodded knowingly. "Remember when I was mending your shoulder? I asked you why you had a chip on it, like you wanted to get even with somebody. So that somebody, it turns out, is her husband. You exact your revenge and you are rewarded with his wife, a beautiful woman who, if you don't mind my adding, is way out of your league."

Merrie bristled. "I do mind."

He resented the charge that Chloe was more than he could handle, even if it was true. Maybe he didn't like hearing it from Harriet who could see his world better than he could see it himself, or wanted to see it. He was confused, his clarity of purpose fogged by the intersection of these two women, both of whom he needed but neither of whom needed him. Tethered together, the three of them, a ménage a trois if you will (not to mention a troubled son) sharing a 40-foot sailboat for several days at sea, nothing to separate them but their personal desires, vendettas, jealousies, fears, anxieties. Would they make it through whole, or even make it at all? Because none of this took into account the inherent danger of a small boat on the high seas. Was this the ultimate folly that Merrie was engaged in, putting others at risk because of his...he wanted to say magnificent plan, but in truth it wasn't that at all. If anything it was a petty obsession.

Harriet was studying his face, as if she were looking in a dictionary for a fuller meaning of his words. Finding only a blank stare she turned away.

"I'm sorry if I stepped out of bounds."

Merrie felt he was the one who should apologize, that he was acting irrationally, defensively, that Chloe represented a make-believe world he bought into and did not know how to bow out of. Harriet represented the real one, the manageable one, the one you could bank your existence on. He was ready to tell her this but Chloe and Jon returned from their ablutions and the words suffocated in his throat.

39

If his plan was not magnificent at least the boat was. Because of her length she was tied up next to the dock rather than in a slip. Even with sails furled she seemed in motion. The cabin portholes were square instead of round, adding to the impression of low-slung sleekness. The boat's name across the stern was Paradise Alley, the lettering painted in script. Harriet had completed all the necessary paper work, registration and insurance. The master license she earned while living in Havana plus her nonpareil Spanish went a long way for the owners, Caribbean Cruises in the Virgin Islands, to hand over a bareboat charter. In addition to the cost of the charter there was an advanced provisionary allowance and a delivery and redelivery charge, but Merrie didn't mind. Enrico was paying for it.

They left the Malibu parked in the marine lot. Harriet had rented it for the month and no one at the marina would be suspicious since sailors often left vehicles on the lot to use when ashore. National would not miss it until long after they were back in Minneapolis, mission accomplished.

Everything was falling into place Merrie wanted to believe, but his training told him to be on alert. They climbed aboard, changed into the dungarees and chambray shirts Harriet had brought for them, and left port a little after eight, Harriet at the helm as she powered Paradise Alley into open water with the inboard diesel rumbling under the deck. The Nicaraguan coast receding behind them, Harriet hoisted sail from the cockpit, using power equipment beyond Merrie's ability to understand. It was evident to him she could handle the boat all by herself if need be.

Jon was the most pleasant surprise. He inspected the electronic gear with the eagerness and curiosity of a 4.0 student. He asked about the pods on either side of the wheel containing the radar and gyrocompass. He wanted to find out how to set the sails, especially the jib that gave the boat its ultimately powerful look. He grilled Harriet with endless questions about sailing and, even though she answered with arcane phrases like inner forestay, roller furling and hanks on (Merrie thought she said hands on), Jon was taking it all in. It became clear he was an earnest and serious sailor. By the time they reached Miami, Harriet told him, he'd have enough experience to take the test for captain's license. Jon glowed with newfound energy; he was finally doing something that challenged him. This change in her son did not go unnoticed by Chloe who was getting into the spirit of sea travel and took charge of meals in the impressively laid-out galley.

Merrie was beginning to believe this would turn out to be a pleasant cruise. The forecast called for sanguine weather, and Nicaragua, with the inherent personal dangers it represented, was receding behind them, now a blot on the horizon. Meanwhile the four had instinctively formed themselves into a crew--the sea did that, survival depended on tight discipline, taking orders and looking out for your fellow crewmember.

It was nearly noon. The sun was over the port beam, its heat dissipated by the cool sea air. Merrie was in the cockpit with Harriet and Jon, Chloe in the cabin taking salmon out of the refrigerator in preparation for their first lunch underway, nothing to break the peacefulness of the moment except for the sudden ring of a cellphone, so unexpected, so intrusive, so obscene that the sound of it shattered the serenity of their isolated world like a hammer through glass. Merrie watched in a kind of stupid horror as

Chloe grabbed her handbag and pulled out her iPhone to answer it. He thought he had covered all the bases but forgot one simple thing, so ridiculously obvious that it went by him. He had not told Chloe to get rid of her cell phone.

It was on speaker and after her tentative hello, Buddy's voice boomed out, trembling with impotent fury. "Goddamn you, Chloe, you think you can get away with this? Running off with Jon?"

"Hang up!" Merrie called out. "Don't talk to him!"

"I heard that, fireman! I knew she couldn't do this alone. You helped set this up with that phony fire!"

Chloe looked up from the cabin doorway, holding the phone as if it were a live hand grenade. Her face was ashen, full of fear.

Buddy continued shouting, "You were smart enough not to try to fly out of here. I would have got you at the airport. You may think you're clever, but you're not clever enough. You had to charter a boat to be where you are and I'll find you. Say your prayers, fireman, because this time you really will be a dead man. Dead in the water!" Buddy laughed maniacally and hung up.

Chloe collapsed on the daybed. Jon ran down to the cabin and sat next to her, his arms around her. He was trembling. "How did dad know where we are?" he asked.

Merrie cursed himself royally. "You have tracking software on your phone. Buddy knows where we are. He can follow us all the way to Miami."

He breathed deeply. He could not allow himself to panic, which is exactly what Buddy wanted him to do. Desperation leads to desperate decisions. He had to think this through and try to fool Buddy at his own game. First of all, what was he capable of doing right now besides bluster? How could he attack them at sea? That was absurd. He'd need a helicopter or a speed boat and he'd have to know what boat he was searching for. There had to be hundreds of them in the Caribbean. He'd first have to find the marina they sailed from, and look at the manifest before he could find them and devise a plan of attack. Maybe there was enough time to reach Miami before Buddy learned that's where they were heading, but first things first.

"Ok, Chloe," he commanded, "You know what to do."

"What?"

"Get rid of it."

She stared dumbly.

"You know what I'm talking about. Your phone. Drop it over the side."

Disbelief scoured her words. "You can't be serious, Merrie. My cellphone? I absolutely refuse!"

"It has to go, don't you understand? If you keep it you might as well call up Buddy and tell him where we're going."

Chloe held the phone to her chest like a child clutching her teddy bear.

The stress was really getting to him. He was ready to throw both the phone and Chloe over the side when Harriet pushed Merrie out of the way and stared down at Chloe sitting on the daybed in the cabin.

"Either the phone goes or that suitcase full of jewels. Take your goddamned pick!"

Harriet was not wearing her white coat and stethoscope but she might as well have been. Her commanding authority was unmistakable. "I've had enough of your cry-baby attitude!" she shouted. "Do you think this is some kind of drill? Your attitude is undermining the safety of everyone aboard. I've had enough of your tantrums. I really don't understand what Merrie sees in you."

The last sentence did it. Chloe stiffened and glared back at Harriet, their eyes locked in an ocular arm wrestle. After what appeared to be an unyielding stalemate, Chloe rose royally, climbed the steps out of the cabin and, with an arm worthy of a starting pitcher, threw the phone into the air. It flew in a long arc and hit the water so far away, the sound was as light as a finger splashing.

Jon, standing next to his mother, had not cringed from the confrontation as Merrie had expected. This experience was probably toughening him up. The boy gripped his mother's shoulders.

"Mom," he said, "I'm glad you threw it away. It had to be done."

Chloe patted his hand and returned to the cabin.

Harriet went back to steering the boat, her hands gripping the wheel with the tenacity of a bulldog to keep them from shaking.

"How fast can this boat go?" Merrie asked after what he thought was a decent enough interval to give everyone time for their heart rates to return to normal.

"If we're lucky seven knots."

"Only seven?" he said, "A boat like this should fly."

"We would if the ocean was flat. We are going up and down as well as forward and there's extra drag on the hull. The rule of thumb is, add twenty-five per cent to your distance to account for wave action."

"It's about a thousand nautical miles to Miami, right?"

"Plus two-fifty to account for the wave action."

"How many days?"

"Seven or eight."

Buddy had the upper hand after all. "Can we use the engine to get there faster?"

"It has a range of 500 miles, not near enough, and we need power to get into port."

"So Buddy and his goons will probably be in Miami waiting for us?"

Harriet nodded. "He already knows we had to have sailed from a west coast marina, and that would take him straight to Puerto Cabezas which is the closest jumping off point to the US. He wouldn't have any trouble finding out we left this morning for Miami. All our names are on the manifest, including mine. I don't have any cover now."

"We can't go to Miami anymore."

"We have to. We can't change our plans now. There's the plane waiting for us at Miami International."

Chloe overheard their conversation. "It's over," she sighed, crestfallen and defeated. "We've lost."

Merrie fell into deep thought. Trying to outwit Buddy was like playing chess with a grandmaster. He had checked Merrie with the unexpected phone call. The rules of chess are that if you have nowhere else to go, the game is over. Well the game wasn't over, not yet. There was a move Merrie could make that would escape Buddy's checkmate. He smiled.

Harriet was staring at him. "What's so funny?"

"Seeing Buddy's face when we don't show up in Miami."

"We have to, we don't have anyplace else to go."

"That's what we want Buddy to keep thinking. But he'll be wrong. Turn the boat around. We're heading back to Puerto Cabezas."

"Coming about!" Harriet shouted as she pulled in the sails, emptying them of their wind. There was a momentary loss of speed, like a plane losing lift, until the boom shifted to the starboard side and the sails made a loud snapping sound as they filled out again.

"Are you sure you know what you're doing?" Harriet asked after she had established a new heading.

Merrie was not sure, but he wasn't going to admit it. The first decision, to sail back to port, was made on the fly but now that they were committed he had time to think.

"I will lay it all out," he said, "but let's eat first."

It was close to midnight when they saw the faint aura of Puerto Cabezas street lights on the horizon. Harriet hove to, let go the sea anchor about a quarter-mile offshore and spent several minutes securing the sails to their booms. Paradise Alley rocked gently in the surf as though awaiting further instructions.

Merrie had earlier checked the boat's manual to locate the seacock; it was portside in the forward head under the sink drain. From the doorway Harriet held a flashlight while Merrie got on his knees. It was cramped with little room to maneuver. The seacock was a black plastic disc about eight inches in diameter with a discharge valve to rid waste into the ocean. Only seagoing boats had this system. Freshwater sailboats were equipped with storage tanks that were emptied on shore. He opened the valve and kept yanking on it hoping to break it open but he couldn't apply sufficient torque.

"Won't come loose," he said. "I need a pry bar."

Harriet pulled out the tool drawer under the settee. Behind his back Merrie heard metal banging as she rummaged through the tools. "All kinds of wrenches and screw drivers. Some clamps. Here's a drill. What's this?" she said and the noise stopped. "A hatchet."

"A hatchet?" Merrie asked, surprised. "Give it to me."

It proved to be just what he needed. Even in the restricted space he could strike the valve with the butt end until the fitting broke off. Water began flowing but not enough to suit him. Using the sharp edge of the hatchet he now began to pry the plastic cover. After a few grunts it popped open and a big gush of water hit the under-side of the sink. He got soaked but it was a relief to see so much water pouring in. The boat would go down in an hour.

"She's worth a quarter of a million," Harriet said clearly suffering from second thoughts. "I wanted to sail a boat, not sink it." Her expression was a mixture of guilt and sadness. Her dream of an ocean cruise was listing to port.

Merrie wondered how this would affect their relationship, which at the moment seemed a bit tenuous. Her main reason for joining him in this enterprise was the opportunity to captain a sailboat at sea, and that lasted only a day. Now she was complicit in scuttling it. He didn't know if this might jeopardize her license but he didn't want to bring it up.

Chloe, on the other hand, was docile like a lamb to slaughter, agreeing to it all because it was clear to Merrie now how truly afraid she was of Buddy who was so deranged he would probably not hesitate to kill her if he felt it was necessary. More than ever Merrie had to get everyone safely back to Minneapolis and, if sinking the boat was a necessary evil, so be it, collateral damage. He tried to explain this to Harriet when they were back in the cockpit, speaking softly so that Chloe could not hear him from the saloon where she and Jon were packing their belongings.

"I know this is an extreme decision, Harriet, but it's our only option. When we don't turn up in Miami, Buddy will no doubt contact the charter company. They'll do a search and not finding Paradise Alley they will declare the boat lost at sea with all hands on board. That's what we want Buddy to believe."

He felt the boat lean more as the water began to flood the forward compartments. He called down to Chloe. "Bring everything up to the cockpit while I inflate the dinghy."

He had hauled the compact package of reinforced canvas out of the storage locker and laid it on top of the cabin. Now it was time to pull the pin. A steady hiss of air snapped the folds apart and in a few seconds, the dinghy took shape. Tucked under the thwart seat were two oars, which Merrie attached to the oarlocks. The raft measured 4x8 feet; a tight fit but they only had half a mile to shore. He slipped the dinghy off the sloping deck into the water, now lapping at the port gunwale, and tied it to the aft taffrail with the towrope. Jon helped Merrie load their backpacks.

Chloe reached around Merrie as if she no longer trusted him and handed Jon her carryon. "I'm not going to leave this behind."

"Ok", Merrie said with a sigh of finality, "abandon ship."

Squeezing into the four-person dinghy with extra baggage, not only Chloe's carry-on but also the animus between the two women, was nearly enough to sink them. Merrie sat in the thwart seat and rowed with his back to Harriet, her knees pressed against his waist. Face-on were Chloe and Jon sitting on the stern outboard motor bracket. Stuffed between them were the bags. As he crossed-stroked his oars, Merrie kept an eye on the shadowy hull of Paradise Alley finally lying on her side, the boat's masts and keel providing unwanted buoyancy. She seemed to be resting. Merrie was concerned the boat would keep on floating and eventually drift to shore.

Chloe and Jon followed his stare and turned.

"Will it go down?" Jon asked with concern.

"We'll have to wait and see."

Merrie held the dinghy steady for several minutes watching Paradise Alley fight for her life. It was a prolonged process, far longer than Merrie imagined, before the boat finally sighed a farewell and disappeared beneath the waves, turning upright in a final show of stubbornness, and surprising Merrie who anxiously waited to see if the ocean was deep enough where they were so that the 50-foot mast would not poke up like a periscope. He needn't have worried. Nothing broke the surface. Is she in Davy Jones locker now, he wondered as he imagined Paradise Alley settling on the bottom of her wet grave.

He began rowing in earnest. Ten minutes later the dinghy pushed onto sand with a small scraping sound. Merrie shipped the oars and they jumped out, hauling the dinghy up the beach where he deflated it, folded the oars into it and tied it with the towline. He walked twenty yards into a field of guinea grass behind the beach and dropped the canvas clump, stomping on so it would wedge in the almost impenetrable thicket that grew well over his head. Only an archaeologist will ever find this, he said to himself.

In single file, the group edged its way alongside the tropical grass, finally reaching a chain link fence bordering the marina. Merrie was lugging Chloe's carry-on over his shoulder because dragging it on the sand proved next to impossible. He whispered to the others to stay in the shadows while he scoped the area for dogs or night watchmen.

Nothing stirred. There were no signs of life but theirs. Apparently Nicaraguans took their security casually. The only illumination was coming from metal-shaded lamps high up on poles casting small pools of light as in a film noir scene. They followed the fence past a line of cradled boats in various stages of repair or cleaning, their rudders and keels hanging below the hulls like giant mechanistic genitalia.

At the main entrance, Merrie set Chloe's bag on the ground.

"Wait here," he said, and walked to the parking lot to fetch the Chevy. Never expecting to see the rental again, he came to respect the unique irony it represented: the car they abandoned turned out to be their means of escape, while their means of escape, their chartered boat, had been abandoned.

40

Sitting at Gate 29 in Dallas Fort Worth International waiting for Delta flight 316 to Minneapolis, Merrie could finally relax and let his mind flow over the last twenty-four hours, what under ordinary circumstances would have been a forgettably short interval but had been filled with such intensity it seemed like a lifetime. They had left the marina with Harriet behind the wheel because she knew the route, and ended their odyssey where it began—the Managua fire station. Juan Carlos met them at the door after Merrie's pounding roused the night crew. When Merrie explained their surprising reappearance, Juan Carlos called Abelardo and, while waiting for him to arrive, turned on the coffee pot and prepared breakfast for the exhausted travelers. They sat around the big table in the common room immersed in their own thoughts. Juan Carlos then led the women and Jon to where they could wash up and take naps. Although equally exhausted, Merrie could not sleep and sat at the table with Abelardo exchanging experiences, Merrie's scuttling the boat, and Abelardo's fighting the fire.

"You should have seen the look on Buddy's face when he discovered his wife and son were missing," Abelardo said. "He would have killed you on the spot. I fear you have disturbed a very big hornet's nest."

"How did your father react?"

"Relieved at first that his cars were safe, but when he realized it was a diversion he became upset. But I have seen him more upset than that, and so it was not for him the end of the world."

"I promised your father I would get rid of Buddy but I didn't tell him how."

"Buddy is not gone yet."

"Give me two days and he will be." They reflected a moment. "Did Enrico see you put out the fire?"

"My father is a man of faint praise especially when it comes to his own son, but he did manage a grudging compliment on my performance, for me a major victory." He leaned back in his chair. "Tell me about the boat you lost."

Merrie described it to him.

Abelardo whistled. "Quite a craft. How far from the beach did you scuttle it?"

"Half a mile out, just south of the Marina."

"Can't be too deep there. I know people in the salvage business. It is possible the boat can be raised and reconditioned."

That was hopeful news. "Captains don't like losing their ships." He was talking about Harriet.

"How are Jon and his mother doing?"

"Taking a nap. It was harder on Chloe but I was surprised how easily Jon adapted to sea life."

"When he is tested, he is full of surprises."

"He is a different person."

"I am happy to hear that," Abelardo replied. "Now, my friend, what comes next?"

Next was getting out of Managua. "We had a chartered jet lined up in Miami. The money for that is out the window. I don't think your father will shell out more. Besides we can't reveal to him what happened. Our only option is to fly home commercially."

Abelardo went to work quickly, booking airline tickets to Minneapolis on his cellphone in rapid no-nonsense Spanish. Merrie asked him to avoid Miami just in case, and they settled for economy with intermediate stops in Dallas and Chicago. That was not an issue but paying for it was. "I don't think your father is in any mood to buy tickets now that he had to swallow fourteen thousand dollars for the jet."

Abelardo put the cost on his Visa and Merrie promised to pay him back, in installments of course.

They landed in Minneapolis late in the afternoon. Harriet had her Prius parked in the long-term lot. Merrie accompanied her to her car while Chloe and Jon waited for him at the National rental office.

"So this is it?" Harriet asked.

"I'll see you again."

"I'm not so sure."

"After what we've been through together, how can you say that?"

"I can say that, but can you?"

He knew where she was going with the question. "Are you talking about Chloe and me?"

Harriet nodded.

"She seems to think I can fit in her world."

"It's never the other way around is it?"

"You mean Chloe fitting into mine?" He laughed at the inanity of the suggestion. "Regardless, I told her no."

"For what it's worth, she really does love you."

"How can you tell?"

"She needs you. She needs your protection, your strength, your—what is the word I'm looking for?—your permanence."

"Permanence?"

"You are solid, Merrie, always there, always ready to help someone. That's what I saw in you when we first met, when we went sailing..." It was almost wistful the way she said it. "It's what I most admire about you." She looked into his eyes as though searching for her reflection in them. "Now that I've become involved with you, it's a pity I won't get to see the final act."

"What final act?"

"Your epic morality tale. How will it end?"

"Oh," he said, "that depends on Buddy Boynton. If he wants to see his son he will have to meet me where it all started, where I found his canoe, Lake Harriet."

"Why there?"

Merrie shrugged. "Symbolism, I guess. Full circle. That's where my story started and that's where I want it to end."

"Are you sure it will end? Really end, I mean, where everyone lives happily ever after?"

"Like in a fairy tale?" Merrie thought about that. "Maybe nothing really ends, happily or not. Let's just say it will come to a close."

"I hope so."

Harriet climbed into the Prius and shut the door. She backed out and drove down the ramp, her departure as silent as the car she was driving.

He told the man behind the National counter not to give him a Chevy Malibu. He didn't want anything to remind him of what he went through the last three days. He upgraded to a cream-colored Cadillac SRX, hang the expense, a car he would probably choose for himself if he were ever to get rid of the old Coupe Deville sitting in the parking ramp of his condo building. God, but it seemed like forever since he drove that car. Would he even recognize it or, anthropomorphically speaking, would the car even recognize him?

Merrie drove out of the airport and got on the Crosstown. Chloe and Jon chose to sit in the back seat together, making Merrie for all the world their chauffeur. Harriet was probably right. She said Chloe needed him, yeah, like she needed a servant. That's what he really was to her, not the rock Harriet alluded to but a pebble Chloe could kick around. He checked her image in the rearview mirror. She was staring blankly out the window at the freeway traffic. Since throwing her phone away she had been stoic, reflective, responding listlessly when spoken to but not initiating conversation. That was fine with him. The less she demanded of him the better. He needed the down time. He ramped off the Crosstown to 35W northbound. Ahead the hazy-summer skyscrapers of Minneapolis looked like Oz. He would bypass the city and continue north, destination Karl Mittelstadt's cabin on Lake Vermilion. He had not told Chloe where they were going. She could figure that out for herself. What she did not know was that Karl would be there waiting for them. There, in the seclusion of the north woods, Jon would find out that Karl was his real father. Jon had to know if he was going to be on Merrie's side. Otherwise why would a son stand by and see his father hauled off to jail? It was a bitter pill, but the son had to become the enemy of the man he thought was his father. I'm not a nice person, Merrie told himself, regardless of what Harriet had said. He had become a cold, calculating human being, pitting one family member against another, and for what? Revenge. Merrie was out to get even, screw any noble cause of justice. He wanted to see Buddy pay for what he did to him. Let Buddy lie on that metaphorical highway bleeding to death.

"Slow down," Chloe said from the back seat, "you're driving too fast."

They arrived late; it was nearly midnight when Merrie turned into the drive of Karl's hideaway. The last time he had seen the cabin he was lurking in the shrubs to rescue Chloe. Imagine that, as if she ever really needed rescuing. Headlights illuminated the unusual design of Karl's entryway, the tree trunk shaved of bark that held up the peaked overhang. Karl heard the car and opened the front door before Merrie doused the lights of the SRX.

Jon had fallen asleep in the back seat and Chloe was unbuckling his seatbelt. The boy looked around, disoriented at first.

"You're at Uncle Karl's," she said softly.

Uncle Karl's? She was talking to the kid as if he were eight years old. This was the first overtly parental interaction Merrie had witnessed between mother and son and it made him wonder just how mature Jon really was. Was he a case of arrested development? The longest conversation Merrie had had with him was in the dark farmhouse where the kid talked like the brainwashed Manchurian candidate.

Chloe gripped Jon around the shoulders as they walked into what Merrie came to realize was a surprisingly well-appointed interior, more like a country house than a cabin. Chloe turned into a bedroom off the main hallway and shut the door.

"That's it?" Merrie said. "Not even goodnight?"

Karl shrugged. "She is that way sometimes."

"How about all the time."

"You're tired," Karl said, more critical of Merrie's impatience than Chloe's brusqueness.

As Merrie looked around, Karl waited for an opinion of his design like an expectant father. The walls were paneled in high quality Norway pine, with hardly any knotholes and stained a light yellow. The pine boards were laid sideways and curved so that they gave the impression of logs without the bulkiness. Merrie wondered how the wood was shaped, a planer with a curved blade no doubt. The firehouse workshop had some pretty impressive woodworking equipment including a 12-inch planer, but not a curved cutter head.

The hallway was like a catwalk leading to a stairway. The balusters supporting the handrail were tightly fitted panels of pine, and there were actual-size cutouts of leaves randomly jig sawed out of the wood to look like peekaboo forms. Merrie followed Karl down the stairway to the first level. A double fireplace separated the parlor from the dining room. Like the tree holding up the entry roof, the beams supporting the kitchen's header were actual trunks of small trees. Casement windows were cranked open to let in the northland breeze. Merrie could hear water lapping the shore somewhere in the dark.

"Nice place you have here," he said. "Not my first visit, but the first time I've been inside."

Karl smiled. "Can I offer you a drink?"

Merrie shook his head. "Got any coffee? I can't sleep anyway." He sat down at the dining room table of white oak while Karl went to work in the kitchen, grinding fresh beans out of a bag labeled 100% Kona, and pouring water into a shiny black Cuisinart. Presently he poured the dark steaming nectar into a mug.

"I won't join you because I do want to sleep."

The coffee reconnected the synapses in Merrie's brain and he began a rambling discourse of their escape from Nicaragua. The images in his head sequenced like a Movietone newsreel. He probably was still in a state of shock. Harriet suggested it takes time for harrowing events to sink in. Later, he thought, a form of post-traumatic shock may come, like a combat veteran coming home to discover how impossible it is to resume a normal life. How the hell, Merrie asked himself, will I ever be able to go back to hanging around in the firehouse waiting for the alarm to go off?

But sitting now in the secure comfort of an elegantly designed cabin drinking Kona coffee, he was cushioned from the impact of what he had set in motion, beginning with the diversionary fire he set and ending with his scuttling a chartered sailboat. Even in the retelling none of it made sense, calamitous things out of your control rarely make sense anyway.

"Thanks for letting us hide out in your cabin."

"I am only too happy to help. But how long do you think before Buddy finds out you are back in Minnesota?"

"For all he knows we were lost at sea, presumably we're dead. If I know Buddy, he is thanking his lucky stars that there is no one in the way to Chloe's fortune. He is probably thinking that he couldn't have done a better job himself. It wouldn't surprise me at all if he isn't toasting me posthumously for saving his ass. I can't wait to hear the surprise in his voice when I call him."

"When do you propose to do that?"

"I want this over and done with, but first we have to make sure Jon is prepared."

"Is that why you wanted me here?"

Merrie nodded. "It's up to you and Chloe to tell him."

Karl seemed less certain. "I worry about his well being. He has been through so much."

"He will go through a lot more if he thinks the man carted off to jail is his father. You're not getting cold feet are you?"

"All these years I waited for this moment but now that it's here..." he stopped talking. The door to the bedroom at the front of the cabin opened. Chloe padded down the stairs in slippers. She was wearing a caftan over silk pajamas. "Is anyone having a drink?" she asked, sitting at the table.

For a moment Merrie was stunned to see Chloe appear in such elegant garb with the casual attitude of the lady of the house playing hostess. The image was in sharp contrast to recent events, but then he remembered this was a familiar place for her and no doubt she kept a supply of clothing.

Merrie held up his cup. "Coffee?"

"Brandy."

Karl went to the kitchen, opened a cabinet and held up a bottle for them to see. The label read Schladerer Kirschwasser.

"Black Forest" he said proudly and returned with a snifter of amber fluid. Chloe rolled the brandy around in the bell of the glass before taking a sip.

"How is Jon doing?" Merrie asked.

She lingered with her gaze on the brandy before setting the glass down. "Asleep."

"That's what we all should be doing," Karl suggested.

Even as tired and as emotionally drained as he was, Merrie did not want the night to end, not yet. "We need to talk."

"Can't it wait till morning?"

"We're alone. Now is the best time."

"You never give up do you?" Chloe said.

"We're down to the final act, we can't let up now. Tomorrow you have to tell him that Buddy is not his real father."

Chloe gave Karl a nervous glance. "After the dust settles and we get back to a normal life, we can tell him then."

"Earlier I saw some gumption in him. Somewhere there's a real human being wanting to get out and express himself, but you keep smothering the kid, Chloe. You owe it to him, both of you, to tell him who he really is. Only then can he get his life in order. Can't you see that?"

Chloe shook her head. "He'll have a breakdown."

"It will be the best thing that ever happened to him."

"I don't want him to hate me," Chloe said, and added almost remorsefully, "more than he already does."

Karl wrung his hands. "Don't blame yourself, Chloe. I'm responsible, too."

Merrie was too tired to listen to any more of this self-effacing tripe. "Stop feeling sorry for yourselves. It's time to do what's right for a change."

Karl and Chloe became silent, steeped in their own thoughts. Presently they exchanged glances as though each instinctively knew what the other was thinking.

Merrie waited for one of them to say something. Exasperated that neither seemed willing to take responsibility, he asked gruffly, "Well, who's going to tell him?"

Chloe coolly stared him down. "You are."

41

The day dawned as only a day in the north woods could dawn, brilliantly, with a promise of cool temperatures and nature showing off her intense colors. It was the morning sun that woke Merrie up, not the smell of coffee, eggs and bacon in the air. He got up and climbed into the shower. He felt surprisingly good, reasonably rested and having a sense of completion that his long trek was about to end.

He came downstairs just as Karl and Chloe were finishing breakfast. "We decided to get out of here so you can be alone with Jon," Karl said.

"You still want me to do this?"

They ignored his question. "There are scrambled eggs and bacon in the warming oven and I just put on another pot of coffee."

Ok," Merrie said. "So where are you going?"

"I'm taking the boat out. We'll cruise around for an hour or so. If you need us I have my cell phone..."

Karl's comment, meant to be helpful, instead felt as if a fissure suddenly widened the ice drift between Merrie and Chloe. Would she ever get over it, he wondered, or was this the beginning of the end of their relationship?

He was nursing his third cup when Jon came down the stairs. He was in his stockinged feet and Merrie did not notice his presence until he entered the dining room.

"Where is mom?"

"She and Karl went for a boat ride. It's just you and me, kid," he added, making an effort to be casual and disarming.

Jon was wearing jeans and an oversized t-shirt that hung loosely on his thin frame. He felt Merrie's gaze and pulled the shirt from his chest as if it was itching him. "Found it in a drawer. I didn't want to wear anything I brought along."

"Like you want to put it all behind you?" Merrie said

"Something like that."

Merrie got up and brought a plate of eggs and bacon, and a cup of coffee. "I'll put on some toast."

"Thanks," Jon said.

Merrie remained quiet while Jon ate, staring out an open casement window at the blue Vermilion down below. The elevation provided a bird's eye view that, if you liked the outdoors, was breathtaking. But to Merrie, a city dweller, it was unrelenting wilderness. Karl's cabin was tucked into the end of a narrow inlet so that the main body of water was hidden by a promontory of land, making the site appear more remote than it really was. The lake had to be busy this time of year yet they were protected from the noise of motorboats and jet skis.

When Jon finished his breakfast, Merrie said, "This is the first time we've been alone together since that night in the farmhouse." He laughed trying to ease into a transition. "It was so dark the only time I saw you was when you lighted a cigarette. I didn't know you smoked."

"I don't. That was just for effect."

"Effect?"

"Playing the tough guy, you know? Part of the image, the remote farmhouse, being in the dark. It was done to make you feel ill at ease."

"Well, it worked."

"There was more going on than you knew." He hesitated with his coffee cup to his lips; then he put it down. "I don't know if I should tell you this, but so much has happened I guess it doesn't matter anymore. All I ask is that you don't bring this up with mom. She's really sensitive about my coming into the open."

Merrie pulled himself up and leaned forward. "What are you talking about?"

"Abelardo's father set up the kidnapping. You weren't supposed to be hurt but things got out of hand."

"You mean it wasn't Buddy's hired thugs who threw the sack over my head?"

"No, they were Esperidon's men. You were set up."

Merrie's mind shot back to that night, reconstructing in a rapid, even frantic, flashback the events that took him to the farmhouse, to rescue Chloe's son from the brainwashing grip of El Grupo. He recalled covering his trail, having Abelardo meet him on the upper floor of the parking ramp. "You mean Abelardo knew about this?"

"He not only knew, he arranged everything."

Merrie was stunned, his morale pummeled by another double cross. "But why?"

"This is the hardest part to tell you about. Abelardo's father was trying to break us up."

"Us?"

"Abelardo and me."

Merrie sat for a long time not saying anything, still trying to make sense of what he just heard. "Because of your involvement with El Grupo?"

Jon shook his head. "That was a sideshow to everything else. El Grupo was nothing more than a bunch of us staying up late in a coffee shop trying to solve the world's problems. I got hooked on lofty ideals. It was an adventure and I guess I was vulnerable because I'd led such a protected life growing up. As a child, mother treated me like a piece of expensive porcelain, terrified I might break I guess. I was totally transformed when I met Abelardo at the National University in Zurich. He was sophisticated, clever, urbane, and handsome. We...well...we hit it off. I mean in a big way."

Finally Merrie was getting it. "Is that what you meant by coming into the open, you and Abelardo?"

Jon nodded. "That's why I went to Managua after college. Not to be a revolutionary. I wanted to be with him."

Merrie let out pent-up breath. No wonder Chloe was upset that day by the hotel pool when he told her he was going to meet Abelardo.

Jon's gaze became distant. "We had to be discreet, but around our small circle of friends we felt comfortable and unrestrained. Word got out, someone told someone, you know how it is, and pretty soon Abelardo's father found out about us. Family pressure was brutal. His mother was getting dementia and Esperidon blamed Abelardo for being responsible for her mental condition. To admit to the world that his only son was gay was beyond, well, beyond anything you can imagine, the humiliation, family honor, position in society, a respectable businessman, all those things..."

"What about you? How did your parents take it?"

"Mom accepted it but dad was upset, not so much because I was gay but because it interfered with his grand plan, his magnum opus, to take control of MetroCentre." Jon made a large gesture with his hands. He was getting more animated, a different persona was emerging from the thin-faced, troubled youth Merrie had always thought he was. Maybe that's what confession does to a person. It releases trapped feelings, like a dam bursting and water long stagnant begins to flow again.

Merrie, who was primed to broach the subject of fatherhood, now began to wonder what, if anything, would be gained by telling Jon who Karl really was. Maybe that's why Chloe and Karl left it up to Merrie. They probably reasoned, correctly, that once Jon told Merrie he was gay, Merrie would have second thoughts. If that was their motive, they were right.

Besides, revealing a family secret should really be up to them, regardless of their reluctance, not some fucking fireman, right? Merrie did not want to appear to Jon as if he was piling on; it wasn't fair to take it out on the one person who was being truly honest with him.

"What's the matter?" Jon asked.

"Oh, nothing," Merrie replied, "I just wondered if this changed how you felt about your dad, that's all."

"He's my dad. I'll always love him."

That ends the debate, Merrie thought, let it lie.

"Anyway," Jon continued, "Esperidon told Abelardo that if he didn't stop seeing me, he'd be disowned, kicked out of the family."

"I thought it was because he wanted to be a fireman."

"If you believed that all the better because Esperidon wanted to make it look as if I was being rescued from El Grupo, not Abelardo."

"You and your parents flew to Minneapolis the very next morning, leaving me high and dry."

"There was no time to explain. Besides you couldn't be told, you were a pawn, Mr. Gilbert."

"I'd appreciate it if you didn't refer to me as a pawn and Mr. in the same breath."

"I'm sorry. I understand how frustrated you must feel."

No you don't, Merrie said to himself, no you don't. "Finish your story. What happened after you got to Minneapolis?"

"You know most of it. You caught up to us really fast, faster than dad expected even though he knew you'd never stop going after him, but he thought at least he had a few days to wind up his business affairs."

Jon got up to replenish his coffee from the pot on the counter and sat back down again. "Anyway, Karl met us at the airport. The whole time mom and dad were arguing. Dad wanted me to move in with Karl but mom insisted she would not leave me alone. Things got heated. I never heard so many mean words being thrown back and forth. Dad even threatened mom and that's when she called you for help. The whole thing blew up when dad discovered you were following us and he ended up shooting you. Mom was convinced you had died. Now there was no longer any hope that either of them could ever come back to Minnesota. We flew first to Zurich so she could transfer her assets to dad, and then to Nicaragua. Dad promised Esperidon there would be no contact between Abelardo and me. I wasn't even to come to dinner in case he turned up."

"I kept asking your mother if I could see you and she kept putting me off. Were you happy with that?"

"Of course not but I was too depressed to give a damn."

"No one told me, not even Abelardo."

Jon pushed his coffee cup aside and leaned toward Merrie across the table. "No one respects you more than he does. He was in a delicate situation and could not show his hand, even the second time around, taking a boat to Miami, everyone got what he wanted and no one was the wiser."

"Including me?"

"Not unless you still want to arrest dad."

"Are you saying that I should forget the whole thing?"

"Dad was angry at you for messing up his plans, but not for getting me out of Nicaragua."

"You mean he won't come here to get you?"

"Why should he?"

Merrie sighed a sigh of defeat. There would be no final act. "What about your mom?"

"I guess what happens to her depends on you, that is, if you help her clear her name. Financially she will be fine. She has her art collection, the house, the farm, some bonds tucked away at R&S Bank."

R&S Bank, Merrie, thought. We're back to the beginning, full circle.

He leaned into his chair staring at the twenty-two-year-old he had written off as a weak-willed, mother-smothered dependent who hung around in the wings, never onstage, and yet turning out to be the principal actor in Merrie's own theater of the absurd. A tragi-comedy whose plot, looking at it now in the harsh light of reality and in the past tense, was corny, amateurish and blindly romantic. Enrico Esperidon hires an impressionable fireman to rid him of Buddy Boynton but, in a second act twist, it turns out that the person he wants gone is not Buddy but Buddy's son in order to keep hidden an embarrassing family secret. A simple plot, really, but if there ever was a story with crueler irony, Merrie could not imagine it.

42

Merrie expected Buddy to answer his cell phone right away and he was right.

"So, fireman, you are not dead after all."

"Alive," Merrie said, thinking to add, "and well," but it rang hollow. He was far from well.

"Chloe and Jon?"

"The same. Were you worried?"

"I never believed that you died at sea. You had to ditch that boat somewhere. We're still looking for it. Where did you hide it?"

"Under water."

"Under water?"

"I scuttled it."

A roar of laughter exploded out of the phone like amps at a rock concert.

"You find that amusing."

"You got more brass than the Statue of Liberty, fireman, I'll give you that. How did you sail that fucker alone? You're not capable, and we could not find any trace of a crew. And who chartered the boat? It wasn't you. How the hell did you do it?"

"I had help."

"Whoever it was, the guy had to be a licensed captain."

Merrie let the gender error ride. No sense volunteering information.

"Where are you, Minneapolis?"

"Vermilion, sitting on the dock of Karl's cabin, soaking in the sun."

"So that's where you ended up. Where are Chloe and Jon?"

"Up in the cabin, talking."

"About what?'

"You'll have to ask them."

"I can't call her, she doesn't have a cell phone." More laughter.

Merrie's stomach was grinding. "We ditched it after you called."

"At least I figured that out, and the fire, but not the boat." Buddy laughed again. "Wait'll the underwriters hear about this, a scuttled boat and arson both at the hands of a mad fireman."

It irked Merrie that he, of all people, was guilty of arson. "Only the storage shed," he said in his own defense. "As for the boat, Abelardo thought it could be raised."

"Oh, so he had a hand in this, too?"

"He got us on a commercial flight."

"As simple as that? Fireman, you are one shrewd cookie. Going to the airport like a bunch of tourists."

"I know how to blend in a crowd."

Buddy mused for a moment. "I'll miss you. You really made my life exciting. Too bad it's over, life is going to be dull without you around."

"You know why I went to all this trouble, don't you?"

"Sure. You stole my idea to kidnap my own kid. Well, it didn't work then and it won't work now."

"So the pursuit is over?"

"As far as I'm concerned. The U S of A and I have parted company for good."

"What if I let Jon know that you are not his real father."

"What's that?"

"Karl told me that he is Jon's father, not you."

There was a sharp intake of breath and the sardonic humor in Buddy's voice vanished. "That sonofabitch promised me he'd never say anything! If you mention one word to Jon I will follow you to the ends of the earth and this time I will finish you off."

"The pursuit is not really over, after all, is it?"

"Goddamn you!"

"You know, Buddy, in a way I have won because I can always use that against you. And you will never know when or if I do until it's too late."

Merrie knew in his own heart that he could no longer be the one to tell Jon, even if it meant getting even with his arch enemy, Buddy Boynton. Revenge tastes best when served cold, he recalled reading once upon a time, but does it still taste best when it becomes stale? Maybe too much time had passed, too many bridges burned to give a damn any longer that Buddy pay for killing Jim Thorpe.

He sighed audibly.

"Does that sound like you're weakening, fireman?"

"If I keep my mouth shut, it won't be because of you, it will be because I don't want to hurt Jon. He doesn't deserve more crap in his life. He's not a bad kid. He just needs some breathing space between him and his mother."

"You see that, too? Well, fireman, maybe we're not so far apart after all."

"I wouldn't be too sure. I still want to beat the shit out of you."

"Anytime." The humor was back in Buddy's voice and this time the sardonic tone was gone. "Tell me, what's your first name? I never could remember it."

"My friends call me Merrie."

"Ok, Merrie," he said. "Now, does that make me your friend?"

"No."

Merrie pulled out Enrico's business card from his wallet one last time, or so he thought. He dialed the private number and the response was immediate as though the Nicaraguan mogul was expecting his call.

"You set me up," Merrie said without preamble. "Your goons almost killed me. When I showed up at your house looking like road kill you still let me into your private splendor. I should have figured my visit was too perfect. You knew I was coming all along."

"My little ruse worked, Mr. Gilbert. Jon is in America and my son is working for Metro Centre."

"You still have Buddy on your hands."

"And you took fifty thousand of my money."

"I'll pay you back."

"On a fireman's salary?"

"It will take a few years."

"Consider it a business loss or, better yet, the spoils of war."

"What do you mean?"

"You set me up, too, or have you forgotten the clever deception of setting fire to the outbuilding? I feared for my cars before learning you were the instigator, a fireman of all people, and so I needn't have worried. However dangerous it appeared to me, you knew what you were doing. It was a frightening experience but also invigorating. I have to hand it to you, Mr. Gilbert, you are a worthy adversary."

"But I didn't get rid of Buddy as promised."

"Nevertheless, I would still like to keep you in my employ--placed, as you say in America, on administrative leave."

"Why should I continue working for you?"

"To take care of unfinished business perhaps?"

"You still want Buddy out of your hair?"

"And Chloe in it, if I had my wish."

His next call was to Ben whom he did not expect to answer and he was right about that, too. Merrie left a message on his voice mail.

An hour later his cell rang and Ben's number appeared in the window.

"Finally I hear from you," Ben said. "How long has it been, two months?"

"Closer to three."

"How time flies. Some day you'll have to tell me about it."

"I can tell you now."

"Speak."

Merrie gave as detailed an account as he could without involving Harriet. She didn't have to be part of the story as far as Ben was concerned. "I let you down," Merrie concluded. "I didn't get Buddy for you."

"It's out of my hands anyway. The case has been turned over to the BCA in St. Paul as an open file. We have a suspect but even if we did apprehend him it might be hard to prove murder charges. Even harder as time goes on. No prosecutor will bother to touch it."

"What about Chloe?"

"There's nothing to go after her for if her husband is still a fugitive. If she wants to she can contact the Bureau and be deposed, tell them what she knows, but that's up to her. So we might as well forget about it and get on with our lives."

Merrie didn't say anything.

"Think you can do it?"

"I hate loose ends."

43

A cool fall breeze was blowing off Lake Harriet, and yellowing trees were starting to drop their leaves. The concession next to the bandstand was still open but serving less ice cream and more hot chocolate. The summer concert season was long over and the empty benches in front of the stage were lonely reminders of warm summer nights and happy crowds listening to rousing Sousa marches. Wearing his fireman-issue, dark blue jacket imprinted on the back with MFD, Merrie sat on one of the benches, a solitary figure looking down at the expanse of maroon-colored patio bricks, many inscribed with memorials for which people paid one hundred dollars each to express remembrance, gratitude, or tribute. He tried to think of one for himself, something reflecting his own private feelings, and all he could come up with was: DON'T STEP ON ME.

He told her seven a.m. and it was approaching seven forty-five. He knew she would be late and that was why he said seven because she would not show up until eight, which was the time he wanted to walk around the lake anyway. Presently he heard the commanding sound of a Cadillac horn, a short toot really but nevertheless announcing an authoritative presence. He looked over to the parking lot. The big Escalade was pulling into a parking space, its black finish shiny and spotless in the bright morning sun. Chloe got out and walked over to him, ignoring the parking sign that directed payment at a central depository. She was wearing designer jeans, a designer windbreaker with a hood and designer shades. She was a designing woman all right.

"Were you waiting long?"

"Not bad."

"This is early."

"Eight is not early."

She squeezed his arm as she sat next to him. "Brr, it's chilly."

"We're protected by the band shell. Wait'll we get in the open where the wind picks up speed as it crosses open water and..."

"Please!" she interrupted, nudging him playfully. "You'll discourage me from walking." She gave him a private glance. "I'm only doing this for you, you know."

"Let's go then."

They got up and began to walk. The paths and biking lanes around Lake Harriet were busy, as usual.

"Do you know it's shorter around the lake walking in this direction," he said, trying to be lighthearted,

"Why?"

"Because we're going clockwise, on the inside lane. If we walked the other way, counterclockwise, we'd be in the outside lane."

Chloe stared uncomprehendingly. "How much shorter is that?"

Merrie shrugged inside his jacket. "Maybe twenty steps."

Chloe laughed and enclosed his arm within hers, leaning into him and stretching her gait to keep up with his longer stride. "I never know when you are serious or when you are joking."

He did not reply.

They passed the rose gardens across the road, now dormant, the many species of rose bushes covered in hay. The sight exaggerated his feeling of emptiness.

Sensing his emotional barometer falling, Chloe removed her arm from his and walked alongside, not saying anything until they got to the lake's South East

Beach, the wood sign and lifeguard stand the only remnants of summer days. The wind had picked up just as Merrie had predicted, and Chloe pulled the cord of her hood and tightened it around her head. The hood framed her face, a perfect oval accented by elegant cheekbones Michelangelo could not have carved more exquisitely. She was so ineffably beautiful he wanted to hold her tight until he could feel her body warming his.

"You have a funny look on your face."

"It's the wind."

She changed the subject. "Oh, I forgot to tell you, Jon has decided to go back to school. He wants to get a master's in psychology."

"Where?"

"Carleton. He plans to start winter quarter."

"That's great," Merrie said, truly meaning it. If anyone deserved a break, Jon did. "Sounds like he's getting his life together."

"He's moving to Northfield. No more living with mom." She smiled, her cheeks glowing from the brisk air. "Let's walk faster. You're right about the wind."

They continued to the leeward side of the lake, protected from the wind by a steep hill of valuable real estate. The backyards of three-story homes faced easterly and looked out on the lake, their front entrances three floors up faced westerly and fronted on Upton Avenue, a block over. The rear walls of these two-million-dollar homes boasted tall windows and balconies with enviable views of the lake and downtown Minneapolis.

The wind was now cut off and Chloe undid her hood and let if fall across her shoulders. The vegetation thickened here and trees and shrubs lined the walkway. An occasional runner passed them using the dirt path alongside the asphalt lane, the grass once growing there carved away by countless Nikes, Reeboks and Adidas. They walked on, passing the tennis courts and Plaisance Park and then, around the corner, the band shell reappeared ahead of them in the distance.

Fifty yards from the band shell, Merrie said, "Here's a bench. Let's stop for awhile."

Chloe sat to Merrie's left, turning away from the band shell.

"Did you talk to Ben?" he asked, finally bringing to the forefront the subject he wanted to talk to her about.

"I don't want to go to that office in St. Paul, what is it called?"

"The Bureau of Criminal Apprehension."

She gave an involuntary shudder. "That is so ominous sounding." She looked at him. "You told me your lieutenant friend said I didn't have to unless I wanted."

"Yes, it's up to you."

Chloe studied the bobbing buoy markers where sailboats had once been tied up for the summer. "All the boats are out of the water."

"The cutoff was October 15." Merrie pointed with his head. "The canoe rack is empty too."

"Oh." Chloe said, glancing briefly at the metal framing farther down.

Merrie said, "I wonder if the police are still storing Buddy's canoe as evidence."

Chloe seemed discomfited by the question. "Why bring that up? We need to look ahead, not back."

Merrie nodded.

"Have you thought about early retirement?" she asked him.

"I'd lose a lot of pension."

"You really don't have to worry about that, Merrie." She inched closer until her knees touched his thigh. "Remember the Maxfield Parrish you saw that day you came to my house, when we first met? I was so impressed you knew who the artist was."

"As I told you, the Benedictines beat an education into me."

"I had the painting appraised at over a million. And that's just one work worth a lot of money. I have a Warhol Jackie, one of Jasper Johns' diagonal series, two

Oldenburg signed sketches and a wonderful Rauschenberg, a 1965 collage. "

"You would not want to sell those."

"I'd do it for us."

"Us?"

"Get rid of that place you live in and move in with me. I'm not talking about marriage. We can just live together. Jon will be leaving soon. I need company."

"What about Hank?"

Chloe shifted away from him. "Hank?"

"Riker."

She tensed. "What on earth has Hank got anything to do with me?"

"Jon said he is taking care of your investments."

"Oh that," she said, obviously relieved. "A few CDs. Nothing to crow about. You know how little the interest rate is on those, around a per cent."

"Not much of a return. You told me once you barely knew him."

"I didn't, but after Jim Thorpe died, Hank has been taking care of my finances. I understand he was promoted to senior vice president. I expect he'll take over the bank one day."

"That doesn't surprise me."

"Let's move on, I'm getting chilled."

"In a minute. I want to talk."

"About what?"

"I've had a lot of time to think, Chloe, since we got back. That's all I've been doing, thinking about you and me, about us as you say. About how much my life changed since last summer when I was running around the lake and right about here, where we are sitting now, I spotted Buddy's canoe bumping against those boulders. See them over there?"

She would not look.

"I could have continued to my car and gone to work as I usually did, but I was curious and called the station and found out the canoe belonged to Buddy...Buddy's empty canoe."

She interrupted. "Why are you bringing this up? It's over, Merrie; can't you get that into your head? It's over, just like the sailboat season." She glanced at the buoys bobbing in the water.

He shook the head he was unable to get things into. "It's not over. In a way it's just beginning."

She stared around as if she was looking for something she'd misplaced.

"Beginning of what?"

"The end."

A couple walked by, glancing briefly as they passed, their attention grabbed by the obvious tension between the man and the woman sitting on the bench. Probably the opening salvo of a domestic argument.

"From the very beginning I was on the wrong track," Merrie continued. "Every time I thought I had the answer I learned, mostly the hard way, that I had been set up." Merrie's eyes were drawn to Chloe's hands, her fingers intertwined so tightly her knuckles were white.

"And now I've been hit by the biggest set-up of all." He looked into her eyes, trying to get her stare to meet his but she was concentrating on her hands. Her thumbs rubbing against each other reminded Merrie of Lady Macbeth obsessed by a bloodstain.

Chloe finally spoke. "You are being very theatrical."

"It wouldn't seem theatrical to you if you had been smothered by a gunny sack and shot on a lonely highway."

"I told you it's not wise to keep bringing up the past."

"The only way to get the present straight is to figure out what happened in the past. All this time I've been chasing the wrong person. Buddy did not kill Jim Thorpe."

Chloe took her eyes off her hands and stared at Merrie, challenging him, daring him to commit himself. "Then who did?"

"Hank Riker."

She drew back as suddenly as if a locomotive had brushed her. "What on earth are you talking about, Merrie? This is crazy."

"Buddy could not have killed Thorpe somewhere else, brought his body to Lake Harriet and dumped it in the water. There was not enough time to do all that and get out of town. The timing is way off."

"Are you saying Hank helped Buddy?"

Merrie shook his head gravely. "No, Chloe, Hank did not help Buddy. He helped someone else."

Her eyes questioned him but she did not say anything.

"The person he was helping was you."

Amazement narrowed her eyes, either because Merrie had figured it out or because she thought he was a lunatic, he was not sure which. But she was clearly caught off guard, stunned into silence.

"You both had plenty of motive. Thorpe had a directive from on high to cut staff and Hank was afraid of losing his job. You wanted Buddy out of your life and the two of you hatched a plan that would satisfy both your desires. Buddy was already in Nicaragua. He didn't know you and Hank were setting him up. Maybe that's how you got good at setting people up, practicing on Buddy and then using it on me.

"By killing Thorpe, Hank eliminated his nemesis and you could pin the murder charge on Buddy, effectively eliminating him from your life, and he would serve a life sentence for a crime he didn't commit. Thorpe was already dead before he was dumped in the lake from blunt force blows to the head, we know that from the coroner's report. His body was brought to the lake, probably in the trunk of Hank's car. He worked alone because I just can't imagine you being that involved, more like a silent partner. In fact,

I think you made sure you had deniability so if anything went wrong you would be full of innocence and let Hank take the fall all by himself. I can't even put that past you, Chloe. Using Buddy's canoe, Hank dumped Thorpe's body into Lake Harriet. He probably banged the oar against the canoe rack to make it looks as if it hit something. The only thing I can't figure out is the blood on the canoe. Has to be an old stain. Buddy was handling the canoe and cut his hand, or maybe he hit a sharp corner on the storage rack. He might have tried to wipe it off, but blood is tough to get out and some of it stained the wood. It doesn't matter, because it worked perfectly in your plot to make a case for murder, suggesting that there was a fight, Buddy slamming the paddle over Thorpe's head, killing him because he stood in the way of Buddy getting the loan he so desperately needed. Another thing I didn't know and I guess I really don't want to know is how involved you were with Hank. To me this was not a casual plan but well thought out over many dinners and glasses of wine, maybe a weekend or two alone. I don't want to know.

"The way I see it is that Hank was the ringleader. He had the bigger motive to get rid of Thorpe, and you were a collaborator perhaps producing the idea of using Buddy's boat since Buddy was already gone. It was a neat plan. Each of you had an alibi. Who would connect you two? And when I got involved, it was the biggest break of all. You wanted me to snoop around. You were happy to have me sneak out a strand of Buddy's hair from your house, and more than happy to see me involved in the recovery of Thorpe's body. All the time I thought it was Buddy we were searching for but everyone else was surprised to see Thorpe come up except you and Hank. How clever it all was.

"So Hank lets the canoe drift as planned, got in his car and drove home. Next morning I happen to run by and find the canoe. It was a fortuitous coincidence for you. I'm sure you decided to wait until the police put one and one together, Thorpe's disappearance and Buddy's empty canoe. What you didn't figure was that I would come along and solve all of your problems. I was a convenient foil. I'm sure you could not believe your good luck when I called you later that morning."

Tears welled in her eyes. "Oh Merrie, you are ruining everything, everything I wanted to create for the both of us. We had such potential; so much we could do together. Why," she asked plaintively "why are you doing this?"

"I have to know, Chloe, is it true?"

She shot him a look of defiance. "And if I said it was, what then? What would you do, have me arrested?"

Merrie shook his head. "I can't prove any of this."

"Then why..."

"Because I love you, and loving you is only possible if I know everything. No secrets, nothing hidden between us. That's the only way we can build something together."

Tears fell freely now. "Oh Merrie, can't you simply love me? The way I am? I love you, you know I do. No one ever kissed me the way you kiss me, no one ever made love to me the way you made love to me. Why can't we just be who we are? None of us is perfect. Is that what you want? Perfection? Well, you will never find it, never. You will lead a lonely life."

"It would be lonely anyway. You hiding this from me would make my life lonelier than it could possibly be otherwise. Maybe we could hide it for a while, months, maybe years, but it would always haunt us, like a poltergeist in a haunted house, we'd be afraid of footsteps in the night, rapping on doors, moaning..."

Chloe slid across the bench and clung to Merrie as though she were over an abyss that she was slowly, inexorably slipping into. She did not notice that she was attracting more attention. To observers they were two lovers who had argued and now could not wait to have make-up love, too needful to be discreet.

She cried into his shoulder, "Am I supposed to confess? Is that what you want me to do? You think everything will be all right then? Can you still love me?"

He was afraid of that question. How would he answer? How could he answer? Knowing was as bad as not knowing. He would agonize constantly over not fulfilling his moral obligation. The Benedictines pounded not only an education into him, but in addition the imperative that he must be moral, truthful, fight wrongs, and not shirk from responsibility. Isn't that what he believed? Giving up seminary to be a fireman, saving people, sometimes from themselves, risking his life to save another. Isn't that what he decided to do? And now how in hell could he be any different living with Chloe? Could he ignore his sense of right and wrong, submerge it in the deepest recesses of his being, hoping to hide it from himself, never letting it bubble up to taunt him, torture him? It was a moral dilemma that had no answer, no yes or no, just fog and mist and uncertainty.

Chloe pulled away so she could look at him fully, directly, nothing between them but the cool air of late autumn. He loved her, he would always love her, but he could not live with her.

She saw it in his eyes; he didn't have to express it. Slowly, with great deliberation, she unwound herself and stood. She looked at the lake, the trees losing their leaves, the blue sky patterned with gray clouds, the sun in its nether mode. Then she turned and walked away, toward the parking lot. Merrie waited a moment or two before looking at her receding figure. He saw the Escalade's lights flash momentarily as she remotely unlocked the doors, and watched as she climbed in, turned on the engine and backed out, a brief flash of brake lights coming on.

Merrie sat on the bench for nearly an hour, his mind not functioning at all, simply marking time. Finally he got up and walked to his Caddie, which he had parked on Queen Avenue across the tracks from the Streetcar Museum. He climbed in and looked out the windshield.

The car was hardly any different from him, worn, aging, a bullet hole through it, and still running.

He decided to call brother Tad and see if he wanted to play a round of golf this afternoon, only nine holes because the sun goes down earlier now and he also wanted to hit Bunny's Happy Hour for a bump or two. Maybe have Vicki meet him there. He had not called her for a while, but it didn't matter. She was always available.

Acknowledgments

A number of people to thank for this effort and, in no particular order, they are:

Zoe Johnson, my daughter, who did the computer work to get the story into book form.

Emily Johnson, my granddaughter, who helped Pedro Rodriguez in finalizing the cover design.

Peggy Georgas, my wife, who provided invaluable editing and copy changes.

Dale Mulfinger who provided the prototype for the cover design.

Marc Burgett, whose canoe on the cover represents the empty one in question, and who took the cover photo. I also am indebted to Marc for providing the spark for this story.

The Waimea Writer's Group on the Big Island of Hawaii—fellow writers who provided constructive help during readings of various chapters.

Mark Sorenson for allowing me to use the name of his 27-year-old company, Boa Constructors, for my fictional builder's firm. It is so wonderfully original I could not think of anything better.

Finally a confession of sorts. I borrowed five words from the greatest detective writer of all time, Raymond Chandler. His memorable character, Philip Marlowe, uttered those words in The Long Goodbye. Just five words. I hope this doesn't amount to plagiarism but they were so good I could not help myself. Mea Culpa.

CPSIA information can be obtained
at www.ICGtesting.com
Printed in the USA
LVHW082015111221
705947LV00020B/2066